EMINENT MURDER

Joe Crain

EMINENT MURDER

ISBN: 978-0-9842594-5-8

Library of Congress Control Number: 2009913777

Cover photos by: Joe Crain

Cover design by All Things That Matter Press

Published in 2010 by All Things That Matter Press

DEDICATION

To the girls in my life – Donna, Danette and Brittany

Acknowledgments

It is a rare author that completes a book without the aid of others – I sure could not. I owe thanks to those who read through my early drafts to find my many errors and make suggestions for improvements. Those are my wife Donna, friend Forest McNeir of New Orleans, and friend Jonathan Barg of Houston. I also thank my friend, fellow pilot, and firearms instructor Rick Hankel for his assistance with details in relevant areas. For insights on life in Depression era East Texas, I owe my father-in-law, a true-life son of a sharecropper, Woodie Whatley of Linden, Texas. And a really big thanks to ATTM Press editor Marvin Wilson for rewrite suggestions, polishing, and final corrections. *Thank you all.*

CHAPTER ONE

The Houston Live Stock Show and Rodeo is billed as the "Worlds Biggest Rodeo" and it is. The daily attendance is in the hundreds of thousands. The rodeo and the music concerts following each evening's rodeo draw 60 to 70 thousand. The three-week event attracts the best professional cowboys – and cowgirls – and the hottest names in entertainment. James Robert Griggs, Mason's father, Mason and the Gott brothers attended. They sat in the primo chute seats, right above the gates for bronc-riding and bull-riding.

In the bull-riding event, Bob Tallman, the famed rodeo announcer, carried on about 'Bodacious'' and any cowboy's chance of making a qualifying ride – eight seconds. And it was an attraction of a lifetime to see the most famous rodeo bull to ever travel the circuit. A bull that was ridden only ten times out of 135 attempts before being retired, Bodacious was 2,000 pounds of mean-spirited bucking muscle.

The cowboy who attempted to ride Bodacious that night was forgettable. The bull was not. The brown beast jumped from the chute, twisted left 180 degrees, reversed his turn to the right, and then threw his rump so high that his back was near vertical. As the rider fell forward, Bodacious hit the ground with his front hooves and threw his bead back as if sensing he could reach the cowboy, who was slipping down over the bull's front shoulders. Sure enough, the heads came together. The cowboy's head snapped back. Bodacious won again. As the rider slumped and slid off the side, his hand was momentarily hung in the bull rope. Bodacious leaped forward and the hand slipped free, with only a moderate jerk of the arm – lucky rider. Unconscious, he was dragged to safety. He had ridden for 3.9 seconds.

The spectacle made a lasting impression on the boys, especially Rodney Gott. The name and the domineering bull – so appropriate. *Bodacious – Bodacious – Bodacious.* The name was stuck in his head. He kept repeating it silently. He was captivated by the name and what it said. Bold. Audacious. Bold and audacious. The best. The strongest. Dominating. That was him – Rodney Burnette Gott. He knew it. He was bodacious.

"You know we ought to call ourselves the Bodaciouses." It was a couple days later, Rodney was talking to his brother Ray and Mason, still trying to think how he could be or at least use the name.

"Sounds funny to me. Bodaciouses," Ray said.

"Well, 'bodacious' is an adjective. It doesn't have a plural." Mason was thinking too much.

"But it's the name. We'll be named after the bull," Rod said.

"Still sounds funny."

"How about the Bodas?" Mason said. "B-o-d-a-s and you say it like bodays."

"Yeah. We'll know what it means. Bodacious." Rod said the word at every opportunity. He loved the ring of it and the power – always, like the bull.

"We're going to be like a club? How do we get members?" Ray said.

"No! It's us. The Three Musketeers didn't get members. We are the Bodas. Together we are the best. We will rule." Rod had been thinking about this and was expounding. Ray didn't have the vision yet. Mason was taking it in.

"I like it," Mason finally said. "But we don't advertise it. We just let it slip out gradually. Like when we speak to each other, we'll say Hey, Boda."

"That is B-o-d-a. Rhymes with day," Rod said.

"Yeah, long A," Mason said. "Singular, and together we are Bodas. Doesn't rhyme with day, it is day."

"I like it, too, but what's the point?" Ray asked, still a little in the dark.

"Look at our dads. They work together. They run things around here. Nobody else, just them. When our time comes, it'll be just us. We've always heard them talk about 'the makers, the shakers, and the peons.' We're the next makers and shakers of Byar County." Rodney told the other two what he had been contemplating for some time. "Mason, I know you want to be a lawyer like your dad. I want to be a lawyer, too. Ray, that leaves you. You ever thought what you want to be?"

"I always figured we would do the same as Dad. You know, just run businesses."

"Yeah. We can do that. But when we go to college, we can go to law school. Then we know what all the laws are and it helps run the businesses. Running the businesses and making money means we are the 'makers.' To be the 'shakers' we got to be in politics. Most of the politicians are lawyers." For a seventeen year old, Rod Gott had a lot of things figured out. Spending a childhood exposed to the philosophies of their father, Junior Gott, and Mason's father, James Robert Griggs, provided him a practical, though somewhat jaded, education in the ways of Byar County society.

CHAPTER TWO

"This is great whiskey," Leland Griggs, Attorney at Law, said to Junior Gott as they sat under the old evergreen tree behind Junior's rented apartment. "In the old days we only had shine. That stuff would eat your guts out. You weren't around, but I bought it off Old Man Gott…I mean your daddy. He'd get it from the moonshiners that owed on their bills at the old store."

"Old Man Gott." Junior smiled as he said it. "Haven't heard that in a while. And, yeah, I've got plenty of memories of that old store," Junior said as he thought about his father. He had been R. Burnette Gott, Sr. He was sandy-headed, but nearly bald on top, and had to depend upon reading glasses that hung low on his misshapen nose. His father had narrow shoulders and always looked as if he were leaning forward at the waist. "You know, I always think of my father as a prematurely old curmudgeon."

"By the time he married your mother, that was in 1932, I think, folks were already callin' him Old Man Gott."

"Well, he would have been 35 then and Mother was a widow ten years younger." Junior knew about his mother's first husband. He had been killed in a logging accident and left her with an eight year old son. Junior had heard gossip over the years. It seems everyone knew the widow Bessie Gandy caught Gott. She needed a husband and father for her son and R. Burnette Gott needed a legacy – not to mention some built-in labor for his small town general store. It was a match and then Junior was born the next year.

"Well, Junior, it was a different day back then. Different for single women – they didn't have any payin' jobs. Not any proper ones, anyway. They needed a man to take care of them. Byar County, fact, all East Texas in the early 1930s was timber and farming country." Despite being an educated man, Leland Griggs had a lazy East Texas drawl. It stood him well with the locals. "Like most of the nation at the time, we was poor, but even more so. Most of the virgin pine timber was long gone. The second-growth timber was just getting large enough for the tie mills that cut cross-ties for the railroads. That represented most of the pine being harvested. Many of the other sawmills had turned to processing hardwoods. The Depression about destroyed the lumber industry."

"Memories of the Depression are still fresh. I guess we always had more than most people. I don't recall going without." Junior thought back to the days of the small town general store. He remembered spending his days in the storeroom while his parents and half brother worked out front. When the war started and Charlie went off to the Army, he graduated from the storeroom to take Charlie's place up front.

"Yeah, you did, Junior. Your daddy was a hard man to deal with for most folks. We did a lot of business together back then," Leland Griggs said. "Case you don't remember, I'll tell you how things went. Cotton was still the biggest cash crop for those trying to scratch out a living from the land. The terrain is changing, looked far different from today. A hundred and more years ago the land had been cleared for cotton farms and plantations. Even in the Depression it was an agrarian economy, still dependent on cheap labor to turn Mother Nature's land and a few seeds into livelihood. At one time, most of the labor was slaves. Planters brought a lot of slaves to Texas. Later on, it was sharecroppers and some small time farmers. Great Depression lasted until the early 1940s. Cheap labor to work the lands would have started disappearin' as men found other work. Oil was discovered all over Texas, but somehow nothin' here under this dirt. The Depression dramatically slowed the meager industrialization of the South and poor ole Byar County especially. But it did stretch out the days of the sharecroppers."

"Lots of the poor depended on that store for credit and I guess some of them were sharecroppers. I remember my father was hard on them," Junior said.

"Let me tell you a story I bet you never heard. In about 1934, I think it was, late on a Saturday afternoon, two young men in dirty and ragged clothes entered the store. One of them carried a single-barrel shotgun and the other a hand axe. It was armed robbery. They got away in your daddy's old Ford Model T delivery truck. Said they left with almost thirty dollars cash plus a box of chicken eggs that was sittin' on the counter. The truck was recovered. It never had more than a couple gallons of gas in it, but the thirty dollars and the eggs were long gone. It was the last time someone would get away with Gott money. Your daddy built a loft area above the storeroom in the back of the store."

Junior chuckled at the story. "That loft looked out over the store and was entered by ladder from the storeroom. My father sat in the loft behind a low wall doing his ledgers. A double barrel 12-gauge shotgun was visible sticking up over the top of the wall. From the counter, a string trolley was rigged to run up to the loft. If someone paid cash, we put the money in the syrup bucket hanging on the string and my father would pull it up into the loft. Any change he dropped in the bucket and the trolley brought it back to the counter to be handed to the customer. Charge account tickets also went to the loft. We still did that until I was about 14. Never knew that was the result of a robbery."

"Yep. Anybody checked out that store thinking about robbery figgered they had to deal with your daddy and that double-barrel shotgun."

"At night he would bring the cash box and his ledgers down and put them in that old safe. That thing was big and heavy. If there had been a night burglar, they'd never have been able to walk off with that six or eight hundred pounder."

"Your daddy's caution may have led some folks to think there was a lot of cash involved in the business. There wasn't. Most of the regular customers had charge accounts, some paid off only once a year. They were the farmers or sharecroppers. The sawmill workers and the loggers might pay once a week or once a month, if y'all was lucky."

"I think my father hated that store, like some people hate their jobs. He viewed it as a necessity. Remember him telling us, 'We ain't here to make sure people have food to eat, tools to use or seed to plant. We're here to make money. Selling food, tools and seeds is how we make money.' He believed it and he lived by it."

"That he did, Junior. He used that store as a means of acquisition. Not just money, but whatever else he could acquire. First, it was produce, then it was farms. That's where I came in."

"Guess I don't know that much about what went on before the War," Junior said.

"Sunday was collection day. He would get in his Model T, double barrel shotgun for protection, and go visit the customers who had failed to satisfy their charge accounts on time. He would start with the truck loaded with empty baskets. Farmers, and sharecroppers, as well, would always have a small portion of the land set aside for a garden. Occasionally someone would have a fruit tree of some type. They would also likely be keeping a cow for milk and butter, raising a hog to slaughter in the fall, and raising chickens for eggs and special dinners. A few of them even had honey bees. Sometimes laborers or other charge account customers did the same. That was the livelihood of the poor during the Depression."

"A lot of that's still true." Junior thought about the number of childhood friends whose family grew vegetable gardens. His never did.

"Yep. And speakin' of that shine we had to drink, there were a few locals known to keep a whiskey still in the woods. That production didn't go unnoticed as something of value, either. The jars of clear distillate, they call it white lightning now, that your daddy accepted as payment on charge accounts were stashed in the feed room. He'd let me know when he had some and he sold the illegal moonshine to me and some of my in-town associates. That was before Roosevelt fixed it."

"Before my time," Junior said.

"Now, your daddy's method was to first insist on money to settle their tab. He would then negotiate a partial settlement with whatever produce he could squeeze out of the debtor. Whatever food items didn't wind up on the Gott supper table went back into the store."

"Sure," Junior said, remembering more. His father would never give credit for full payment by barter alone. 'Always keep them owing and indebted,' he would tell his mother and Charlie and later on, him.

"Many a time, them poor sharecroppers or laborers would come in the store only to be denied further credit. Once their bill was as much as your old man believed they would ever pay, Bessie or Charlie would look up to that loft to get the sign on whether or not another purchase could be charged. If Burnette shook his head no, there was no appeal. He would turn away and ignore pleadings. Heard that story told many times."

"I never knew him to be anything but heartless. Can't say that I have fond memories working with him," Junior said.

"He was a sly one. Now, the landowners was a different story. They were gladly led down the path of deeper indebtedness. He'd watch carefully what the small farmers were buying. If it looked like they were about to 'take to the road' or 'head for California,' he'd force them to settle up. It meant their land. Whatever they owed plus some additional supplies for the road was the price paid for the farm. On rare occasions, he would have to throw in a few dollars. Me, his lawyer, was just a jingle away and I'd go runnin' with a handful of legal papers to take deeds to property. We had a slick operation."

"But it was all legal?"

"Oh, sure. Sometimes I'd get in on some of the squeezes as my payoff. Heck, that's how I got this house. Cost me about four hundred dollars paying off that widow's grocery bill and givin' her movin' money to go to her son in Arizona. I split the house into two apartments and rent 'em out. This old house has been payin' for itself over and over, year after year. Always told your daddy I didn't care about becomin' a farmer or a logger. Never tried to get any of the land. Took some of the in-town stuff. That was a mistake on my part. He sure grabbed up a lot of land." Griggs paused and took a deep sip of Jack Daniels.

"We're still land rich," Junior said. He wondered how his father, if he were so shrewd a businessman, let things like the old house get away. Real estate that turns a hundred per cent profit every year is a hell of an investment.

"Yeah. Took time, but that land finally started paying off. The old man had a different vision. He saw how some of the landed gentry, such as they were in poor East Texas in the 1930s, had the land working for them. What at one time had been large plantations, that had one way or another stayed in the family, were split up and worked by the sharecroppers – some of them the descendants of the slaves and others just poor whites.

Sometimes a widow with a good size farm had a sharecropper working the land. The landowner would provide 40 or 80 acres, or whatever acreage a sharecropper could handle, in exchange for one third of the crop. That kept taxes paid and turned a little profit."

"Had to be a hard life for sharecroppers," Junior said.

"Most often, the landowner provided not only the land but also a sharecropper house; usually it was just a shack. A sharecropper that was industrious was always looking for a better deal, a better piece of land, a better house, or a larger piece of land as he had older kids to help with the farming. Landowners in turn were looking for the harder-working man who would wrestle a little more production from the land. You'd think that the situation would reach equilibrium, but it never did. The share croppin' life was always in a state of flux as men finally gave up on farming and sought other means to earn a livelihood. But there was always another poor soul to come along."

"How about I freshen up your drink," Junior said and then took the older man's highball glass. Leland Griggs liked it on the rocks, while Junior took his with water. Bourbon and branch water, that was Junior's drink, a taste he had developed while a student at the University of Texas. While he was running in to the house to get ice he thought how enlightening it was to have his father's old business crony providing him details he had never known as a child. With Junior once again seated in the metal yard chair, Leland, with a full glass, picked up where he had left off.

"Even in the turmoil, Burnette aspired to become one of the landed gentry. While he didn't fully appreciate how, he believed that wealth was in the land. He accumulated as much as he could. Then his only means of making the farmland pay was to get him some sharecroppers. He found it meshed well with his general merchandise and feed store. He used the leverage of the store and the credit he extended on charge accounts to entice the men he wanted to come to work for him on the Gott land. Nothing was amicable, just business. He had the knack for cajoling and squeezing just the right amount to keep the sharecroppers he wanted. The old, ill, or lazy he sent packin' as soon as he could line up a replacement."

"It's been years since we had any sharecroppers. Still got land, but my mother depends on selling timber to keep all the taxes up," Junior said.

"By the time World War II started, your daddy had acquired 3,000 acres of farmland and another 4,000 acres of creek and river bottom, land you couldn't hardly give away. He was sellin' some timber but most of the wooded acreage was sitting unproductive. Fortunately, taxes were very low and then the War started. You know, there was a time during the War that they sold lots of timber. Anything big enough to cut and haul, the sawmills and the War Department was buyin'. I'd say most of the money your mama has came from sellin' timber."

Junior briefly thought about the War. His half-brother, Charlie Gott - they had given him the Gott name - was an early draftee for the war effort. He recalled family talk at the time of how his father attempted to have Charlie declared exempt for physical defects that he contrived, but Charlie insisted he go and do his part. After all, he wasn't a real Gott. There was no Gott blood in his veins. The Gotts had never been the type to serve. Junior knew his father avoided WWI service as his ancestors had done before him. His great grandfather had falsely claimed to be a Unionist in Texas during the Civil War as his excuse. Charlie Gott's determination to serve his country cost the Gott store a key piece of labor and ultimately cost Charlie his life. The family received the news of his death in the Fall of 1943.

"During the war, all our business, even the Gott store, was the best it had ever been. Lots of shortages and the rationing, but there was more cash floatin' around. And, your old man picked up a couple thousand more acres of farm and timber land as more people abandoned the country life for the war industry jobs along the Gulf Coast. The War brought an end to the sharecroppers to work all the Gott farm land. They had gone off to war or to jobs in the cities. Junior, they never came back. The era of sharecroppers was over." Leland sighed, denoting the end of his story. He rattled the ice in his glass.

"You have time for another," Junior asked.

"Ain't goin' nowhere but home," Leland said.

While working on the refills Junior toyed with memories of his father. Two days after New Years in 1949, R. Burnette Gott Sr. dropped dead of an apparent heart attack. He was three months shy of being 52 years old.

"All that land with all its potential and my father died kind of young," Junior said as soon as he was back under the tree.

"Your daddy was one of the best known men in Byar County, but attendance at his funeral was embarrassingly sparse. Guess you could say he was neither well liked nor respected. And, you know what, I don't think he would have give a damn."

"I know that's true. Realized that when we were back in the store." Junior thought about a joke he had not known about until years later. *"Do you know how much Old Man Gott left behind?"* The punch line was, *"He left it all!"* Surely it had made the locals cackle and now even gave him an inner smile.

"Mother sold that old store right after my father died," Junior said as he settled back into the old yard chair. "She told me I had better things ahead of me than operate a run-down country store. She bought us a new house and then went to a Houston car dealer and bought a new white Hudson."

"That was her reward. She earned it." Leland nodded.

"After high school graduation she pushed me to enroll in college and took me to Austin to attend the University of Texas. Not sure what I would have done had she not insisted." At the University of Texas he considered the idea of adopting another name – maybe Rufus as most of the professors called him. He finally settled on R. B. Gott, Jr. and signed his name that way the rest of his life. But, back home in Byar after college, his mother, Leland and everyone else called him Junior.

"She did right. Your Mama was still young ... still is, and there's been a number of eligible men in Byar County who wanted to keep company with her...and the Gott money. Heard Bessie's told a number of lady friends that she has no desire to have another man run her life. Several men have tried, but no one's got her to the altar."

"I owe Mother for making me go to Texas and I guess for not marrying some freeloader. I managed to get a degree in Business Administration and she says she's going to turn everything over to me sometime." The other thing Junior acquired while away, though he didn't need to mention it, was the taste for good bourbon whiskey. While his classmates and playmates were trying to enrich the beer distributors, he went for the hard stuff. Bourbon and branch water – that was his drink.

Byar County was still dry when Junior returned home in 1953, but that represented only a minor obstacle. He drove his new Ford Victoria into Houston each month. He returned with two cases of whiskey, one of which was Jack Daniels Black Label. The other was a case of whatever other brand someone had told him was just as good, or better, than Jack Black. He tried them all, but never changed his favorite.

"You're an educated man now. Things you can do with the Gott estate," Leland said.

"Mother and I are in disagreement right now. Of course, she doesn't approve of me drinking and thinks I should be getting a job in a bank or something. That's not for me. Don't see myself being the nine to five type. Not going to punch the clock for anyone."

"You're a fortunate young man, Junior." Leland Griggs had made a substantial portion of his own fortune as a result of being the legal cohort in coercion and confiscation with Junior's father. He had been around the area for years and had the pulse of the city and county. The more they talked, the more ideas Junior developed.

On another early evening whiskey sipping occasion, the elder continued to expound on his philosophies. "You got the makers, the shakers and the peons. People like us are the makers. We got some money and we use it to help our friends out. We kind of stand behind the fence. Nobody is lookin' at us. Our friends that get elected to office become the shakers. Then they have to use their positions to help us out. They're the ones that get things implemented that we want. If you aren't a maker or a shaker, you're a peon. But the peons are important, too. We got to have enough of them peons to go along to make sure the elections come out right."

"I guess you would say Lyndon Johnson is a shaker," Junior said, and thought, this is the kind of valuable education you don't get at any university.

"Yeap. LBJ is a natural. That guy makes things happen. He's got power and he knows how to use it. Heps lots of folks. Makes lots of friends. He's goin' places, makin' lots of money for some friends, and he's gonna be rich himself."

"I don't recall my father ever mentioned giving money to politicians," Junior said.

"Times are changin' Junior. Was a time when we was ignorin' what most politicians was doin.' And we wasn't bein' noticed too much ourselves, but I always had to keep a few around the courthouse and city hall happy. Your daddy didn't believe too much in givin' away money. He didn't ask no favors and he didn't give none." Junior knew what Lawyer Griggs said about his father was true.

"Now, when you got a tight election, our man will need some money. Best to just give him a handful of ten-dollar bills. He's got to go down to the quarter and knock on the doors and tell 'em they got to vote. He gives them a ten for their trouble. Then on election day, we got to hire somebody to go back down there and pick them up and tell them that Mr. So and So sent them to take them to vote. Remember Frank Grimes? He's good at that. Knows every colored and every available vote in the county. Worth ever'thing we ever paid him. They expectin' it. That's the way it's done."

"Well," Junior said, "I've been thinking about getting into real estate development, maybe starting a housing project. I've read about the developments in Houston. I was thinking about trying out a small one here, on a piece of property my father acquired just before he died - out where the Williams Farm was. Will I have to be asking favors to get everything approved?"

"Perfect example, boy. What you want is the City of Byar to foot the bill. There ain't no city water out that way. You want them to put that in. They puttin' in that new sewer system for the town. You want that extended out there to your property. You gonna be wantin' to cut some streets and you want the city to pave them streets. If they don't do it, it's all money out of your pocket," Griggs said, developing the idea.

"I know where you're going. No point in spending money unless you have to."

"See, what we got to do is package this all up pretty and present it to the city council – better to be the city instead of tryin' to make this come under the county. Talk to the city about how this will create more tax revenue; bring some jobs and all that stuff. But first thing we do is get with the members individually. We grease all the skids. Might cost a few dollars, though. They don't owe you anything. They'll be expectin' you to be like your daddy. You're gonna have to be willin' to spread a little around. We gonna have to show them it's a new time."

It looked to Junior like Griggs was including himself in. That was okay. Junior figured he would need Lawyer Griggs for at least a while. He nodded agreement with everything the much older and experienced Griggs had to say.

"When do we get started greasing?" Junior purposely used the word 'we' to indicate the partnership. He would eventually have to work out what part Griggs would receive.

"Junior, you know my nephew, my brother's son from over in Jasper. James Robert is in his last year in law school up at Baylor. He'll be joinin' me in the law office next year. Now, that boy is gonna be a maker and a shaker. Yeah, that boy could sell sand to the A-Rabs. You guys are gonna be great together. I wish I was 30 years younger so I could go along on the ride with you." Leland Griggs held his highball glass up for a toast of sorts and then took a sip of the Jack Black on ice, displaying a wide satisfied grin.

Junior thought, I don't know about the nephew, never met James Robert, but a much younger version of Lawyer Griggs will be a welcome. I might have more in common with James Robert than just sipping whiskey. Leland Griggs had no children of his own, although he had gone through three different wives over the years. "I look forward to meeting James Robert," Junior said.

***

Pecan Estates grew into the nicest housing development in Byar County. It became the place to live in the City of Byar.

Junior and James Robert quickly established themselves, under the tutelage of Leland. Junior was the first to marry. Her daddy was a local politician who felt fortunate to push his daughter off on such an up and coming young businessman. James Robert went back to Jasper for the girlfriend he had strung along for many years. She was delighted to give up her career as a school teacher and move to Pecan Estates, keep house, and start a family.

Pecan Estate neighbors included a dentist, a doctor, a sawmill owner, a couple of local merchants, two more attorneys, and the county judge. In Texas, the county judge is an elected position, the chief executive officer or head of the county government. Even though they have the title "Judge," they are as often as not from the business community and not the legal profession. They are elected and none-the-less, 'shakers' – as Leland Griggs had referred to them.

In 1960 Rodney Burnette Gott was born. The next year saw the birth of his brother Raymond Joseph. There was no possibility they would be saddled with either a name like Rufus or a suffix like Junior or Trey or The Third. A few weeks after Raymond was born, the Griggs saw the birth of their son, Mason Robert Griggs – the 'Mason' was after James Robert's father. Also born that year was Clayton James Longley, son of the youngest shift supervisor at the National Paper Mill. They did not live in Pecan Estates.

CHAPTER THREE

"I don't know why Rod always gets to pitch," Clay said to his dad. "I'm not great, but I know I'm better than Rod. Manuel Rojas is better than both of us and he doesn't get a chance to pitch." Clay had already realized that the sons of the most prominent men in Byar County were treated with favor. "We play sports and attend the same school dances and activities as the Gotts and Mason Griggs and they call the rest of us peons. Nobody says anything about it. Why do the other kids even want to be around them?"

"Don't worry about it son. I'm sure the coach has a reason. Anyway, you're the best first baseman on the team," William Longley said. Ever since little league baseball, Clay thought he knew the coach's reason. The advertising signs along the outfield fence included one that read "Compliments of National Paper Company," which happened to be the employer of the older Longley and a couple hundred other locals. But the largest two signs were "Gott Custom Homes" and "James R. Griggs, Attorney at Law." Even Mason Griggs, who couldn't judge a fly ball or hit anything but a slow pitch, made the starting team. "You'll get your chance, just be patient," his father told Clay.

Just be patient. Clay heard that from his mother and father for years. Tenth grade was the defining time for Clay. William Longley, who always used the name "Will" instead of the more common nickname of "Bill," had been a mill foreman since Clay was five. It was the second time Clay knew of that the production manager, his father's immediate boss, had left. Each time Clay thought his father would be promoted and each time a new, younger man would move into Byar to fill the job.

"See, everything is like that here in Byar," Clay said to his father. "They should have made you the manager."

"Work is different. The production manager is a college man. They're engineers. That's why you have to go to college. Otherwise, you get stuck." Will Longley knew he could easily handle the production manager job. After all, he had trained the last three young engineers.

Even though no one at school had ever mentioned college to Clay, going to college became his private obsession. The assumption in Byar and at Byar High School was that he would follow in his father's footsteps. After all, they were blue collar. It was the curse of living in a small town. Everyone, educators included, knew everyone else and knew their appropriate place in society. Clay felt he could compete intellectually with people like the Gotts and developed a determination to become an engineer.

Even in relatively poor and obscure places like Byar County it seems social strata develops. And so, the Gotts and Griggs were the "upper crust," while Clay Longley, Manuel Rojas and the others were some other form of crust.

"They are always talking about the Bodas and about how they're going to be lawyers," Clay said. "I know Mason is like a genius, but the Gotts aren't that smart. Rodney isn't even that good at quarterback. How does he get voted Best Athlete and them Most Handsome Boy, Most Popular Boy, Most Likely to Succeed and everything else?" Despite Clay's obvious disagreement, the next year when Rod went to the University of Texas, Ray received much the same treatment, except Mason was Most Likely to Succeed and was Class Valedictorian.

Clay started as an end on the football team for three years, continued to play first base during baseball season, but received no other recognition. The popularity contest bore out what he had felt. The Bodas, as they called themselves, were the big fish in the little pond of Byar. Clay had his own goal. It was singular. He would attend college, become an engineer and he would move on.

Clay started college at Texas A & M, while Ray and Mason followed Rod to the University of Texas. At the end of his freshman year, Clay was offered a ROTC scholarship. He accepted and it meant his college was paid for. In return he would be commissioned a 2nd Lieutenant in the U.S. Army and be obligated for four years of active duty.

During his second year at A & M, over the Christmas holidays, Clay started dating Claire Brooks in Byar. The Brooks family descended from one of the first families of Texas, those who were part of Stephen F. Austin's Colony. "We are proud of our family heritage," she told Clay.

"My family has a dubious claim to fame," Clay said as they exchanged background. "My dad, and I guess me too, are relatives of Wild Bill Longley, not a direct descendant, Bill Longley didn't have children, but a relative none-the-less."

"I've heard the name, but don't remember who that is," Claire said. It didn't surprise Clay. It wasn't something his family spoke much about.

"Campbell Longley was one of the Tennessee Volunteers that rushed to Texas to join Sam Houston's army to help win Texas independence." Clay started with the better part of his heritage. "He got a veterans land grant in Lee County, moved there and they say it was a respected family. William Preston Longley was one of Campbell Longley's sons and was the black sheep. He became one of the best known outlaws of the nineteenth century." Clay tried to avoid sounding proud of his background, but at least he and Claire had something in common, the generations of Texas heritage, even though Clay's ancestor, Will Bill Longley, was nothing to brag about.

"What did he do and what ever happened to him," Claire asked. Clay wondered if she were really interested or just making conversation. Clay's father had only casually mentioned their ancestor, so Clay had no real knowledge until he had researched Bill Longley in the library. He recited what he had learned, the bad and the not so bad.

"Well, they hung him. Bill Longley had been too young to serve in the Civil War, but was old enough to harass and kill by the end of the war. As a teenager, the first people he killed were ex-slaves who just happened to cross his path, and later anyone else who may have offended him or his family. It was confirmed that he killed, or more accurately, murdered, eight people. While being held in jail, he first claimed to have killed from 28 to 32 people. At the time, the numbers were slightly more than fellow Texan John Wesley Hardin was supposed to have killed. Bill's bragging probably helped do him in. In 1878, he was hanged down in Giddings – close to his hometown. They say he got religion in the end and took back most of his killing claims. 'It was really only eight,' he supposedly said. The papers and dime novelists of the day glorified his life as they had Jesse James, Billy the Kid and other outlaws like him. They're the ones that started calling him Wild Bill Longley."

"It's still interesting history, something, someday to tell your children and grandchildren."

Claire had been one year behind in high school, was a strikingly beautiful blonde and had been the girlfriend of Ray Gott. Claire was attending college at Sam Houston State University in Huntsville, Texas. They started seeing each other regularly on every possible weekend. The romance continued for a year and a half.

While things were going well between Clay and Claire, Clay began to start feeling trapped. It was nothing in particular, but he was not ready to make a commitment. It wasn't that Claire was putting any pressure on Clay – she wasn't. He felt he needed to cool the relationship because of his military obligation and overriding desire to insure his career. To him, commitment meant a marriage proposal. There was no way that Clay could see himself married any time soon, and that was exactly where he feared he was headed. In his current situation, another year plus of college and then four years in the Army would be too long to ask Claire to wait.

Too late, Clay learned that Claire took his cooling of their relationship as rejection. Clay wasn't good at handling the situation or explaining his motivations. He should have talked with Claire more openly. She felt she was being dumped – albeit gradually. Claire just broke it off. She was not only beautiful, she was also intelligent, self- assured, and had too much pride to allow herself to be cast aside. She as much as told Clay to see others, and she would be doing the same. It wasn't a fight, but it wasn't what Clay was looking for either. Now, Clay had been dumped. Foolish pride would not permit him to attempt to make amends.

When Clay returned to Byar following ROTC summer training at the end of his junior year of college, he found Claire once again dating Ray Gott. Of course Ray had been in Byar all summer, piddling in the family businesses. There was no ROTC, National Guard or military reserve duty for the Gotts.

Clay completed his mechanical engineering degree at A & M in December 1983. He was a "C to B" student, but felt he could have done better had he not been required to work part time to cover room and board, plus a little spending change. Nonetheless, he was commissioned a 2nd Lieutenant in the U.S. Army and reported for active duty in January 1984. As much as he loved engineering and the challenges of solving technical problems, he chose infantry rather than pursue a commission in the Army Corps of Engineers. His immediate interest was in developing his leadership skills. He felt the challenges of being a platoon leader and then a company commander outweighed the experience of being a civil engineer on a construction project or worse, a functionary in some flood control office.

Prior to leaving Byar for Fort Benning, Clay learned that Claire Brooks was engaged to marry Ray Gott. It was over. Nothing would happen to put Claire and him back together. In a small sense, it gave him some closure. He could put Claire behind him and get on with his life.

By this time Rodney Gott was in his second year of law school with Ray Gott and Mason Griggs both in their first year – all three at the University of Texas.

In the summer of 1986, Rodney Gott joined James Robert Griggs' law firm in Byar. Immediately the name was changed to Griggs and Gott, Attorneys at Law to take advantage of the Gott name recognition.

It was just a few months after Rod returned to Byar, November of that year, when Junior Gott was admitted to Byar County hospital. He never left – alive. He died three weeks later as a result of liver and then kidney failure. His taste for fine whiskey led to his death at the relatively young age of 53, about the same age as his father had been at the time of his death.

The Gott business interests had been overseen by hired managers for years. Nothing changed, except Rodney assumed the head of the family. Their mother had never engaged in any of the business activities. The Garden Club, the Historical Society and a couple of other groups consumed her time. With the death of Grandmother Bessie, she had become Mama Gott.

In the summer of '87, the Griggs & Gott law office doubled in size with the addition of Ray and Mason. The growth of Byar County and the legal work for Gott and Griggs business activities, plus the declining participation of James Robert, provided enough work to support the three young attorneys. The elder Griggs was spending more and more time "shaking and grinning" as he called it. He had been elected to the Texas Senate several years before and was spending more time outside Byar County, cementing his influence and contacts. James Robert was an important person in East Texas and would from time to time take one of his protégés with him to meet other "important" people.

Ray and Claire had married the year Claire graduated from college and Ray was in the second year of law school. Upon Ray's graduation, they returned to Byar to live in the Gott home in Pecan Estates. Rod was still enjoying the life of bachelorhood. Mason, also a bachelor, didn't get around as much.

As the senior partner of the Griggs and Gott law firm, James Robert hosted the weekly "Board" meeting, as he called it, at Lake Byar Marina Restaurant. Every Monday night he had a private dining room reserved. The routine was drinks at 6:00 p.m., dining at 7:00, and gone by 8:30. It was men only. Law Office business was discussed throughout, but much of the time was devoted to James Robert passing on his knowledge, experience and philosophies to his young charges. Since Junior Gott had died, he was playing the part of surrogate father and mentor to Rod and Ray.

"I like the Bodacious name you boys use. The Bodas. Yeah. It gives meaning and identity. It holds you together and that's what you need to do. Your granddad, Burnette, and Uncle Leland worked together on lots of deals and made good money," James Robert said, speaking to Rod and Ray primarily. "You boys never knew Burnette and I didn't either – they say he was a good businessman."

"People still remember him as Old Man Gott," Ray said with laughter. "Doubt anybody knew his name was Burnette."

"Guess that's true. But Old Man Gott was what you call apolitical. Uncle Leland was the political connection. He never ran for office, but he used a lot of connections. He knew how to get the politicians owing him and he knew how to cash in on favors. He was even known to spend some money to buy a few favors. He always talked about the makers and the shaker and the peons. He was an unabashed maker. But he knew it was even better to be both maker and shaker. That's what he pushed me to. You got to hold office to be a shaker, to be the one that actually gets something implemented."

"Dad, we've heard this before. We know we are all going to run for some office in Byar," Mason said.

"That's good. Money is spent by the City of Byar and by Byar County. You got to spread out and cover both."

"Don't see how the three of us can hold down that many offices," Ray said.

"True, but really what I wanted to say is about the Party. You boys can start now working in the local political party. You know I'm a Democrat. Guess you are too." It was as much a question as a statement. It got a lukewarm response. "Anyway, locally the party is Democrats. All the civil service workers, whether Federal, State or local are Democrats. Schoolteachers are Democrats. The union mill workers are Democrats. Hell, most of the old people and all of the blacks are Democrats. And, of course, all the poor are Democrats. You control the Democratic Party in the county and you control who gets to run for office."

"What we don't hold, we control. Yeah, Bodas Rule." It was Ray that led the Bodas' high five.

James Robert chuckled quietly. "Now, I'm a careful politician. Most politicians aren't. They are out there because of ego. And Ray, don't do it because of ego." James Robert tried to convey a serious tone to counter the lighthearted jubilation of the younger men.

The elder Griggs continued to expound. "Ego will get you in trouble. Let's keep it business. We have always been about building wealth. Because, in the end, it's wealth that's power. It's real easy to get into trouble in politics. Lot of folks try to make a living out of political office. If you need to make a living, you ought to be working some place, not running for office or getting involved in politics."

"Well, we see plenty of politicians getting fat," Rod said.

"I know, but when guys that need money are the party leaders, they start putting the bite on candidates who run for office. You know, like requiring a kickback of part of office holder's salary. Then the poor slob that gets elected, in turn, has to take money in exchange for favors. Lots of them that take money get caught and anything they thought they would accomplish in political office is down the drain."

"Don't get caught," Ray said to confirm his understanding.

"That's not exactly the point. Politics is a revenue generating profession. It hasn't always been like that, but is becoming more so every day. I have never taken a dollar, not even campaign contributions, from constituents. As long as you're on the local scene, you don't want to make your money that way. It breeds contempt, resentment and disrespect. Besides that, for the most part, it's peanuts." James Robert took a sip of his wine and let his advice sink in.

"The most anyone was ever able to accuse me of was a conflict of interest between political office and the law office. I have a good line that has always served me well. I say, 'Well, I don't take bribes and I don't take campaign contributions, so I have to make a living somehow.' That always gets a chuckle or two and some approving nods. Some other politicians don't like to hear me say that, but that's their problem if they can't say the same thing. Now, it may seem two-faced that I talk about giving money to candidates we support and then say I don't take contributions from constituents. That's not a dichotomy, that's politics." James Robert again paused his sermon.

"Now, if one of you ever makes it to a state wide race or Congress, there is a ton of money flowing in from organizations. Guys in that game build up tremendous re-election funds, war chests they call them. The law is set up so that it is their money. When they finally retire from public office, they get to keep it. On the national scene, you see already rich men taking campaign contributions from labor unions, industrial organizations, the NRA, the NEA, the AARP, the ecologists, big corporate contributors and anybody else that will give. They don't spend their own money for election expenses or even personal travel. Then it's about accumulating wealth."

"Dad made a lot of money in real estate development. A lot of that was the result of Lake Byar being built. How often can we have that kind of luck?" Rod said.

"Different point, boys. We both made a lot of money. And it was all mostly legal." James Robert knew he was stretching it a bit, but he felt he had a caveat by adding the phrase *mostly legal.* "Junior owned a lot of property already. I was in the State Legislature and had advance knowledge. We had opportunity and we had influence. You know we didn't have to pay any money to anybody for that job. We sold off some nice home sites at very favorable prices. Some of them old boys wound up with only a nice weekend camp." It was again time for a silent moment. The younger men waited for James Robert to continue, but his mind had gone back to the frantic days of him and Junior Gott grabbing up all the property they could.

"Let me tell you boys about that. It was shortly after Uncle Leland retired from the firm. Junior and I, with the help of some friends, made the biggest strike of all. The Texas State Legislature was forming the Lake Byar Water Control Authority, a quasi-governmental corporation to develop the water project on Trinity River. One purpose was to conserve water resources and the other was for flood control down river. Of course, that meant the dam built on the river and the water reservoir – the Lake.

"The makers, the guys hiding behind the fence as Uncle Leland always described, got to work. It was surprisingly easy. We supported this campaign that said 'After they build that dam, taxes are going to go up.' That was the line espoused over and over. There was a segment of population that accepted it as gospel. No one had to explain why taxes would go up. It worked. The minor hysteria created by the word of mouth campaign convinced a number of land owners to sell before that happened. Retirees, widows, and absentee owners were particularly anxious to sell. Junior and I were available to take the property off their hands, some at near give away prices."

"Dad never told us about any of that. Kind of dishonest wasn't it," Ray said.

"Freedom of speech," Rod said. "Just like advertising."

"Still not something that needs to be made public. Let me remind you that damage to your reputation affects the business bottom line. It's fair you boys know how it went down, but it goes no further." James Robert looked each of his young lawyers in the eye to assure they understood the confidentiality of the subject.

"By the time the bill was passed in the state legislature and signed by the governor, we had acquired another 5,000 acres of mostly river and creek bottom property. The exact location of the dam was then determined in a small hotel conference room in Austin, rented by Junior and me. We had three state senators and six state representatives, one of which was me. I had just been elected to the State House. Also attending was the appointed head of the Lake Byar Water Control Authority, the consulting engineer, and, of course, Junior was there.

"We used topographical maps so we knew in advance the lake's shoreline. Landowners of property that would be flooded, knew the Water Control Authority would purchase their property, but that wasn't the whole story. The Water Authority purchases required the sale of the adjacent shoreline along with the soon to be submerged property. Some landowners were forced to sell by the courts under eminent domain – taking at a fair price for the public good. Now, we sold a lot of property without any hassle, pieces that would be under the middle of the Lake. Made money on all of it.

"While much of the property in question belonged to Junior, individually, some was owned by me and Junior together. Then we arranged to deed over some submerged property to the Water Authority at no cost. In so doing, we avoided the established shoreline purchase requirements, which incidentally, we had helped to create. Consequently, Junior and I became the owners of miles and miles of waterfront property. Densely wooded, almost worthless bottomland was miraculously converted to prime real estate development property."

James Robert smiled with satisfaction, after all these years still full of pride over the slick scheme he and Junior Gott had pulled off.

"Within a few more years, Byar County paved roads so that a large percentage of the property had good access. Several new developments went in. We did Lake Byar Estates together and Junior did this marina. Lake Byar Restaurant and Marina was Junior's and as you boys know, it became his home away from home. During nice weather, he sipped his Jack Black on the open-air deck, inclement weather drove him indoors to his window seat. Making it a private club restaurant, with the bar overlooking the lake turned out to be a great idea."

"I can imagine why," Ray said, "what with Byar County being dry."

"Exactly," James Robert said, snapping his fingers and beaming at Ray for his astute acumen. "Marina Restaurant, owned by your daddy, then Mama Gott, now you boys, effortlessly made money. Byar County is still dry and this is the only place for thirty miles where someone can pay $5.00 for a one-year membership to a private club and legally indulge. And, your members can also buy beer at the dock."

"Yeah. The manager says sometimes the marina sells more beer than gas," Rod said.

"Some other folks have tried, but so far no one has been able to get all the permits needed or purchase a good site to build another marina on this side of the lake," James Robert said. His message could not have been any clearer had he winked at his charges. "Yeah boys, times had indeed been good for Junior and me. Right from the time we developed Pecan Estates. It grew into the nicest housing development in Byar County. It became the place to live in the City of Byar. The first home was built in '58 and it was upscale for the county, each home costing more than $25,000. We laugh at that price today, but the shakers of Byar County and the City of Byar were all over Junior and me. They couldn't do enough for us.

"You boys' father put up bare land, the old Williams Farm, and the Griggs law firm managed all the sub-dividing, deeds, and the contracts. The first half a dozen houses were built by contractors who provided all of the construction cost. By the end of 1958, the old farm had been annexed into the city limits and the business endeavor was at break-even. Just like Uncle Leland had envisioned, utilities and paved streets were courtesy of the taxpayers. Except for some "public relations" expenses, all sales after that became profit. We reserved a couple of the choice lots back in the pecan orchard where you boys grew up. In 1959, Junior started his own construction company, Gott Custom Homes.

"By the way, this is off the subject, but let me tell you kids something," James Robert said. "Lake Byar was back in the '60s and was different, but was a learning experience for everybody. Today, when politicians start making a lot of noise about a water project, you know a dam – like they are doing up around Dallas now – it ain't about the water. It's about the land. It doesn't matter where, nothing makes land more valuable than having some water. Look at who is pushing for the water project and you'll find out who owns what will become prime waterfront property. You know, it's the spending of taxpayers' money that makes them richer. But you're right, Rod. We aren't going to have another Lake Byar in Byar County. But we may have one in a close by county. We may have something else, you just never know."

Mason said, "No telling what we may get. We have more and more people moving up here from Houston. Most are looking for weekend ranches, lake houses or places to build a retirement home. Byar County is considered a very active real estate market."

James Robert raised an eyebrow. "Be looking for it, a small investment multiplied many times over because someone else spends money to make it so. But that's not the only thing. Back to my original point, when you don't take money directly from folks who want to be your friend, or really want you to be their friend, then they make it a point to throw business your way. It's good business and it's steady. The more influence I have in public life, the more legal work flows into the practice. I expect each of you boys to get to the point where you keep two or three girls busy."

"Girls?" Rod and all three of the Bodas had question marks on their faces.

James Robert smiled and wagged a hand in the air. "By girls I mean the legal secretaries and paralegals employed in the law office. In casual conversation like this, I always call them girls. But in the office, you must always be respectful, addressing them all by Miss and then their first name. It's an old Southern custom carried over from when Uncle Leland ran the law office, and I've maintained his example. As a result, and you can ask any of my staff, as an employer in Byar, I'm considered exemplary. And that's the way you boys should be, too. Treat your hired help with generosity and kindness like I do and you'll have no problem keeping employees long term."

"Guess we'll have to move to a new office," Ray said.

"Get the business first. We'll move when we need to move."

"Then we'll get the girls." It was an odd comment coming from Mason. He was never the lady-killer type, a little on the shy side, and not strikingly handsome like the Gott brothers.

James Robert frowned at Mason's comment. "I can't control how you boys mess around in your private life, but don't screw the hired hands.

There'll be some girls that would like to get you into the sack and get promoted up to the big house, but don't do it. You'll ruin the business. And, I want you to keep in mind, if you boys are going to be in public life, you can't have a lot of dirty laundry hanging out." James addressed his next remark to Raymond. "Ray, you've got a lovely young lady. If these other two do half as well as you, I'll really be proud."

***

In the summer of '88 the board met and the main subject was the big news in Byar County.

"What should we do about this mess? Ray said, "Sheriff Harrell gets arrested for corruption in office. He's been taking in prisoners from other counties with overcrowded jails. Been getting paid a daily rate per prisoner with funds that went directly to his office, and the idiot's been skimming the funds for his own use."

Rod nodded, raised a finger and said, "Yeah – and Harrell's already contacted our law firm for help. What do you think we should do, James? You and Harrell go way back; he's been a crony of yours forever, it seems."

"Best advice is just don't get involved," James Robert said, leaning back in his chair with both palms up. "Keep your distance. Even if you know someone in office is stealing, don't be the one that exposes it – not even if you consider them your political enemy. Now that doesn't mean you don't get someone else to report it. Sometimes it just needs to be done. I've given old Ollie ten grand to repay what he'd taken, but I'm not about to go public in support of him, and neither should you boys. Got that? I told Ollie the best thing for him is to resign and then try to stay out of prison. He is guilty, you know."

"What about a new sheriff," Rod asked.

"Chief Deputy Smith is probably just as involved. He and Ollie are old buddies. County Commission will make him acting until the election in November. Rest of the department is long time deputies with just a few young guys. Won't be any of them. I'm going to talk to Constable Bell. Think he ought to be interested. He'll need some help with a campaign and some money, but that's not a problem. I want you boys to get your feet wet on this."

"What do we do?" Mason said.

"Rod, you be the campaign manager. Behind the fence, as Uncle Leland would say. You set up Bell's campaign schedule. Get him to every ladies' club, every black church and the Chamber of Commerce. Probably going to have to put words in his mouth, too. Mason, you be the bagman.

Whatever money is needed, you take care of it. We'll get the party to put up what they can. We'll spend what we have to. Go see old man Frank Grimes. He'll be expecting somebody. Make sure he knows who he's working for. He knows every vote that can be had in the county. Been doing it for thirty years. Ray, you be the public relations man. Write up a glowing bio on Jimmy Bell and get it in the papers and keep something in the papers until we get this sewed up. You and Rod work out what Jimmy has to say, and coach him. I'll make sure he listens to you. Talk about law and order to the ladies, talk about hiring black deputies to the blacks and talk about honesty and ethics to the Chamber. You know, that kind of stuff."

The Bodas were into it. Ray said, "Who'll be running against our man?"

"If we get a big enough jump on this, nobody else will get in. That is, nobody that would have a chance. Seems like there is always some joker who files just to get some recognition, you know, get his name in the paper. If we keep any serious contenders out of the race, it gets cheaper for us in the long run. No matter, when this is over, Jimmy Bell will owe us big."

CHAPTER FOUR

"Mr. Longley, I've got something we need to talk about," Marvin MacDonald said, sticking his head into Clay's office. Clay had an open-door policy with his immediate staff. There were no egos, and scant office formalities. It had been quite a homecoming for Clayton Longley, the new Corporate Vice President and General Manager of the Paper Products Division of Consolidated Forest Product Industries.

"What do you have, Marvin, union issues?" It seemed most of the time Clay had to deal with his legal eagles was when a personnel issue arose, and Marvin was the senior of the two lawyers resident in Clay's newly formed division office.

"It's the new tax assessment. They just hit us with a 48 % increase in assessed value for property."

"Can't we appeal the reassessment?" Clay felt sure there had to be some due process. After all, Consolidated Industries had to be the largest property tax payer in the county. All of the plant sites, yards, offices, etc. were assessed as improved property. There was also unimproved forest land within the county, but that property was held by a different division of Consolidated.

"Yeah, we can file a request for a hearing on the assessment. I've already contacted the Assessor Office. I thought it had to be some mistake. Problem is, the Tax Assessor told me we needed to hire Griggs & Gott to represent us at the hearing," Marvin said with an expression of dismay and confusion.

Clay looked puzzled. "They can't do that. He just came out and told you that?"

"Let's say he strongly hinted. What he said was, 'most of the successful appeals are handled by Griggs and Gott. You should give them a call.' I've already called home office and they said get with you and basically, no - we don't need an outside counsel for a hearing."

"Griggs & Gott. Crap! No, it isn't a mistake. It's a Byar County shakedown." Recollections of growing up with Rod and Ray Gott and their nerd sidekick, Mason, flashed through Clay's mind. "They gave themselves a nickname. That's another story I'll tell you about sometime. They try to run everything, and I guess they pretty much do. I've bumped into a few of my old schoolmates since I've been back here. They've had plenty to say." Clay knew Mason Griggs had married, and lived in his parents' house. Ray and Claire also lived in the Gotts' childhood home in Pecan Estates. They saw after the boys' mother and had no children. Rodney Gott had become infatuated with a young lady from France he had met in Houston. She was attractive, and with the French accent, strikingly different from the women of Byar. Rod thought she was just enough of a novelty to be an attention grabber, and that fit his plans. They were married and lived on a country estate outside of town, on the other side of the highway from the Longleys and a little closer to Lake Byar.

"They say Rod Gott has a French wife and you should see their house. It's half a mile from the highway and still looks huge. By far the most ostentatious home in all of Byar County. Then again, maybe it's only befitting his position in society."

"The local tall dogs at the trough," Marvin said. He had been transferred from Georgia soon after Clay had gotten to Byar.

"Rod Gott is not only one of the richest men in the county; he has already served as District Attorney and got elected to the Texas Senate when James Robert Griggs, that was Mason's father, retired."

"Griggs and Gott is a big firm for a rural county. They have about twenty young guns working there," Marvin said. That, Clay already knew.

"The Gotts, Rodney and Raymond, are old money now and control all of the local politics. Ray is the District Attorney and the Griggs of the firm is County Judge." Clay thought about the connections he had learned about since his return to Byar and then said, "It sounds like Ray Gott inherited the District Attorney office when Rod moved on to the State Senate. That's the way a dynasty works, and the Bodas intend to be a dynasty. If that isn't enough, the mayor of the City of Byar, and that's a part time job, is held by one of the lawyers at Griggs & Gott. And then there is Jimmy Bell, a Griggs and Gott man, entrenched in the Sheriff's Office where he's been for years. Things seemed to be running well, as long as one considered the Bodas' way as being good."

"Well Clay, this is your territory. You know these people, but Home Office says no outside counsel." The usual practice was for Clay's immediate staff to address him by first name. Marvin was always at odds with himself on what to call his Vice President, and one of the last to only sometimes drop the "Mr. Longley" and acquiesce to Clay's insistence on first names.

Without being asked, Marvin stepped into the office and sat down in one of the brown leather side chairs. It looked like it would be a longer discussion. Clay had stood and had his back to Marvin and was gazing out his third floor windows. He seemed to be looking at nothing in particular. "I would expect there would be some legitimate increase in the tax assessment, but 48%. If we went to a hearing to appeal, it would probably be lowered to something reasonable." Marvin continued to keep the discussion going. "We need to build our case. Gather data on comparable property assessments. That should all be public information."

"I'll talk to Rod Gott. May as well go right to the head shed. How long do we have on this?" Clay asked.

"Things like this are normally 90 days. I'll check, though, and let you know," Marvin said as he lifted himself to his feet. He took his leave while Clay was still facing the windows, arms crossed in front of him, jaw clenched.

***

It was Friday evening. Clay stopped by his parents and then headed for Lake Byar Marina Restaurant. He had paid his $25.00 annual dues to be a member of the private club. He expected to find Rod Gott in either the restaurant or the lounge. He found both Rod and Ray Gott, their wives and Rod Gott's 18 year old son in the restaurant. It looked like they had just gotten there. Clay walked right up to the Gotts' table.

"Good evening, folks. Rod, I've got something I need to speak to you about," Clay said before the diners could respond.

"Clayton, it's good to see you." Rod Gott stood and extended his hand to shake. Rod was over 280 pounds and looked overweight at six feet and one inch. Evidently not the athlete he used to be, round faced and fat hands, Clay thought.

"Hello, Clay," Ray said as he walked around the table from the far side and initiated a handshake with Clay. Clay noted Ray was still trim. Rod's gained 90 to 100 pounds since the high school days, but Ray and I have grown by only 15 to 20 pounds. Rod and Ray both still have more hair than I do though, and neither of them has the gray at the temples like I do. "Ray. I'm sorry to intrude, but this is important," Clay said. He was having second thoughts about his rudeness.

Rod made introductions, not warmly. "Clayton, this is my wife, Margarette, and my son Todd. And you know Claire. This is Clayton Longley; he works at the paper mill."

Works at the paper mill. Clay thought that comment over. That's supposed to put me in my place, I suppose? Cheap dig. Clay's heart skipped a beat as he nodded to Claire. She looked uncomfortable at his presence, but gave him a warm greeting and smile. It was the first time he had seen Claire since he had been back in Byar, though his mother had mentioned her several times.

"Why don't you call the law office and make an appointment for next week?" Rod intended to further tell Clay that he was in control of the situation.

The thought that came to Clay was that Rod Gott should be calling and making an appointment with the Vice President of Consolidated

Industries. "This isn't law office business, Rodney. This is related to the biggest industry in your district, Senator." Clay spit out the title, *Senator*

"If it is that important, let's step over to the lounge a minute," Rod said, and motioned out of the restaurant. "I'll be back in just a minute," Rod said to his dinner party and left Ray standing without invitation to follow.

"What's got you so hot, Longley?" Rod said, in a completely different tone of voice.

"We just received our property tax assessment for next year. It's a preposterous 48% increase. Consolidated Industries will not be shaken down by some small town politicians." As soon as he had said it, Clay realized he could have been more diplomatic in his characterization of those involved.

"I don't have anything to do with tax assessments. That's county business."

"When a public official intimates that a payoff of such will resolve any issues, then it becomes an issue of Texas law, maybe even Federal. You're the lawyer. You'll know what laws are violated." I don't really know what I'm talking about. Hope the bluff works, he thought.

"While I'm sure there was no intent to violate any laws, I'll see what I can do to help a constituent. Everybody needs to pay their fair share, even big companies like Consolidated. What say, you get a 15% increase?" Rod offered.

"Make it 5%. Consolidated hasn't added any improvements this year." I really should have previously done more homework and thought through what a fair increase would be. Clay's thoughts continued to be self critical.

"See what I can do." Rod turned and headed back toward the restaurant. There was no handshake, no departing formalities, and certainly no invitation to join them for dinner.

Clay was left standing in the near empty lounge. He walked out to his car thinking to himself, did I make an enemy, unnecessarily? Did I do Consolidated Industries more harm than good? What kind of crap can be expected in the future? No, Rodney Gott was never a friend. He was an acquaintance – a school mate – a teammate. He was never a friend.

Clay got in his company car and made the brief drive to his house. Shortly after arriving in Byar, Clay bought a two-year old house in Lake Byar Estates, one of the Gott developments. It was close to his parents and far larger than he required. He rationalized that as an executive, he would be obligated to entertain, and besides, it would be a good investment.

The only vehicle Clay owned was his GMC pickup truck. As a corporate executive, Consolidated Industries provided him with a choice of a luxury car. Clay chose a Cadillac. It was just a white sedan – nothing too flashy. Then again, there were only a few Cadillacs in Byar. The Caddy got a spot in the garage and the truck lived in the driveway even though the house had a three-car garage. The kit plane Clay was building and his array of tools got the rest.

There's something else bothering me. Meeting Claire, that's what it is. It's not like I've been pining over a long lost love. Thought about her occasionally over the years - nothing too unusual. Never made a point of keeping track of her, nor have I tried to look her up during the last three months. Why the angst? He shook his head free of the line of thought. She's married - evidently happily married. Put her out of your mind.

Clay prepared himself a meal. Not much – a TV dinner, but with a glass of wine. He was restless and agitated. He kept thinking of the confrontation with Rod Gott. What did Claire think of me barging in like that? There it is again. I'm thinking about Claire. She looked nice. Hasn't aged a bit, still beautiful, pretty much the same as the last time I saw her. I wonder how I looked to her. Where have the years gone?

What had Claire been doing when I was in the Army for four years and then when I started my engineering career at Consolidated? Other than being married to Ray Gott while he finished law school and then moving back to Byar, Clay saw only a blank slate. Even imagination would not fill in the space – the missing years of Claire's life. Himself? He had been occupied, falling naturally into the shirtsleeve work environment and always willing to do whatever was necessary to "get the job done."

Though his first job was as a design engineer for handling equipment at a plywood mill in Georgia, the company made everything from wood panels, to computer paper to baby diapers. Consolidated's production had one thing in common – the reliance on forest products as the primary source of raw material. The next few years saw Clay being promoted and recognized by Consolidated Industries' senior management. He was put on a fast track to bigger and better things. From being a young plant manager, he moved on to the corporate office.

By the end of the millennium, Consolidated Forest Product Industries bought out National Paper Company, the company that Clay's father had worked for in East Texas. Later, reorganization and realignments led to the creation of a division office in, of all places, Byar, Texas.

Clay Longley came to town single. He had been married briefly to a woman who could not grow accustomed to his workaholic life. He was a company man at heart and never seemed to leave work at work. What made Clay successful at work made him a failure at home. He vowed to learn from his failed marriage. If given another opportunity, and he wanted another chance, he would temper his enthusiasm for work and pay more attention at home.

Clay decided it was time to occupy the mind with something else. He went to the garage and started work on his kit plane, his other passion. While in the Army, he had joined the flying club and had earned his private pilot license. Like so many pilots, Clay wanted to fly his own plane and not be limited by the availability of rentals. He had toyed with the idea of designing and building his own airplane, but had never gotten beyond preliminary sketches. It would be just too time consuming – time he never seemed to have. Besides, he wanted to fly sooner rather than later. He settled on building a kit that would be a design someone else had produced and would sell the parts needed to assemble.

Clay surveyed his work-in-progress and re-thought his criteria in selecting the kit he had chosen – good short field capability, two-seater, side by side with a high wing and a pusher propeller. Not the fastest design I could have picked, but I like the sensation of flight more than speed. The longer it takes me to get someplace, the more I will enjoy the flight.

Clay took a look at the construction log he kept, noting he already had 470 hours invested in the project. The kit advertisement claimed assembly in 500 to 600 hours. The partially assembled kit had been shipped to Byar along with his other possessions. He would be ready to move the plane to the airport and attach the wings shortly, having finished the engine installation. As he approached the end of the project, Clay had hired a contractor to build a hangar on airport property to house his pride and joy.

***

Months went by without any other confrontations. Clay had directed Marvin MacDonald to request a hearing before the Tax Assessor and to prepare evidence to support their position. The legal office submitted the request by registered mail and shortly received an amended assessment. It seems Consolidated Industries property tax assessment had been in error and included the correct increase of about 5%. In a way, it puzzled Clay. He wondered why it had been so easy to get the locals to back down. He, Clay Longley, son of a blue-collar mill foreman, was the biggest employer in the county. Do I have the clout to counter Griggs & Gott – or the Bodas? He thought how, in high school, they called themselves *The Bodas.* God, they aren't still doing that, are they?

"Clay, it's your father on line two." It was Clay's secretary, who sat right outside his office. She could talk through the open door – no need to use the intercom.

"Thanks, Millie." Clay seldom received a call from his father, although his mother would call his office a couple of times a week. Since being back in his hometown, Clay had established a routine, becoming an attentive son to his aging parents. When not out of town on business travel, Clay stopped by their house each evening on his way home. The rest of his spare time went into completing his kit plane.

"Hey, Dad. What's up?" Clay said upon picking up his phone. He never used his speakerphone for a one on one conversation.

"We had a visit today from one of the lawyers from Griggs & Gott. She said somebody wants to buy our farm." Although the title of the property was in Elizabeth's name, Will had built the house and invested years in the place. To him, and to Elizabeth, it was "our" farm or often referred to by others as a ranch.

"She say who it was or why they wanted it?" Clay was curious. He knew the property had not been put on the market for sale. His parents would have told him. He saw them almost daily.

"She wouldn't say who. She wouldn't even say how much. She was kind of pushy and ugly about it. She said we need to decide how much we want for the place. We don't want to sell, not for any price."

"What did you tell her?" Clay said.

"Said we weren't interested. That's when she got pushy. We told her it was Mom's home and we intended to stay here."

Clay frowned. Dad's quite upset. Most unusual for him. "Well, I wouldn't worry about it. They can't make you sell."

"When she left, she said we would be hearing from them, and if we didn't set the price, the buyer would. She made it sound like we didn't have a choice."

"Did she leave a card or anything?"

"Yes. Her name is Rebecca Rals. At Griggs and Gott."

"I'll call her and see what I can find out. I'll see you this evening." Clay had not experienced much of this, but realized it was coming. Parents take care of the children for years and then the parents become the children and the children become the caretakers. He was thankful that he could be close by to serve that function.

"Mom says tell you to plan to stay for dinner."

Clay immediately placed a call to the Griggs and Gott law office.

"Yes, Mr. Longley, I did make a presentation to William and Elizabeth today," Rebecca Rals responded after Clay got her on the line.

"They are upset the way the situation was presented to them. They are not interested in selling and we would appreciate it if you would notify your buyer and drop the matter," Clay said, in his most straightforward and business like manner.

"If they are not willing sellers, I will tell you there is a good possibility the property in question will be condemned," she said.

"What do you mean, condemned? There is no reason for that." Clay was mystified. What - was it a hazardous waste dump in the past, or something?

"Actually, there is a public benefit issue at stake here. It's called eminent domain.

"I know what it's called. What is the public benefit?"

"I'm sorry Mr. Longley, I am not at liberty to discuss it at this time."

"Well, our answer is the same. Let me give you my number and if you have any further correspondence, please direct it to me."

"What ever, Mr. Longley. I have your number. Good day."

What a snippy bitch, Clay thought. I have to get involved.

"Marvin, got a minute for some personal stuff?" Clay said at the door to the company lawyer's office.

"If it affects any of the employees, its fair game. If I need to tell you to go hire a lawyer, I'll tell you," Marvin said.

"Okay. What's the likelihood that a 160 acre farm can be condemned for a public benefit?" Clay watched Marvin momentarily contemplate his question.

"Any piece of private real estate can be condemned for public necessity or really for the public good. It takes a legal action. The governing body seeking the condemnation must show just cause, you know like the property lies in the path of a new or expanded right of way; the property is the only site where such and such can be built – those kinds of things." Marvin was good at putting things in layman's terms. "And, they have to show that they are paying a fair price. Quite often, that's the rub. Owners don't agree on what's fair."

"A court has to decree it?"

"Right, if there is an issue. It's a process. You would not just get a notice that your property is being taken by the state – or whatever-- and it's a done deal. Anything in particular you're concerned about?"

"Yeah. Griggs and Gott are threatening my folks that if they don't sell they could lose the farm through eminent domain."

"With the Longhorns?" Marvin knew Clay's parents had the Longhorns on a small farm and had driven by there to show his kids the cattle. He surmised it was the Longley's farm Clay was asking about.

"Yeah. About the time I was getting out of the Army my folks retired to the 160 acre farm that had been my mother's childhood home. Been in her family for generations."

"Looks like they built a new house."

"Grandpa's old wood frame house had to be demolished and they built on the same spot. When I left here the place hadn't been farmed in years and had grown over. Dad got a tractor and started clearing brush and trees. They say it was a full time job to rebuild the barn and clear pastures."

"Wasn't any Longhorns then...I mean your grandparents didn't have cattle?"

"Oh, no. They told me they bought the first three the second year after they moved out there. Just started slowly building a small herd. The cattle were still somewhat of a novelty and people would drive by slowly just to get a look at them. At first, they didn't expect to make anything off the cattle. It was just something Dad wanted to do after all the years working in the mill. He put his welding skills to work building pipe fences to keep the Longhorns corralled, and to keep them from entangling their horns in wire fencing. Mom says she loves being back on the farm."

"Not much you can do until there is some public filing and notice. You have to find out what the public project is and why that particular piece of real estate is required. It may be worth fighting, and maybe not. Frankly, I can't imagine what it would be. How about keeping me posted on it?"

"Thanks, Marvin. I'll let you know if we hear anything else." Clay returned to his office and didn't think much about the subject the rest of the day. He did discuss it with his parents that evening over dinner, and advised them to not be concerned.

About a week and a half later Clay received another call from his father. Will Longley reported that the lady lawyer, Rals, had called again. She was very brief and only asked had they decided. Will said he had told her they were not selling, and she ended the conversation. Again, Clay advised his father to not worry about it.

***

The Bodas continued their Monday board meeting at the Lake Byar Marina Restaurant, even after James Robert Griggs had retired and no longer attended. Rod Gott assumed the elder role. As often was the case, he allowed his son, Todd to attend. Rod was the only one of the three with a child, and he had only one. Rod enticed Todd along for the dinner, but his ulterior motive was to indoctrinate Todd in the doings of the family. Todd was attentive to the conversations and enjoyed a cola while the others indulged in alcoholic beverages. Rod had over the years picked up some of his father's taste for hard liquor. Ray and Mason were predominately wine drinkers. While they had a couple of glasses of wine, Rod would easily down three to four highballs.

"Looks like Will Longley will resist any efforts to sell and that's what I expected," Rod said, starting the discussion of his current issue.

"My understanding is that no specific money offer has been tendered." It was Mason.

"No point in getting specific when they are totally unreceptive. Besides, giving them an offer shows our hand. We're not going to pay what the future value or potential value of the property will justify. Hell, it's just a little house, a couple of barns, 80 acres of pasture and 80 acres of woods. Our granddaddy would have picked that up for the grocery bill," Rod said. Acquiring other peoples' land for cheap still ran in the blood. Just making an open attempt to purchase the Longley's place ran against his nature.

Todd had heard a lot of this type of discussion before. He knew all about the Bodas and where the name came from. 'You're going to be a Boda. You've got to know what's happening. But what we say here, stays here,' his father had told him several times. Todd had listened to them regale with stories about his great grandfather, Rufus Burnette, and Uncle Leland. He was always referred to as Uncle Leland, even though he had been only Mason's great uncle. Uncle Leland's reference to *the makers, the shakers and the peons* was often heard. It was a litany. There were stories and recollections of grandfather, Junior, and James Robert. Todd never knew Uncle Leland, or his grandfather, Junior, and had only vague memories of James Robert, but he knew well their legacy.

"We threatened them with condemnation, let's do it. Have the County Commissioners pass an ordinance precluding the keeping of livestock on property adjoining to the Estates. It's a residential area and the livestock creates a health hazard to the public. Get the entire Longley place included." Rod addressed his instruction to Mason, since Mason was the County Judge and head of the Board of County Commissioners. When he talked about the Estates, it was understood to be Lake Byar Estates. Where Clay lived was now the most exclusive neighborhood in the county, outstripping the older Pecan Estates.

"What will we accomplish by this restriction," Ray asked.

"Well, if the peons really want to keep those damn cows, maybe they'll move. We just want to get that place the easiest and quickest way we can."

"The Board will pass that, no problem. I'll have some maps done up and get it introduced next week. Want to make sure everybody is signed up prior to the meeting. We would rather not have much discussion on the item, just bring it to a vote. Now, this is just my legal opinion and it's the downside. If the property owner fights this, that is, files suit against the county, and they can show that they are singled out by this ordinance, that would be a winner." Mason was thinking ahead. Even though he held an office that was totally political, he did have the best legal mind of the group. He would rather be District Attorney, but Rod had passed that office on to brother Ray. Mason saw himself eventually becoming a real judge, maybe on the Texas Supreme Court.

"Okay. Include all that property to the north and northwest of the Estates, all the way down to the Lake. We own just about all of it anyway," Rod said with ease.

"Why not all the way around the Estates?" Ray said, not thinking.

"Hell no, Ray. That would be my place. I got all those horses.

"Yeah. That wouldn't be part of the project anyway." Ray referred to "the project'" currently the closest held secret of the Bodas. It was the next bonanza. It would mean millions. But the mention of 'the project' earned Ray a frown from Rod. This was something that had not been discussed in front of Todd. It was too confidential. Ray got the message and decided to speak no further.

"If the plaintiff can show a financial loss of value to the property, the county may be found liable." Mason was still mulling over the legal issues associated with the scheme and thinking out loud. "Most of the cases on these types of condemnations have been in Federal Court and the burden of proof has been on the plaintiff."

"Well, I'm not worrying about winning or losing in court. Doesn't matter. We're just trying to motivate the seller. Give him reason to move on. Okay. Enough of this. Mason, you just do your thing with the commissioners. Todd, you ready to order? Go find us a waiter."

CHAPTER FIVE

Clay was finishing the last of the at-home work on his kit plane when the phone extension in his garage rang. It was Marcus Franks, a reporter for the Byar County News, the local weekly. Marcus had visited Clay at his office shortly after his return to Byar and had written a brief but nice piece on the hometown boy who had done well and returned to his roots. They had bumped into each other a number of times and shared a number of interests, including flying. Clay promised Marcus a flight after the kit plane was all signed off.

"I'm at the County Commissioners Meeting. I just stepped out to call you." Marcus was excited and blurting out all he had to say without allowing Clay to interrupt. "The Board just passed an ordinance that prohibits the keeping of livestock on property surrounding Lake Byar Estates. It was a slam-dunk. Almost no discussion. One commissioner wanted to debate it, but Mason Griggs brought it to a vote and it passed four to one. It was over in five minutes. That's your folks' Longhorn ranch."

"How can they do that?" Clay said. Just as quickly, he thought about the threat from the lawyer bitch to have the Longley property condemned. That was it.

"I don't know what it is, but something is up here."

"Thanks Marcus. I've got an idea what it is. I appreciate your call. You didn't call my parents, did you?"

"No, just you."

"Please don't call them. I'll stop by in the morning and talk to them. Thanks Marcus." Clay hung up and called Marvin MacDonald at home. He relayed to Marvin what he had just learned.

"That's not what I was thinking when we talked about condemnation. It's one of the aspects of it. It is depriving someone of property rights rather than just taking the property. I think your parents will need to get counsel. I'll get you a name in the morning."

Clay continued to ponder the revelation. He felt the offer to buy conveyed by Griggs and Gott, and the ordinance rammed through by Mason Griggs was tainted by the same stink. Is this how Rodney Gott is getting even for the tax assessment flap?

***

Clay stopped by his parents on the way to work. It was unusual, but Will and Elizabeth were early risers and glad for the visit anytime. Clay caught his father out at the barn. He broke the news and then assured his father that it was not the last of it. They would be consulting with an attorney to determine their recourse. "It ain't right. It ain't right," Will continued to say. "Why would they do that?"

"They, someone is trying to get you and Mom to sell this place. They want it for some reason. The other possibility is that it is a vendetta orchestrated by Rod Gott because of the Consolidated tax issue I told you about. He's trying to get back at me. Anyway, don't do anything. We will be talking to a lawyer about what we can do."

"We haven't saved enough off the cattle to justify paying some lawyer just to keep them. Everything has gone back into the herd to build it up."

"Don't worry about the lawyer. I'll take care of that. I'll let you know when we can set up a meeting." Clay reassured his parents again and headed off to his work.

At work, Clay was involved in a couple meetings and did not have time to think about the problem his parents faced. It was late morning before Marvin MacDonald stuck his head in.

"Got a few minutes?"

As often as not, the mid portion of Clay's day was consumed by a lunch meeting or some type of civic or business luncheon. This day was one of the free days. "Yeah. You want to go to lunch?"

"Sure. Any place in particular?"

"Nah. Bar-B-Que? Seafood? Mexican?"

"Okay. Bar-b-que," Marvin said.

"The Kings? Have you been there?"

"Let's give it a try." Marvin had not gotten to Byar until after Clay's return and was less familiar with the restaurants than Clay.

Clay made the quick drive in his company car. At The Kings' Bar-B-Que, owned by a husband and wife, last name of King, Clay and Marvin took a back booth.

"I've spoken to a couple of classmate friends and have a referral. He is a friend of a friend. I don't know him, but spoke to him briefly a while ago. He's from Austin and comes highly recommended. I briefly told him what it's about. He's interested. Frankly, I'd love to argue the case myself. But this guy is a specialist. He goes all over the country. His name's Forest Donovan."

"Sounds expensive," Clay said.

"We didn't discuss his fee. I did tell him it was an elderly couple. Maybe he'll take that into account. He wants to come and meet with you."

"I guess it won't cost too much to meet him," Clay said.

"Say when. I think he's anxious. "

"Whenever he can make it over. An afternoon would be best," Clay said, as Marvin whipped out his cell phone and pocket notebook.

Marvin punched in the number and spoke directly to the lawyer. After some brief conversation, he asked Clay if Monday afternoon was good. Clay nodded agreement and Marvin confirmed the time and place. They would start at Clay's office and then go out to his parents.

***

Forest Donovan had an average build, just under six feet with thinning blond hair and thick glasses. Clay's first impression of him was that he was intense. He was friendly, but he really wanted to talk the issue. Marvin had asked if he could sit in, just as a friend. Clay and Forest agreed.

"Before we go too far, we would like some idea of your fee," Clay said.

"Fair enough. Sorry, I didn't get to that first. Okay, today is free. Nothing. No expenses or anything. I'm a one-man shop. Just me, so I can't do this pro bono. If this is what Marvin told me and you choose to engage me, I'll work cheap. It sounds like a perfect case of government encroachment on private property rights. Believe it or not, there are some people in this profession who have a fundamental belief in the Constitution, and that protecting individual rights is the most important legal issue before us today. I'm familiar with Griggs and Gott. I've met Rod Gott. What an asshole. Somebody needs to chop that prick off at the knees, and...."

"You're hired," Clay said. "I don't need to hear more."

Forest returned his comment with an agreeing smile, and then continued. "Mr. Longley, let me recite a portion of the Fifth Amendment to the Constitution."

"Please, I'm Clay, that's what everyone calls me."

"Great. I'm called lot of things, but I prefer to be called Forest. Okay Clay, the Fifth Amendment is the one about double jeopardy and giving testimony against yourself. It is also the one that is called the taking clause. It says, 'nor be deprived of life, liberty, or property, without due process of law; nor shall private property be taken for public use, without just compensation.' I would love to make the argument that this condemnation is exactly that. It deprives your family of the liberty to continue with a business endeavor that has been longstanding. The farm was there long before the adjoining developments. There has also been no due process exercised. The action of the County Commissioners was arbitrary. Furthermore, no compensation has been offered for the deprivation of the private property. You see, it is not the physical property itself, it is the economic use of that property that the county is taking."

"I appreciate your explanation. You make it sound simple. What do we do next?" Clay asked.

"First, we wait for the County to issue the ordinance. I expect it gets published in the local paper as legal notices. The first thing will be to get a restraining order to preclude any immediate enforcement action or penalty. Next, we will get a hearing to get an injunction. Then we file suit and try to get the case to court. If we can get to court with a jury of peers, we will not lose. Unless of course, we are somehow waylaid by the judiciary. Then we will continue our appeals all the way to the Supreme Court if necessary." Forest Donovan finally caught his breath. "And don't worry; you won't be billed for any legal research. I'm absolutely familiar with all the case law on this issue. I've been the plaintiff attorney in a large portion of it in recent years."

Clay was nodding agreement with everything, even though he didn't know the difference between a restraining order and an injunction. He thought he may as well ask. "Forest, you said we get a restraining order first and then an injunction. What's the difference?"

"A restraining order is essentially a temporary injunction. It is typically issued from the bench without a hearing, and may be in effect until a hearing can be held. The injunction would be a more permanent court order, until the issue is resolved. Now, all of this being said, I doubt we get that far. From what Marvin told me, this property is used for business purposes, a Longhorn cattle ranch. It belongs to your parents. Are you the only heir?"

"Correct, it is a business. Although, to be honest, it's a hobby type business. My father has basically been retired for a number of years."

"They do derive income by periodically taking product to market?"

"Yes, they do sell off older cows and a number of calves each year. I really can't at this time tell you how profitable the Longhorns are. And yes – I am an only child. My mother was an only child and sole heir to the property from her family. I'm the only heir to the property. And, what do you mean we won't get that far?" Clay was puzzled by the long explanations that sounded like a preview of coming events.

"You say your parents received some type of offer to purchase the property and the threat of condemnation. Being familiar with Griggs & Gott, and Rod Gott especially, it's not about the livestock. The offer to buy was never made in writing and no specific dollar amount has ever been mentioned. Marvin told me you believe they just want the land. I agree with you. Why, I don't know. The Gotts are already land rich. What do they need another 160 acres for? I think this ordinance, this condemnation, is nothing more than a harassment tactic. They may be trying to devalue the land, to buy it cheaply or maybe they are just trying to cause you to have to spend a lot of money on legal fees to fight them." Forest stopped his theorizing long enough to get Clay's response.

Clay thought for a few moments before speaking. "Not far away is a Gott development, Lake Byar Estates. It is where I live. It is a fairly exclusive neighborhood." Clay suddenly wondered if it sounded that he had just bragged about his status and felt a little embarrassed. It wasn't his nature. He had bought in Lake Byar Estates for a number of reasons. It was close to his parents, it was nice, there was the three-car garage, and he felt it was a good investment. After all, he still had a big mortgage on the property, so he couldn't be too uppity. "Of the 160 acres, about half is un-cleared. It used to be my grandfather's farm, but it has three decades worth of scattered trees and undergrowth. There is a lot of Lake Byar Estates property not yet developed, before the subdivision would need to expand into Mom's property."

"Do you mind if we drive out there and take a look? I would just like to see what we are talking about. Also, I guess I would like to meet your parents. Or perhaps more importantly, I would like your parents to meet me. Maybe I can reassure them in some way. If I thought this was some run-of-the-mill real estate dealing, I wouldn't get mixed up in it. But when a government entity is involved in the taking of private property or property rights, it piques my interest. I don't expect this to be a one-shot assault. The Gotts will eventually back down on this condemnation. The County will never pay for the indefinite denial of private property rights. The County Commissioners will repeal the ordinance before it comes to that. That will be a victory for us. But the Gotts will come back with something else."

Clay left instructions with Millie to contact him on his cell phone if necessary, and took Forest to meet his parents and see the property. Clay pointed out the property lines from the highway. He also took a drive through Lake Byar Estates before stopping at his parents' house.

Forest was intrigued by the 20 head of Longhorn cattle and by the two donkeys that roamed the Longley's little ranch. Clay explained to him that, although once the dominant breed of cattle grazing throughout much of Texas, the Longhorns had become scarce. They made a significant comeback, thanks primarily to novelty ranchers like Will and Elizabeth Longley.

While strolling about the land, Will filled city boy Forest in on some Longhorn history. He told him the Longhorns were descendants of the first Spanish cattle brought to America in 1493. For years cattle ranged wild in Texas and the first recorded cattle drive out of Texas was at the time of the Texas Revolution in 1836. That drive went to Louisiana, long before the glamorized cattle drives up the Loving-Goodnight and Chisholm trails to the Kansas markets.

By the end of the Civil War there were estimated to be five million Longhorns in Texas. The Longhorns were well suited to the cattle drives because of their hardiness. Once the days of cattle drives were over, other breeds of cattle were favored for their beef and the Longhorns almost disappeared. More recently, the Longhorns became highly prized animals. A registry is maintained and some stock of admired bloodlines were selling for more than $10,000.

Will told how he had bought his first three cows for $400 each and now each head was worth a minimum of $3,000. He pointed out two cows that had exceptionally long horns, looking in excess of 60 inches tip to tip, that he felt were worth $8,000 to $10,000 each. Will planned to keep his herd in the range of 20 head and his future stock would come from those two cows. Each year he sold off the steers or male calves and planned to slowly sell off the less valuable cows as they were replaced by better pedigrees. The Longhorns were about to become a significant subsidy to their retirement income. What had started as their retirement hobby had become a business.

Forest took time to explain to Clay's parents the applicable legal principle and reiterated much of what he had told Clay. He said, "Our laws stem from British common law where no ownership of real property is absolute. Our real property titles are said to be held 'in fee' and that means 'subject to the King's prerogative.' Now, we don't have a king since the American Revolution, so what that means today is 'at the government's prerogative.' Can Byar County, that is the government, do this? In a legal sense, yes they can. However, it is also our tradition that citizens are due justice and simple fairness."

Forest thought the Longleys were the perfect example of traditional America. They truly had a Mom and Pop business. It was nothing like the little corner grocery store some would typically think about, but was nonetheless the American tradition. They collected no subsidy or redistribution of someone else's tax money; just the two of them working the business, building little by little each year, not hurting anyone and needing only to be left alone by the government. What a wonderful argument he could make before a jury. The message Forest left with the Longleys was to not worry.

CHAPTER SIX

It was Mason Griggs' practice to arrive at Griggs and Gott law office at 8:00 each morning. He would usually make it to the Byar County Courthouse and his County Judge Office by 9:30. By then his secretary had already sorted the mail by what she perceived as priority, and placed it in the center of his desk. That day the item on top was a simple piece of correspondence. The top letterhead read – *Forest Donovan, Attorney at Law*.

Mason's eyes immediately fell upon the line that said, 'I have been retained by Mr. and Mrs. William Longley for legal matters pertaining to Byar County ordinances that effectively result in condemnation of their property. Address all future matters to this office of record.'

Mason got on the phone to Rod Gott. State Senator Gott had his public office in the same building as the law office, even though it had a separate entrance and phone number. "The Longleys have hired Donovan. When I said I didn't think this would hold up, now I can say for a certainty, this ordinance will be struck," Mason said.

"That's fine. Let them spend some money. We'll play it out for a while and then we'll change horses." Rod Gott wasn't the least bit concerned, having already thought of Joshua Simmons, the Byar County Attorney. The county attorney was a contracted position, the attorney being selected by the County Board of Commissioners with Mason Griggs as its head. Josh Simmons was a former member of Griggs & Gott who they had set off to appear to be a separate practice. He was not only dependent on Griggs & Gott for his county appointment, but also the largest of his prior firm for most of the referred business he received. Josh Simmons did as he was told.

Gott said, "Let's get Josh to go ahead and gin up a suit to enforce the livestock ordinance."

Since the ordinance had already appeared in the legal notices of the local newspaper, Josh Simmons sent a letter of specific notification to the Longleys. He threatened suit to enforce if the Longleys did not comply within 30 days. Even though he had been copied on the Forest Donovan letter for office of record, he directed the registered letter to be delivered to the Longley residence.

Clay contacted Forest when Clay's father called upon receiving the letter from the Byar County Attorney's Office.

"It is exactly as I suspected. Fax me the letter and I'll take care of it," Forest said. "The request for a temporary restraining order is already prepared. I'll meet with a judge tomorrow. We'll get a hearing scheduled as soon as possible. Again, tell your folks to not worry about it. I feel really good about this case."

"I'll tell them, but you can imagine how old people are." Clay had begun to view his parents as old. His father had taken early retirement from the mill when he was 55. His mother, three years younger, left her hospital job at the same time. They had lived a relatively frugal lifestyle, had saved, and had his small pension plus their social security. They could survive without the Longhorn business, financially. Clay could always provide any essentials. Liquidating the livestock would replace most of the savings that had gone into the farm and breeding stock. But the Longhorns were important to them. For some retirees it is fishing, boating, golf or grandchildren. For the Longleys, it was the farm and the cattle. That's what kept them going.

Forest had no difficulty in obtaining the restraining order. Even the district judge for Byar County, another Bodas wannabe, was not going to refuse a temporary injunction. However, he was in no hurry to schedule a hearing to make a permanent ruling. Rod Gott had suggested to the judge that the issue should be dragged out to allow all the dust to settle. Rod figured the clock was running on the Longleys' legal fees.

It was four months before the hearing. The elder Longleys, Clay and Forest, listened as Josh Simmons made a half-hearted argument in support of the Byar County ordinance to eliminate the keeping of livestock near the premier residential area. He noted that the Longleys were the only property owners presently not in compliance with the ordinance. He neglected to mention that the Gotts owned the bulk of the other property covered by the ordinance, and their property had not been used for any purpose other than timber harvesting for the last 60 years. Also, a few weekend homes closer to the lake fell under the ordinance. Again, there was no livestock involved.

Forest Donovan was more than a match. He started with the Bill of Rights, the Fifth Amendment. He cited every case law, all of which had been within the last 40 years dealing with depriving individuals of property rights. He pointed out to the judge that in all instances where the courts had upheld a condemnation depriving property rights, the issue had been the preservation of endangered species. The government was also required to adequately compensate the individuals. He also presented as a clincher that should the case go to trial, the Longleys would be seeking a settlement of seven figures.

Clay was amazed at the passion Forest brought to the courtroom. He had spoken for over an hour without benefit of notes and was finally asked to summarize by the judge. Evidently, the judge observed the same passion. Seeing a sure loser for Byar County should a permanent injunction be denied, the judge reluctantly ruled in favor of the Longleys. Byar

County would be prohibited from enforcing the ordinance against the Longley Family, to include descendants, as long as a livestock operation was continuously maintained on the property.

Mason Griggs and Ray Gott were present for the final ruling. Neither Mason nor Ray looked surprised or disappointed. They were in cordial appearing conversation with Josh Simmons as Forest and the Longleys left the courtroom.

The Longleys were elated with the outcome. On the way home in Clay's Caddy, Forest tried to bring them back down from their high. "If I know Rod Gott, this is not over. This is only the first step. Remember, what we had talked about in the beginning. What they really want is your property. This was only the first round."

"Well, we won this round," Will Longley said.

"What would you anticipate to be the next round," Clay asked.

"Don't know that. This was just to wear you down a little. It didn't cost Griggs and Gott anything. The County, or the taxpayers, paid for this little tiff. I think they figured it cost you a lot to win something they expected to lose anyway."

"We haven't talked about your fee. What does it cost us?" It was Elizabeth's question.

"Not to worry. And there are no expenses except filing fees. Clay here asked me to spend the night at his house, which is good for me. I don't have to spend the night in a motel. He even promised to take me to the best catfish dinner in East Texas." Forest was turning out to be as much a family friend as he was their trusted attorney.

***

On Monday evening, Rod Gott made it to the Bodas' weekly drinks and dinner at the Lake Byar Marina Restaurant. As usual, he brought his son Todd along. Rod had been out of town the previous week during the ruling on the Longley injunction hearing. He had expected the outcome and would have been surprised by anything else. This following Monday was the first opportunity for the next strategy meeting.

"My opinion is there is nothing to gain from an appeal," Mason said.

"No. I think we should just go ahead and do a complete condemnation – a taking for public benefit."

"But the injunctions said something like 'as long as there is a continuously operated livestock,' aah business, I guess. What if they went out of business…temporarily?" Ray said.

"Why would they do that? That would be too obvious a flaw to their defense," Mason said.

"Of course they would be helped," Ray said with a wink.

"What do you mean? Like, they sold all of the cattle at one time or all the cattle died?" Rod threw it out. He didn't know what else Ray could be thinking.

"Mitigating circumstances. The old people still win," Mason said. "If you are thinking about killing the cattle, you had just as soon kill the Longleys." Mason intended his comment in jest. No one laughed, nobody giggled. The solemnity of the moment gave Mason a shudder. This was more than strategic planning. Mason was thinking of the legal implications. The Bodas could be found guilty of conspiracy to commit a crime. He had uttered the words 'kill the Longleys.'

"No. Remember, the objective here is to gain control of the property. We're getting sidetracked. Winning this condemnation, and the county paying off the Longleys, would not motivate them to sell. In fact, with lots of money in the bank, why would they sell?" Rod paused and then continued. "This first condemnation was to soften them up. Let them know the pressure is on to sell. Show them that it is going to cost them money to fight it out. I think it is time to play the next eminent domain card. So far, everything has been quiet. We've bought up every piece of property in the area that has become available over the last year. I'm sure there are some folks who suspect something is in the works. Let's go ahead and file the corporate charter for the convention center. Mason, in the morning, tell Rebecca to file the papers with the State."

"How much do we divulge at this time?" Ray said.

"As soon as the Lake Byar Convention Center corporate charter is filed, we'll get a tax ID, set up bank accounts and an office, and then make a request to the County for eminent domain. At that point we have to say that the property is required for the necessary amenities to make the convention center viable. We've got to tell them about the new golf course."

"We're going to need to get a lot of local media support. Let's not talk about the golf course any more than we have to. We'll emphasize jobs, jobs, jobs. The way these hicks think around here is that golf is frivolous – it's for people with money. They'll say 'we already got a golf course – what we need another one for?' Of course, we will be right. It will represent a lot of jobs. Construction jobs, hotel jobs, restaurant jobs and everything else that trickles down." Rodney got excited every time he thought about the grand plan. It was going to be bigger than anything their father and James Robert ever did. "And we are going to have a piece of every bit of it."

"What do you think about getting the PR guys on board," Mason asked.

"Good idea." Ray said.

"Agree. This is too big a deal to try to save pennies," Rod said. "I'll call Riley from Riley Associates. Best public relations firm in Houston. You all know what a fine job they've done for us in recent political campaigns. No need for us to do all the leg work ourselves anymore like we had to do back when we first got Jimmy Bell elected sheriff. Hire the pros to write the press releases and such. We all in agreement?"

They all were.

***

The Byar County Board of Commissioners was made up of four members, each representing a geographical precinct of the county. The Bodas considered three of the four to be political associates or friends, meaning Griggs & Gott held significant influence over their votes on county issues. Of the three cronies, one owned a construction company and one owned a real estate agency. The third was an attorney in a small private practice. As far as the Bodas were concerned, it was a near synergistic arrangement. If only the forth commissioner were something like a plumbing contractor, or maybe another lawyer, instead of a physician's assistant, it would be perfect. Everyone could be funneling business to each other, but most of all, everyone would have the same financial interest as the Bodas.

At the next meeting of the Board, County Judge Mason Griggs introduced J. Truman Smith. His first name was John, but why be known as John Smith when J. Truman Smith sounded much more substantial? Mr. Smith represented a firm he identified as International Resorts Development. He made a computer slide presentation to the Commissioners that promoted the construction of a 200-room hotel, multiple restaurants, a convention center and a 36-hole championship golf course. The site for the proposed 100 million dollar plus project was around and about the Lake Byar Marina.

J. Truman's presentation, he being a skilled salesman, included many references to a 'million dollar this' and 'million dollar that' – a technique he knew would tend to get the average person giddy over the repeated mentioning of large sums of money. He dropped the name of the PGA pro who was designing the golf courses and included a strong hint that Byar County would one day host a championship tournament. He had everyone seeing dollar signs. When the slide of a map showing the areas to be included was finally presented, there it was. The Longley's Longhorn ranch would make up a portion of the golf course, plus some additional upscale home sites.

Mason Griggs followed up with comments on the importance to the economic prosperity of Byar County for this proposed development to go though. He provided estimates for the number of construction jobs that would be created over the next ten years. He also estimated the number of permanent jobs that would be created. Then there were the millions of dollars that would flow into Byar County each year by attracting travelers, conventioneers, and golfers. There would be increased property and sales tax revenues for the County, the City of Byar, and the surrounding small municipalities.

Mason was playing to both sides of the County Commissioners – the businessmen and the political office holder. The businessmen saw where they were going to benefit personally from the economic development. As an office holder, they would have more of other people's money to spend for the betterment of their constituency through increased tax revenues. This they loved, knowing it would help them increase their "business."

Even Ralph Pender, the Physician Assistant, thought about an increase in population, meaning expansion at Byar Regional Medical Hospital. Everyone in Byar County would benefit – at least in theory. Without repealing the livestock ordinance, or even discussing it, the Commissioners were ready to move forward on the convention center.

Josh Simmons, County Attorney, read aloud the prepared resolution required for vote by the County Commissioners.

"I make the motion to approve the action as presented." It was the construction contractor. The motion was about to receive an immediate second by the lawyer. It was so fast it was as if it had been scripted.

"Call for discussion," said Ralph Pender. His comment was not part of the script. "First, I have to say that I am in favor of the development. However, I have reservations about the taking of private property and turning it over to someone else." Pender had noted in the action read aloud by the County Attorney that once Byar County assumed ownership of the seized property, the real estate would be turned over to Lake Byar Convention Center, Inc.

"Technically, we can say it is turned over, but it will be turned over to what will be a publicly held corporation with stock owned by what we anticipate to be Byar County residents," Simmons said. "The initial shares of stock will be offered to the public at $10 each, so you see, almost anyone can afford to own stock in the corporation."

His comment was greeted with lots of positive head shaking from the other commissioners. What was not said though, and was not for publication, was that the corporation had been chartered by Byar County citizens Rodney Gott, Raymond Gott, and Mason Griggs. The corporation was initially capitalized with the state minimum of $1,000. For that amount, the Bodas received 50 percent of the authorized million shares of stock. The remaining 500,000 shares would be retained by the corporation for later sale to the public. There was without a doubt no one in attendance who wasn't thinking about obtaining some of the shares for themselves.

The lawyer commissioner tapped his pen on the desk a few times and said, "Let me make my position clear. This project is important for Byar County we need to move quickly. These developers...International Resorts Development, can go someplace else. I second the motion on the table to approve the resolution as read."

Another scripted endorsement came next from the real estate commissioner. "These kinds of developments don't come along very often. We can't afford to not take advantage of this opportunity."

Pender, the physician assistant, was overwhelmed by the enthusiasm and eagerness of the businessmen and attorneys. He fell silent.

"The motion has been made and seconded to approve the resolution as read by the County Attorney to proceed with an eminent domain action to acquire real property for the purpose of creating the Lake Byar Convention Center. Gentlemen, what is your pleasure? All those in favor ...." Mason Griggs followed the script and immediately obtained a vote of the Board of Commissioners. Ralph Pender slowly raised his right hand along with the other three commissioners. "Miss Secretary, please record in the official minutes that the resolution was approved unanimously."

***

Clay Longley was browsing some production reports he had brought home that evening. It was 9:00 p.m. when he was disturbed by the ringing phone. He answered another alerting call from Marcus Franks, the reporter.

"Clay, you won't believe this. The County Commissioners just voted to approve filing an eminent domain action for all property within the boundaries of a proposed Lake Byar Convention Center. That is what all the deal is about to get your folks property."

"That answers the big question. Again, Marcus, you didn't call my parents, did you," asked Clay.

"No, I'm just calling you. But if you want to get to them first, better hurry. This news will travel fast."

"Thanks. Let me call them now. Talk to you later," Clay said, and hung up. He left his homework and decided to drive over to his parents. Since his pickup was still living in the driveway, he took it. It was only a few minutes over to the elder Longleys'. Clay caught them still up as he suspected. Their habit was to catch the late evening news at 10 o'clock before retiring.

"What's wrong, son?" Elizabeth Longley said when she answered the doorbell and realized it was Clay.

"Not a big problem, Mom," Clay said as he barged on into the den. He thought to himself that he had mischaracterized the situation. It was a big problem. Donovan warned me it was unlikely to be the end of the conflict with Rod Gott, but I had sure hoped otherwise.

Once he got both parents together, Clay told them about the vote by the County Commissioners. Again, he tried to reassure them that Forest Donovan would represent them to fight the action. "I'll call Forest first thing in the morning. He'll know what we need to do." Clay sensed that his parents were now more upset over the news than they had been with the previous attempt to put them out of business. Before it was the loss of their precious Longhorns, this time it was also the loss of their home and land.

"I don't know what we're gonna do," Will Longley said with resignation. Clay thought he detected defeat in his father's comment.

"It's not right and people will see that." Clay tried to console his parents, but he would have been even less sure had he fully understood the magnitude of the planned development that would take in his family's little Longhorn cattle ranch. The phone rang and it was a close friend of Elizabeth. After a brief exchange, Clay knew it was someone calling to break the bad news. He was glad that he had rushed over to talk before that call. Elizabeth assured her caller that they would not worry too much about the situation and ended the call. Clay stayed until the TV news came on before returning to his own home.

Driving back to his house, Clay thought about Marcus Franks, who always covered the County Board of Commissioners meetings for the local newspaper and was thankful he had again immediately called. Clay and Marcus had become good friends, and after Clay had flown off the required solo test hours on his homebuilt aircraft, had taken Marcus on a number of local flights. On Saturdays, when Clay was working on his plane, or just hanging out at the Byar County Airport, Marcus would stop by and they would talk flying. Sometimes the conversation would drift off to local issues.

Marcus was ten years younger than Clay. Although he had never left Byar, he was by local standards a crack journalist. But he had opted to ply his trade in the hometown he loved instead of seeking fame and fortune in Houston or Dallas. He filled Clay in on the political goings on in Byar County since Clay had been gone. Marcus knew about the Bodas and thought the way they tried to perpetuate the macho trio was childish.

There was no question the Gotts and Mason Griggs held near absolute political control over the county. Their influence extended beyond the county to adjoining counties since Rod was also a State Senator. Marcus had said that it was rumored that Rod Gott would be running for a statewide office in two years, probably Texas Attorney General. Clay knew he owed Marcus, much like he owed Forest Donovan, not just for help, but also for being a friend.

CHAPTER SEVEN

The next day the first order of business for Clay was to place a call to Forest Donovan. He explained the situation from the information he had.

"Of course we knew there was ulterior motive. We knew someone wanted the property and now we know why. I'll tell you, Clay; this can be a tough fight. If the county was planning on retaining ownership of the property, they would have a stronger case. The biggest weakness in their case, from what you're telling me, is that the title will be transferred to private industry for development."

"That's what was in the resolution that passed. The corporation is Lake Byar Convention Center, Inc. They said they would be selling stock to local residents for ownership of the convention center. I don't know how this all works. If my parents have to sell their property, who is buying it? The County?"

"Initially the county. Then for some nominal sum, the property title will be transferred to the corporation formed to build the convention center. There are a lot of things we need to know. I'll be digging in Austin for the corporate charter and anything else I can find out. You do the same there. Remember, I explained about real estate titles being 'in fee.' That means 'subject to and at the sufferance of the king,' or Byar County in this case. If the king decides he can get better rents, or today it is taxes, from another tenant, he has the right to throw one tenant off the land in favor of another. If that is strictly applied, then we are a nation of sharecroppers. The recent Supreme Court decision in the New London, Connecticut case ruled that the city could take by eminent domain private property for redevelopment. Creating a larger tax base for the city was ruled to be a legitimate justification, satisfying the constitutional requirement that the private property being seized was for public use. In the past, local governments have successfully used eminent domain to take private property that was considered to be blighted. In New London, the ruling was that declaring the property to be in a blighted condition was not necessary. This seizure was of well-kept middle class homes and small businesses. In that case they were taking private homes, turning the property over to a development company for $1.00 a year for 99 years, essentially free, and it was intended to create jobs and expand the tax base."

"Yeah Forest, I've been reading about that. It still doesn't seem right."

"The point I'm making is that the Supreme Court ruling does not overturn a time honored constitutional principle. Until this ruling, the doctrine of eminent domain, as applied to economic development, has been ill defined. It has gotten a lot of people excited, but the decision is by no means revolutionary."

As was Forest's intent, he conveyed a measure of uncertainty to Clay. Even though he felt strongly that it should be unconstitutional for the taking of private property and the conveying of that private property to another, it was happening across the country. It happened in instances where property was taken for industrial development. It even happened in New York City where private property was taken and given to the New York Times for a new office building. There were successes against this kind of taking, but there were also failures.

"It is not right, it is just not right." Clay shook his head in resignation. "What do we do about it?"

"Remember, we are seeking fairness. That is also the American tradition. The majority of our founding fathers were not only Christians, but Christians from a specific vein of Christianity. They were Calvinists. As Calvinists, they subscribed to the notion of the utter depravity of man. The notions of separation of powers and judicial restraint stemmed from these men's distrust of excessive government intrusion into the lives of ordinary citizens by those in power."

"Then we still have a defense?"

"Absolutely. The biggest deterrent to this type of condemnation is the reluctance of some political office holders to offend the voting public. But the citizens have to let them know they do not support this. The intent of the Bill of Rights of the Constitution, including the Fifth Amendment, is to protect the citizens from the excesses of government. It is not to give powers to the government. With this New London ruling, it is now up to the states to pass legislation to protect the citizens from the Supreme Court. On the down side in our case, there aren't many property owners to squeal, just a handful. A large part of the land is already owned by the Gotts and they are behind this scheme."

"I guess my folks own the largest remaining portion, 160 acres," Clay said.

"Right. The rest are a few scattered small plots and a few week-ender cabins along the lake. There aren't enough voters to get the politicians' attention. If we get this to court, we have a good argument that an orderly and open process was not followed. There has been no long-term plan and there have been no public hearings. It all seems arbitrary and many of the cases nationwide are, also. There are a slew of abuses."

"I can imagine there are," Clay said.

"You are hearing a lot of developers and their political office holder cronies saying in public that there won't be a rush of eminent domain cases as a result of the Supreme Court decision, but let me tell you, they are beside themselves with giddiness. They will be looking at every opportunity. There is nothing to stop them but the relative influence of the current property owner as opposed to the influence and resources of the coveting property owner."

"Well, it's Rodney Gott behind this. I believe that, unless someone proves to me otherwise. They will sell their land to the county and then the county will turn around and give it back to them. Forest, if you are still willing, we want to fight this." After he'd said that, Clay was overcome with self-doubt. Am I asking Forest, as well as my parents, to wage a heartbreaking, losing battle with the Byar County political elite?

"Clay, let me guarantee you and your parents that I will be in this to the end. Don't let what I say give you any doubts about my commitment. Those of us who believe in personal rights and freedoms have to wage every fight that is presented. We can't afford to sit back and pick our battles and only object when we think we can win. Whenever we don't fight, we lose something. We are not only fighting the big government socialist mentality here, I sincerely believe we will also be going up against political corruption. Let me warn you about that. It can get nasty."

"I've known the Gotts and Mason Griggs since elementary school. Griggs is a follower. He may have been an okay guy had it not been for the Gotts. Rodney Gott is the problem. I imagine Ray and Mason just dance to his beat."

"As soon as there is a legal notice, we'll file for a restraining order and go from there," Forest said as he ended the phone call.

***

The Byar County News ran a front-page story under Marcus Franks' byline. The headline read "Lake Byar Convention Center Planned." A smaller subheading read, "Eminent Domain Abuse or Economic Development?" It reported the actions of the Byar County Commissioners and the proposed Lake Byar Convention Center with the promise of jobs and economic prosperity. The story went on to give some background on eminent domain and the Fifth Amendment to the Constitution. It recounted the recent Supreme Court ruling and gave a brief description of the private property being seized by the county. It did not name the individual property owners affected. It did mention that the nearby Rodney Gott mansion and horse ranch was not included in the private property to be included in the new development. It was a fair story, but Clay would have rather seen it more focused on the taking of private property.

Marcus Franks called Clay after being sure there was ample opportunity to view the paper. "I'm not finished," Marcus said. "There's a lot of story to report here. I think it all smells." Marcus was fortunate to be as free as he was to write and report in Byar County. The Byar County News was the only local paper in the county, and some years before had been purchased by a national chain. The editor, who had been sent in to manage the paper, had no allegiances to the local politicos, and seemed to be more focused on increasing advertising revenues than on news content. Marcus was the only full-time real news reporter on the staff, and the editor relied heavily upon his judgment on news items. Marcus even wrote many of the weekly editorials, although they appeared without his name. He had generally tried to stay politically neutral and not offend the local power structure.

"I'm beginning to think that everything the Gotts touch stinks," Clay said.

"There's a lot of excitement about all the new jobs they promise. They're promising more money for schools, roads and everything else anyone can think of to spend the new tax revenue on. People aren't thinking about how the local government can seize your property. If it doesn't affect them, they don't seem to care. That is my story for next week. Got a lot of research to do and you'll like next week."

Clay's daily visits with his parents became more subdued. Clay told them not to worry, but his waning confidence was becoming obvious to the elderly couple. They started talking about what they were going to do – where they were going to live. Clay tried to reassure them, but his attempts lacked enthusiasm.

"I've got a big house if you're worried about where to live. Live with me and really be retired. You don't have to do this. Those cows are a lot of work anyway," Clay said.

"This is retirement. This is what we want to do for our twilight years. Some people volunteer, some people live in a RV and travel, and some people work at Wal-Mart. We raise Longhorns, not many, just a few. We like to have people stop and look at them. We love to show them off and talk about them to folks we don't even know. It's our life; like that airplane is yours. You made it with your own hands. How would you like it if someone took it away from you?"

Clay submitted to that compelling argument and committed to himself that he would not try to talk them out of resisting. He would stand by them for whatever they desired. No, he wouldn't want anyone to tell him he had to give up his homebuilt plane. Not that it was worth that much money, but it was his and it provided him a great deal of joy. *Clay Longley, we the government have decided that you no longer have a right to your joy. We, in our infinite wisdom, hereby rule that we take your joy and give it to someone else. Hell no. No way.*

In a couple of days, Clay read Marcus' new article. It was noon on a Wednesday when the small weekly paper came out. Clay got his copy delivered to his office. The headline read, "Golf Course To Take Home." There was no question where Marcus stood. Clay thought Marcus' views to be unusual, since he assumed most current day journalists to be on the liberal side of big government issues. Marcus, in previous discussions with Clay, had intimated that he was a Libertarian. There seemed to be a number of issues where Marcus thought the government had no business meddling in the lives of citizens. Marcus, for example, felt there should be no laws concerning an individual's growth and consumption of marijuana. He also felt the income tax to be unconstitutional – he would abolish Social Security, as well as most other Federal services.

In the article, Marcus identified the land and landowners affected by the seizure. He said most of the Longley ranch would be the location of a golf course with some portion reserved for executive style housing for the very affluent. He also pointed out several instances where private property had been taken, and then the redevelopment project, for one reason or another, went bust. As often as not the economic prosperity promised never materialized.

When those redevelopments that featured hotel, restaurant and retail establishments were completed, after the early-phase good-paying construction jobs, the community was left with mostly low paying hotel maid, waitress, and clerk jobs. Those kind of jobs resulted in attracting transients and others on the lower half of the economic scale.

Marcus presented historical quotes on the protection of private property and the pursuit of happiness. He also cited a case where property owners successfully defeated an attempt to take their property to provide for the construction of a golf course. He ended the article with a quote attributed to Elizabeth Longley, Clay's mother. "This farm has been in my family for over 130 years. If they can take our home so that some already rich people can become even richer, then they will take your home or your business too when some influential person promises to build something bigger in its place."

Clay thought the article very compelling. He did not see how the average guy, who really thought about the issue, could come down on the side of Byar County. Then he recalled what Marcus had said previously. There was a lot of excitement over the new jobs and the new schools and everything the increased tax revenues would bring. He wondered how many, if they even bothered to read the article, would consider it to be a deprivation of liberty of a citizen. The Griggs and Gott faction would not bother defending the condemning of the private property. They would never want to put individual faces to the victims, or even intimate there were any victims. Clay expected them to only talk up the economic boom that was coming.

CHAPTER EIGHT

It was later in the afternoon, a couple of hours before Clay would leave his office for the day, when he received the phone call. It was his mother.

"Daddy is talking to a deputy sheriff. Someone shot four of our herd." Elizabeth was excited and infuriated.

"No! Who would do that?"

"Daddy found them this afternoon. They were all fine early this morning."

"Let me wrap up things here and I'll be there in a little while. Go find out what the deputy is going to do. I'll see you in a bit." Clay wanted to get off the phone and get going. He stuck his head into Marvin MacDonald's office to reschedule a contracts meeting that was to begin in a few minutes. Marvin had been keeping up with the ongoing legal saga and had displayed interest in the Longley's plight, so Clay told him of the phone call before leaving the office. He told Millie to get him by cell phone if necessary, and left.

When Clay arrived at the Longley ranch, the Sheriff's Office patrol car was still there. His father and a deputy were just walking back from the pasture where, evidently, the dead cattle were found.

"This is our son Clayton," Will said, introducing Clay to the deputy. "This is Deputy Sheriff Gilcrest."

"Richard Gilcrest," the deputy said, extending his right hand while holding a notebook in his left. The deputy was fortyish, lean, and gray-headed with a thick mustache. He wore a cream-colored western straw hat, a blue-gray uniform, and a black police belt with pistol and all the police equipment hanging from it. "Looks like someone took a few shots at some animals," the deputy reported. "Not a big deal. Happens every once in a while. No tellin' where the shots came from."

"Yeah, we have four dead purebred Longhorns," Will said.

"Well, I suggest you butcher those animals while you can salvage something," Deputy Gilcrest spat out what sounded like instructions to Will.

"That doesn't salvage anything. Those animals are worth thousands each," Clay said.

Will was getting heated. "A couple of those Longhorns were worth up to $10,000 each. The other two were about $4,000 each. This is more than a prank."

"All I can do is fill out this investigative report. You can pick up a copy at the Sheriff's Office in a couple of days." Deputy Gilcrest excused himself, got into his patrol car and left.

"Hell! They aren't going to do anything," Will said in disgust.

"Do you have insurance that covers this kind of loss," Clay asked his father.

"Insurance? We have homeowners and vehicles. No, I don't guess."

"It's a casualty loss. You can take it off your taxes. You need to get an appraisal to document your loss. Who can do that?" Clay wanted to take care of as much as possible before evidence was lost.

"I'll call the Perry Brothers over at the auction barn. They'll know what these cows were worth."

"Go do that now, Dad, and I want to take a look for myself. Where are they – the downed cattle?"

"Down past the hill by the west stock pond," Will said, pointing. "Take the four-wheeler." Will turned toward the house to go in and make the phone call.

Clay returned to his company car where he had a small digital camera. He took the camera, mounted his father's green four-wheel ATV and headed down toward the stock pond. It was over a small rise, and then at the bottom of the slope, about a quarter of a mile away. Clay had ridden around the property a few times recently and knew where he was going. He parked the ATV some fifty feet away from the carcasses, and approached on foot.

Two of the animals were the Longleys' most prized Longhorns. Clay had not been this close to them previously. Their horns were impressive, over five feet, tip to tip. Clay noted the animals were facing the same direction, although about 30 feet apart. There was little grass near the edge of the pond. It was mostly dry ground, with a little mud near the water's edge. There was no indication on the ground that the animals thrashed around prior to falling to the ground. One of the animals had dropped to its knees and looked as if it were sleeping, with its head stretched out in front. The other was on its side. Clay took several photos.

Clay thought about Marcus Franks and the news worthiness of the story. He pulled his cell phone from his belt and placed a call to his cell number. Marcus was at his desk, immediately agreed it was a story, and promised to be right out.

Clay continued to take more pictures. The other two carcasses were further away from the water hole. They were in the grass and appeared to have been grazing. Again, each had a single gunshot entry wound in the front quarter area. Clay looked in the direction he thought the shots would have come from. It was less than two hundred yards to the tree line that ran along a fence. The fence was a cross fence that cattlemen typically use to separate grazing areas. This particular fence separated the hay meadow from the pasture. The meadow of approximately 20 acres was where Will grew and cut hay for the winter feeding of his cattle.

Clay got back on the ATV and rode back up the fence line toward the gate to the meadow. He opened the gate, drove through and closed the gate behind him. The cattle were kept out of the meadow until the fall when the last of the hay was cut. He eased along the edge of the meadow, until reaching the nearest point to the downed cattle in the pasture.

He got off and looked around. There it was – plain for anyone to see. The grass was trampled down at the fence. Nearby, at the edge of the meadow, another ATV had been. The meadow had been plowed in the last year, and the soil at the edge was relatively soft. The knobby tire tracks were visible. The vehicle had come across the green Bahia grass; the trail through the depressed grass was clearly visible. The tire tracks turned and went back across the meadow in the same direction. Clay shot some pictures.

Clay saw his father, Marcus Franks, and another person walking over the hill toward the pond. He yelled to get their attention, and then waived to them to come to him. They altered their course and came through the same meadow gate Clay had come through. Clay met them at the gate on the ATV and turned it over to his father. The third member of the group turned out to be a young woman who was introduced to Clay as Rita, a photographer for the newspaper. She had two cameras on straps hanging around her neck. Each camera sported a substantial lens. Clay then led the trio back along the fence line to the spot he had been scouting.

"I'm pretty sure this is the spot from which someone took the shots. It looks like they came across the meadow from over there and left the same way," Clay said, pointing diagonally across the meadow. The far side was heavily wooded. The fence and the property line of the Longley property was another hundred yards into the trees. At the suspicious point, Clay pointed out the tire tracks and the trail left across the long lush grass.

"There is no way anyone could get in from there unless they cut my fence," Will said.

"They probably did," Marcus said. "Rita, can you get pictures where that will show up?" Marcus indicated the grass trail. "And these tracks, too."

"Yes, I think that will come out," Rita said while adjusting one of her cameras. She started snapping pictures.

"Look over here. See all this grass mashed down. Someone stomped around in here," Clay showed the area closest to the fence. Will and Marcus examined the ground.

"Look here!" Marcus pointed to the ground off to the right of the trampled grass. "Rita, come get this." Clay and Will both looked before they stepped back to let Rita by. In the deep grass was a brass shell casing – just one. Rita followed Marcus' pointing finger with her camera at the ready. She snapped several pictures, with each one moving in closer to the shiny brass bullet case until the last shot was no more than 18 inches away.

"Get this grass area too," Clay said.

"How about you all back up and let me get the full area." Rita also backed up and took pictures of the full area that included the edge of the meadow, the ATV tracks and the spot where the shooter was surmised to have stood. She then moved in and started taking more shots across the fence toward the stock pond and the downed animals. Marcus produced a white handkerchief from his hip pocket and gently picked up the spent cartridge, being careful not to rub it. He wrapped it loosely and placed it in his front shirt pocket.

"This may be good evidence," Marcus said. "There ought to be more around if he shot four cows." All four started scouring the tall grass, pushing it aside with hands and sticks looking for additional brass. After a minute or so they were satisfied there were no more spent cartridges.

"Whoever it was must have picked up the rest of the brass and for some reason wasn't able to find this one. Let's get some shots of the Longhorns before it gets too dark," Marcus said to Rita.

"I'm going to see where these tracks go," Will said, getting back on his own ATV.

Will headed out across the meadow, riding his four-wheeler, as the other three walked back toward the meadow gate. By the time they got to the gate, Will came roaring back. "Cut the fence right out by that old logging road," he said. "Guess they went back up to the highway from there and could have gone anywhere."

While Rita shot a number of photos of the dead Longhorns, Will rode back up toward the house to meet another man he saw coming over the rise. It was one of the Perry brothers, from the auction barn, who Will was expecting. They rode double back down to the stock pond. Mr. Perry was dressed in jeans and cowboy boots and was just as old, if not older, than Clay's father.

"I don't see how that deputy you said was out here could have missed that spot over by the fence," Marcus said.

"I'll tell you how," Will said. "He wasn't interested in investigating anything. He just looked at the cattle and said, 'yeah, they're dead.'" Will flung an exasperated hand in the air.

"Will, you got some pedigree papers on these animals don't you," Mr. Perry asked.

"Sure. They are all registered with TLBAA. Got good paper on all four," Will said. "You know, the Texas Longhorn?"

"Breeders Association of America," Perry said with a hand raised to stop Will, finishing his unneeded explanation. He was very familiar with the historic association that registered the early Longhorn cattle. "Get me those papers and, in a day or so, I'll have some close estimates on the value of these cows. You know we ought to take the heads of these two for mounting. These are prize animals. I'd say just save the horns from the other two."

"Guess I'll do that," Will said with resignation in his voice.

"You know, since the Sheriff's Department is not really investigating this crime, I think you should call in someone else," Marcus said.

"Who do you call? It didn't happen on the highway, so we wouldn't call Department of Public Safety," Clay said, referring to the Texas highway patrol.

"Maybe, call the Texas Rangers. This is kind of like cattle rustlings."

"Probably a good idea. Think I'll call Forest Donovan first and see what he says." Clay pulled out his cell phone, pulled up Forest's office number and placed the call. By then, it was after most peoples' regular office hours, but he got Forest in a couple of rings. He quickly briefed Forest on the events of the afternoon. Clay described the scene, the ATV tracks and the found shell cartridge.

"I agree. Texas Rangers would be good. We are talking about a lot of money – a major felony," Forest replied. "Mind if I make a call here in Austin, first? This all smells of something bigger than random vandalism. Sounds like y'all are doing the right things. Keep the brass shell clean. Don't touch it."

"Sure. Whatever you think is the best course," Clay said, and they exchanged goodbyes. Clay relayed to the others what the lawyer had said.

"You keep this," Marcus said, taking his handkerchief containing the shell from his shirt pocket and handing it gently to Clay. I got a story to start working on. How about you e-mail me the pictures you took and between you and Rita we'll pick a couple of good ones for the paper." Marcus and Rita walked back toward the house while Mr. Perry, Will and Clay thought about what to do with the carcasses.

"Can't leave 'em out here overnight," Mr. Perry said. "The coyotes or wolves will ruin those heads."

"Let's call Jonsey and see if he can get a couple of his guys from the slaughterhouse out here. Let me go make some calls," Will said. Will and Mr. Perry doubled up on the ATV again, and headed for the house. Clay took off walking.

By the time Clay reached the house, Mr. Perry was gone. His father had been on the phone and was waiting for a call back. In a short time, the phone rang. After a brief conversation Will came back into the kitchen where Clay was talking with his mother and said that two men would be out shortly. They would load the carcasses and take them to the slaughterhouse. Jonsey would even take care of the heads and horns and get it all to Huntsville to a taxidermist. Will would have to get with the taxidermist to tell him what he wanted done. The rest of the carcasses would go to the rendering plant. He would have to pay for their overtime, but they would take care of everything. It would be worth it. Otherwise, it was limited what he would be able to do with four 1,200 to 1,800 pound animals. Clay left letting them know he would call as soon as he heard from Forest.

It was mid morning the next day before Clay received a call-back.

Forest was excited. "I talked to the Texas Rangers here in Austin. They referred me to Company A, that's the office located in Houston. I finally tagged up with a Lieutenant Rojas. I started telling him about what is going on in Byar and believe it or not, he says he knows you. Said he was originally from Byar and went to high school with you."

"Rojas? Manny Rojas is a Texas Ranger?"

"He said Manuel, but guess that is him. Anyway, he wants to meet with you. Can he meet you at your office? He wants to come up there next week."

"Great. Anytime. I'll make time."

"Here is his phone number. Give him a call and set up the time." Forest gave Clay the number and further told Clay that based on what he had told the Ranger, the circumstances were enough to warrant an investigation.

Clay had not been the type to keep up with his high school classmates. He had gone off to college, to the Army, and then had his work career. He had received a couple of invitations to class reunions over the years, but had never felt he had the time to attend. Once out of college, he had been back to Byar only once or twice a year, and that was to visit his parents. Since being back in Byar he had realized most of his old acquaintances had left the area, as he now knew Manny Rojas had. He and Clay had been good friends, teammates in football and baseball. Clay surprised himself at the amount of pleasant anticipation he had at the thought of seeing his old pal.

Once Clay got Ranger Lieutenant Rojas on the phone, it was like their own private reunion. First item was to catch up on each other's life after leaving Byar. Manny told Clay he had joined the Air Force following high school. He was an Air Police, and had been stationed in North Carolina and Germany during his service. He had also picked up an Associate

Degree while in the Air Force and had finished college following his discharge, receiving a degree in Criminal Justice. Manny said he was a patrolman for the Texas Department of Public Safety for seven years before being selected for the Texas Rangers.

Clay was delighted to hear how well his old teammate had done; a young Hispanic from a small East Texas town, to the Air Force, college degree, state highway patrolman and now among the ranks of the 100 or so officers in the Texas Rangers – an illustrious organization with a long and glorious past, beginning in the early days of Texas defending against raiding Native Americans, to the current status as a State Police force. Clay knew all about them. A certain measure of relief swept over him as he considered the implications of possibly having the State's premier law enforcement team involved. His musings were interrupted as Rojas continued to speak.

"Look, Clay, I have to be in Byar anyway on other business. I'll include looking into this potential investigation in the same trip."

"Manny, you're the best. Call me when you get in town and we can talk."

"You bet." The click of Manny's cell phone in Clay's ear was a punctuation to end the best conversation he'd had in a long time on this subject.

***

Rod called a special Bodas meeting for Friday evening. In times past, James Robert had called it the Board meeting. Now, Rod just called it the Bodas. He was clearly hyped. Earlier in the day, Rod had emphasized the importance of the meeting. Word had quickly spread about the shooting of the Longley cattle and his gut feeling was that it was bad news.

"Even with this week's newspaper story on eminent domain, we still had things going our way. While I had rather seen a more supportive reporting on the economic development opportunity, that crap didn't hurt us too bad. Now you add this story to it and it's going to look like someone is after the Longleys. If I knew who did this, I'd be kicking his ass through next year." Rod was on a rant. His son Todd was fixated on his soft drink, not looking up.

"Maybe we can get a favorable spin on the story in next week's News," Ray said, referring to the Byar County News that would be due out next Wednesday. "I'm thinking that the D.A.'s Office and the Sheriff's Office can get a jump on this. Maybe we can tag this to some personal vendetta against the Longleys. You know, something that has nothing to do with the condemnation."

Mason offered caution. "I would low key it with the Sheriff. We got another problem brewing there. You heard about the trusties getting the gun cabinet open last week. It was just fortunate they couldn't get their hands on any ammunition. Sheriff Bell has problems at the jail,"

"Yeah, ain't that just a pisser. How hard can it be to run a damn county jail. Hell, they don't ever have more than a dozen locked up down there. But, Ray, you're probably on the right track. Get with the editor or that reporter and get out front on this. Write the story for them if you have to. We don't want this thing stirring up sympathy for those old people." Even though Rod generally ran roughshod on the other Bodas, he was not usually the type to pretend he was the only one with a good idea.

"Had we known the newspaper was for sale a couple years ago, we could have bought it and we wouldn't be worrying about what they are going to print.," Mason said. "Now, just in case this gets picked up by the Houston Chronicle, or the Huntsville paper, and they make some inquiries, we need to be prepared. We have to let Sheriff Bell know to refer all reporters to the D.A.'s Office.

"What's that reporter's name? – the one from here," Rod said.

"Marcus Franks. He is from Byar. He's at all the Board of Commissioners, City Council, everything."

"We got anything on the guy? Can we put a little pressure on him if necessary?"

"No." Mason shook his head. "He's young – seems like a pretty good writer. I'm sure he doesn't make much at that little paper."

"Why don't we start talking to him about some fancy job somewhere out there, in the future. Get him on our side. Something like Public Relations Director for the Convention Center?" Rod was thinking out loud.

Ray snapped his fingers. "Yeah! We can string him along for quite a while on that. Doesn't mean we ever have to hire him."

"Okay. I'm going to get with Riley and try to get some positive PR stuff in the papers and maybe on the Houston TV stations. Probably more people up here see the TV news than read our little county rag anyway. I want us to double up on this. Ray, you get with Sheriff Bell and Mason, you contact that reporter. Don't let him write the story by himself. Kind of get to know him and dangle the idea of that job. I just thought of another angle. What about moving our legal notices? I don't mean actually moving them; I mean hint to the editor that the News may be losing the County legal notice business."

"We are required by law to post legal notices in the local paper. We might rationalize that the News lacks adequate circulation to serve that function. Frankly, I don't know if we can get away with it. We can solicit bids from the News and some surrounding papers. Maybe that will get the attention of the managing editor. Make them more attuned to not offending us." Mason said it like "us" and Byar County were one in the same. As far as the brokering of power, the Bodas all knew it was true.

"Looks like we all have something to work on the next few days. I have to head to Austin on Monday. I'll be doing my thing from there. Y'all ready to eat? Todd, find us a waiter," Rod said without waiting for a response.

CHAPTER NINE

Ray called the Sheriff after he got home from the Friday night meeting. No point in waiting and he certainly didn't mind infringing on Jimmy Bell after hours. If it had been anyone other than one of the Gotts or Judge Griggs, Sheriff Bell would have blown them off until Monday. Bell thought of himself as part of the politically elite of Byar County and in full alliance with the Bodas. He'd never realized that the Bodas had no allegiance to him. It was a one-way street.

"You had a deputy out at the Longley's place for an investigation on those dead cows. I want the original of that report. Don't keep any copies. Get your hands on it in the morning and lock it up. Bring it to my office first thing Monday morning. Make sure everyone in your department knows to refer questions to the D.A.'s Office. And, whoever that deputy was, send him on vacation – out of town. I don't want anyone talking to him."

"Yes, sir," Sheriff Bell said, "I'll go take care of that first thing. That was Deputy Gilcrest. He'll be happy to get an unexpected fishing trip."

"And get that report to me early Monday."

***

There wasn't much Clay could do for his parents on Saturday morning. He stopped by their house for coffee and then headed on over to the Byar County Airport. After the initial test flights, Clay had started adding goodies to his plane. He installed position and anti-collision lights and flight instruments for night flying, and had plans for a Global Position System (GPS). Often it was near dark before he had a chance to get airborne during the work-week. Weekends would find Clay at the airport for at least part of each day. His hangar was equipped with a toilet and shower, something most hangars at the small field did not enjoy. The airport consisted of a single paved and lighted runway, a fuel pump that accepted credit cards for self-fueling, and a dozen private hangars. There was no full time attendant. The primary task of the so-called airport manager was to collect rents and to keep the grass mowed. Marcus had said he would be by later in the morning. Clay was studying the wiring hookup for the new GPS when Marcus arrived.

"Can't stay long. You'll never guess who I have an appointment with. County Judge Mason Griggs. He called me early this morning and wants to give me an interview for the paper. Wants to talk about the Convention Center."

"That ought to be interesting." Clay pondered why Griggs would call

Marcus.

"I tried to call him last week and couldn't even get through. He never called back and now he wants to meet with me." Marcus said it as much as a question as a statement.

"Meet you today, huh? Can't even wait until Monday? Must be something hot or something really bothering them."

"Only one way to find out," Marcus said. "I'll give you a call and if you're still out here, I'll swing back by."

"I'll be here," Clay said as he dug his money clip from his jeans pocket. He handed Marcus a twenty and said, "How about running by King's and get us a couple of bar-b-que sandwiches. If we don't get any thunderstorms, we'll get up and bounce around the county this afternoon."

Both offers were agreeable to Marcus. He took the money and left for his appointment at the courthouse.

***

The Byar County Courthouse was old and outwardly appeared the same as when it had been built in the 1930s. The internal modifications were the addition of elevators and a new heating and air conditioning system. Like so many small town courthouses, it sat on the square in the center of the oldest part of the business district. The site of the old Gott General Merchandise Store was nine or ten blocks away.

Except for a Deputy stationed at a desk inside the front door, the building looked to be empty. Marcus greeted the elderly deputy whom he had seen around the courthouse for years. He told the deputy he had an appointment with the judge and the deputy replied that Judge Griggs was up in his office. Marcus knew well where the County Judge Office was located on the third floor, but had never been inside. He opened the eight foot mahogany door and entered into what was a well-appointed outer office, obviously equipped for clerical support of Byar County business. It was empty.

"Judge Griggs," Marcus called out. He felt the Judge was in his office off to the left with the door open, but could not see him.

"Come on in, Marcus," came the greeting from the open door. It sounded friendly.

"Good morning, Judge," Marcus said as he cautiously stepped into the private chamber. It was an impressive office furnished with massive mahogany furniture. Marcus thought, such a poor county – such a rich office? Nothing is too good for our government officials.

"Glad you could come by, Marcus," Mason said as he came forward to shake hands. It was an uncharacteristic greeting from the county judge, who had never more than nodded to the younger small town reporter. Marcus had not been aware that the judge even knew his name. He invited Marcus to sit at the conference table placed perpendicular to the judge's enormous desk.

"I've been wanting to get together with you, Marcus," Mason said, fingering the manila folder in front of him. "It looks like you are 'the man' down at the paper."

He's patronizing me, Marcus thought, but let him go on.

"We have accumulated a lot of economic data on the proposed Byar County Convention Center that we feel is important to the citizens. We want to share that with you so you can present a balanced view of what this means to our future. We are not an affluent county and this is our chance to grab the brass ring. It is literally the rising tide that will lift all boats."

Marcus thought about the overuse of metaphors – something a writer would not do.

"We have complete data on the investments to be made here in Byar County. You'll be able to see in these reports that we are talking about millions of dollars. Professional golf courses are costing a million dollars a hole. That's $36 million on just the golf course. Here is a report prepared by International Resorts on the number of jobs that will be created. Here is the amount for the new salaries that will be created. These are the permanent jobs for people right here in Byar County. And you know, we need these jobs." The judge paused and looked at the reporter to gauge his agreement. Marcus was non-committal in comment and expression.

He continued, "With all these folks having money to spend, it means a flow down to not only the existing small businesses, but also new business opportunities in Byar. With this comes increased revenue to the public coffers in the form of sales taxes and, of course, property taxes. That will be a huge benefit to all the citizens of Byar County. This is so big that even surrounding counties and municipalities will benefit."

Marcus tugged on his cheek, settled back in his chair. "Judge, I appreciate you asking me here, and for providing this information. However, I would like to ask some questions and perhaps get some quotes that I can use in an article." He pulled a miniature tape recorder from his shirt pocket and held it up for Mason to see.

"Absolutely," Mason said, grinning. He felt the interview was going the way he intended.

Marcus punched the recorder on and placed it on the table between him and the judge, thinking, I'll start off easy on him. "Well first, let's do some background. How did this whole project come about?"

"Actually we owe a lot of the credit to State Senator Gott. He is responsible for bringing the Byar County opportunity to the attention of International Resorts. Hosting national business conventions is a big and lucrative business, but you must have facilities that are attractive. We already have Lake Byar, a phenomenal asset. We have great fishing or just boating of any type. We are close enough to Houston to attract national and international travelers – it is a pleasant limo ride up here from Bush Intercontinental. But everyone doesn't go for the water. Therefore, we will also have a 36-hole championship class golf course. I can see Byar becoming a vacation destination." Mason's expression showed he thought he had provided good material for the reporter to work with.

Marcus gave a small nod, but no smile. "In previous statements, it was indicated that Lake Byar Convention Center would be owned by the citizens of Byar County through stock offering. If that is the case, exactly what part does International Resorts play?"

"The forte of International Resorts is resort development and operations. They will provide the facilities design, the engineering, and manage construction. Once complete, and understand, we are talking about something that will take four to six years, they will manage maintenance and operations."

"And Byar County?"

"Under the auspices of the County Government, all of the property to be dedicated to this development is being consolidated. That property will be turned over to Lake Byar Convention Center for a token fee on a 99-year lease, and as we said, that is a corporation principally owned by the stockholders, the citizens of Byar County."

"Thank you, Judge. I understand so far. But what is fuzzy to me is the whole financial scheme. I mean, where is the money coming from to make this all happen?" Marcus raised an eyebrow and noticed a slight wince on the judge's face.

That's not the question I want, the judge thought. I need to soft shoe. The county must do a bond offering and there'll be a whole array of new taxes. That tidbit hasn't yet been sprung on the public. Plus the fact that the Bodas already have half of the shares of stock in the convention center corporation and will be paying International Resorts a 20% ownership. Think, Mason, think.

The judge managed a smiley face. "We will be joining the world of high finance. That will be something new for Byar County. The Byar County Convention Center will be issuing long-term bonds that will be liquidated through operations. Beyond that, I cannot get into the financial details." Mason leaned back and thought, God I hope he swallows that and leaves well enough alone.

"One last topic, if you don't mind Judge – the Will and Elizabeth Longley farm. It is 160 acres and it is by far the largest track of land that the county is attempting to seize for this project."

Mason knew this was a flat statement, not yet a question, and he had to deal with it before it became one. "The particular piece of property in question is integral to the entire project. The public benefit from this development is far more significant than the operation of what is essentially a hobby farm for the raising of a few head of cattle. An effort was made to purchase the property in question. The owners refused the offer, which left the county with no alternative."

Marcus started boring in. "My understanding is that a representative from Griggs and Gott Law Firm, Ms. Rebecca Rals, threatened the Longleys with condemnation if they refused to sell."

"Certainly Ms. Rals never intended that to be a threat. It was an explanation."

"Who was Ms. Rals representing? Who was the intended purchaser?"

"I ah – wouldn't know that," Mason said.

Not a very good liar, Marcus thought.

Mason cleared his throat and continued. "That is a client confidentiality issue and even though I am a partner in the law firm, I excuse myself from those details when there may be a conflict with county business."

Marcus' voice was low and calm. "And then you passed a county ordinance to prohibit livestock on that particular piece of property that would preclude a portion of the income of the property owners. It was all in an effort to force the Longleys into selling." The look in Marcus' eyes was as accusatory as his words.

"I don't recall the time line of all of the events, so let's say the county needs to obtain ownership of the property in question for the success of this project, a development that is the future of Byar County." Mason squirmed a bit in his chair.

Marcus folded his arms and leaned back. "When the Longleys continued to refuse to rollover, the County decided to take their property by eminent domain. That isn't enough, so someone cut their fence, entered their property, and killed four of their prized Longhorn cattle."

Marcus detected another slight wince on Mason's face at that last statement. Mason said, "I have heard that. It is a very unfortunate event. I assure you it had absolutely nothing to do with this project. In fact it has the appearance of some personal grudge that someone holds against the Longleys." That last statement was supposed to be the D.A.'s assessment. It was another lie, but Mason figured the more it was repeated, the more it would be believed. He looked at his watch and faked surprise. "Oh my, look at the time. I do have another appointment, so we will need to cut this short."

Marcus noticed that Mason broke eye contact each time he lied. The interview had gotten out of hand as far as Mason was concerned. He did not feel like he had said anything that would come out too bad in print, but wanted to wrap it up before any more was said. He then recalled the second part of his assignment – dangle the job.

"Marcus, one last thing, right quick. I have been reading your articles for some time. You're a talented reporter and writer. Have you considered moving on to greener pastures, so to speak?"

"What do you mean by that?" The tape was still running.

"The Convention Center. Remember, I said there are going to be a number of excellent positions. The Center will need a Public Relations Director – writing press releases, advertising, and maybe some type of newsletter. What would you think about something like that?"

"Well, that really sounds interesting." It would sound interesting to most reporters at a small-time paper, but Marcus recognized it for what it was. He knew that he was a bit of a muckraker at heart and signing on with the bad guys would not be what a muckraker does. Griggs and Gott were trying to co-op him.

"I want you to think about it. You could have a very bright future and be a leader in the future of Byar County." Marcus noted that the judge broke eye contact once again.

"Thank you Judge Griggs. This will be very helpful in my next report." Marcus stood and retrieved his tape recorder. He clicked it off, returned it to his pocket, and shook hands with Mason, taking the economic data folder prepared for him.

***

When Marcus arrived with the bar-b-que sandwiches and Cokes his first words to Clay were, "Do I look like a Public Relations Director?"

"Yeah, but you don't act like one." Clay wanted to get the details on the interview and didn't know what the P.R. banter was about.

"I think they believe they can buy me off with a fancy job offer. I got it all on tape," Marcus said. Clay had already rolled the plane out of his hangar, anticipating Marcus' return to the airport and their afternoon flight. They retreated to the back of the south-facing hangar to get out of the direct sun. With the help of a floor fan, the temperature was bearable and the seating for lunch was the concrete floor. Marcus pulled the tape recorder from his pocket and let it play while they enjoyed brisket sandwiches.

"I hate to burst your bubble, but they didn't give you a firm job offer,"

Clay said laughing after the tape finished.

"Yeah, I know. Hey, did you know that Mason can't look you in the eye when he is telling a lie?"

"I never noticed. Haven't had any contact with him in years."

"In a way, I think that is an admirable trait. Surprising about a lawyer, but good."

***

Mason scripted the call for the Byar County Purchasing Office to make to Samuel Collins, the managing editor of the News. It included a statement that Byar County would be taking bids for future publication of County Legal Notices and solicited a bid from the News.

The call was a total surprise to the editor who had been struggling to increase advertising and circulation and had considerable pressure from the national media company that had bought the local paper. Collins asked to meet with Judge Griggs to discuss the impending change. Loss of the County business would be devastating to the small paper, already in a tenuous financial situation. After being placed on hold for a minute, the agent returned to the line with the message that Judge Griggs could meet with Mr. Collins that afternoon at two at the Judge's office. The response from Collins fit Mason's plan exactly. He wanted to get head to head with the editor and in one manner or another let him know that the paper should be fully supporting the county concerning the proposed convention center.

Collins arrived at the courthouse a few minutes early. He briefly reviewed the folder of material he had hastily assembled before entering the Byar County Judge's office. He had a News financial statement and hoped to convince the Judge that the paper was on shaky grounds. He included reports from other local papers owned by the parent company showing advertising rates and that the News' rates were right in line.

"Mr. Collins, Mason Griggs," was the greeting from the Judge – they had not previously met.

"Pleased to meet you, Judge Griggs, and thank you for seeing me this afternoon."

"Well, I understand your concern. Let me tell you, this is just a business matter. It is something our County Treasurer initiated." Mason briefly looked away and pointed to a chair at the conference table. They exchanged small talk for a couple of minutes, then Collins started his pitch.

"I have some data here that I would like to review with you. I feel it is important to Byar County to maintain a local paper, and feel that we have served the County well over the years."

"You know, I completely agree with you, Mr. Collins." Mason knew he had to be careful. How does a public official go about abridging the freedom of press? He didn't need to review any of the data. It wasn't necessary for what he was doing. "It is important that Byar County and our local paper work together for the betterment of our constituency. There are significant events happening in the County where full support of the News would be appreciated." Mason didn't feel he had yet said anything that would make him guilty of abuse of his official duties. He waited for a response from Collins. He felt uncomfortable with the next thing he had to say.

"Are you referring to the proposed convention center and the seizure of private property by the County?" The editor was well informed on the current events and he had already approved the lead story written by Marcus that would appear in the Wednesday edition.

Mason hesitated and kept his eyes on his fingertips rubbing the polished surface of the mahogany table. "I suppose I am. I can't over emphasize how important the Byar County News is in forming public opinion. Any news items printed in your paper that cast doubt on this project creates, ah, a strain between the County and the newspaper. We would like to see positive support from the News."

"Judge, I know there are many in the media who believe it is their mission to influence public opinion. They first decide how they want their readers to react to a news story and then manipulate their reporting accordingly." Collins wasn't through with his thought, but Mason interrupted.

"Correct, Mr. Collins. How something is reported makes all the difference in the world." Mason was so deep in his own thoughts he had only half heard what Collins had said, and in fact misinterpreted the comment. "I am prepared to intercede on behalf of the News to ensure there is no change in the posting of County legal notices."

He's going to conclude like that? Collins thought. How very unlike a lawyer. He assumes wrongly we're of the same mind. "Thank you very much, Judge Griggs. I know you have Byar County's best interest at heart. I know the News and I are dedicated to the future of Byar County." Collins stood, exchanged a handshake with the Judge and again thanked him for seeing him so promptly. The editor left the courthouse rethinking the brief meeting. There was no question in his mind what had transpired. The Byar County Judge had offered a *quid pro quo* – something for something in exchange. Collins had already met with Marcus in the morning and had listened to his taped interview with Judge Griggs. He was wishing he had the forethought to have brought a concealed tape recorder to this meeting.

The choice was clear for Samuel Collins. He was 59 years old, had been bumping around newsrooms for 35 years, and had never made it to the big time. He took the job as managing editor of the News and figured it was his last assignment. He could easily go along and get along. There was also no question in his mind that if the fragile finances of the News grew any worse, he would be dismissed – canned – fired.

He had developed a jaded view of his chosen profession. Journalism had become that ex-girlfriend who had cheated on him. He had gotten into the business when reporting ethics meant something. Collins had observed what was happening and saw who was getting ahead. For the most part, it was the broadcast journalist these days. He had met some of the pretty faces who he had thought were quite good, and discovered most of them were not. Far too often, he had encountered so-called journalist who believed it was his or her job to create the news, not report the "Ws" in a clear, concise and understandable form. He had never sold out and he would not do it now.

***

The first stop for Ranger Lieutenant Manuel Rojas was the Byar County Sheriff's Office. He spent over an hour with Sheriff Jimmy Bell gathering details on the recent breach of procedures at the jail. Two of the trusties in jail on burglary charges had broken into the Sheriff's office, forced open a cabinet and got possession of three handguns. Fortunately, there was no ammunition stored in the cabinet. The trusties had hidden the guns in the jail kitchen. A number of violations of jail standards were noted and discussed with the sheriff.

"One last item before I go," Ranger Rojas said, "I would like a copy of the investigation report on the incident at the Longley Ranch from last week."

"Don't have one," Sheriff Bell said. You'll have to get that from the D.A. It went over at eight o'clock this morning. D.A. asked for it."

"Surely, you have a copy." The Ranger was floored by the Sheriff's claim.

"The D.A. was very specific that he get the original."

"Is the investigating officer available?"

"Sorry, he is on vacation this week." Sheriff Bell was playing it out, even though he had not expected these questions from the Texas Rangers. He had figured he would be blowing off just the Longleys, or maybe that nosey reporter from the News.

"Sheriff Bell, I am concerned with the operations of your department. I believe at the conclusion of this investigation there is a strong possibility that the State will shut down your jail for safety concerns. I am also conducting an investigation of the shooting at the Longley Ranch. If I find any obstruction of justice, your lack of adequate supervision at the jail will be the very least of your problems."

***

It was afternoon before the Ranger arrived at Clay's office.

"Manny. Goodness. You look great, and it's great to see you." The Ranger did look good. At high school graduation, Clay and Manny were about the same size – six-feet tall, average build, at165 pounds or thereabout. Now they were both a good 15 pounds heavier, but Manny's additional bulk looked all muscle, Clay noticed. Though not overweight, he thought about the soft pounds he had collected around his waist since leaving the Army. The Ranger was dressed in tan trousers, white short sleeve uniform shirt, pistol on his belt, cowboy boots and carried his white Stetson. Besides the distinctive Texas Ranger badge over the left breast pocket, he wore a nametag on the right breast and had lieutenant bars on his collar.

"It is good to see you too, Clay. You're a big cheese now. That's great." Both were sincere in their mutual admiration. Considering where each had come from to their present positions, admiration was justified.

After Manny sat down across from the desk, Clay handed over the manila envelope he had been saving for the Ranger. "Here are photos I took out at my parents' place, and also the shell casing we found. Marcus Franks, a reporter for the paper, will have some more pictures they took."

Manny took the envelope and emptied the contents onto the desk. He picked up the plastic baggie now containing the shell casing. Clay had immediately taken the shell from Marcus's handkerchief and dropped it into the plastic container, as he had often seen on TV.

"This is good, Clay. You think the shooter picked up all the other casings except this one? And, you don't have any bullets – you know, slugs?"

"Yeah. We did a thorough search. He had to shoot at least four times. We only found one shell. No one saved any slugs. I don't know if they were even found."

"This is a .308. Makes a good deer rifle. Not rare, but also not as common as a .30-.30 or .30.06. Small town like this, it won't be that difficult to find out who owns .308's. Might even get a print. We'll see. Also, we might be able to match it to a particular rifle. Sometimes a gun will leave microscopic markings on the case as a result of being chambered and ejected. Other times, there is nothing distinctive. I'll get this to the lab. Y'all did the right thing. This might help us solve the crime, but I doubt we can get a conviction with this."

"What do you mean by that," Clay asked.

"We probably will never be able to get the shell admitted as evidence. It has to do with the chain of custody. If the investigating officer had found the casing, secured it, and law enforcement had maintained custody, yes, it would be good evidence. But we'll just have to see how it plays out."

"You want to go out and see the site?" Clay said. Ranger Rojas nodded in the affirmative. Before leaving, Clay placed a call to Marcus to see if the other photos were available. Marcus agreed to meet them at the Longleys to deliver the pictures.

***

Manny had just completed the re-acquaintance with Will and Elizabeth Longley when Marcus and Samuel Collins drove up. It was the first time Clay had met Marcus' boss, but had heard Marcus often speak favorably of him.

Clay led the entourage into the pasture, over the rise and down to the vicinity of the stock pond. Marcus not only provided a copy of all the pictures taken, but also a copy of the taped interview with Mason Griggs. Collins had wanted to tag along so he could relay to the Ranger his encounter with the County Judge that morning.

"Lieutenant Rojas, I've been around breaking news stories a long time," Collins said after getting comfortable with the Ranger. "I think all hell is about to break loose here."

CHAPTER TEN

Two different Houston television channels carried interviews with State Senator Rodney Gott on Monday evening. It demonstrated how fast a high-powered public relations firm can work. Senator Gott hawked the proposed Lake Byar Convention Center project. He recited the litany – jobs, millions of dollars invested, future growth - like the politician he was, the senator took full credit for the coming bonanza.

Sheriff Bell had called the D.A. and asked if he could drop by to see him that evening. Ray was sitting in his den in Pecan Estates and the interviews were running on the TV when the sheriff arrived.

"That Texas Ranger is investigating the cattle shooting at the Longleys, too. He mentioned obstruction of justice and real trouble." Sheriff Bell had already conveyed to the D.A. that the jail problem had the attention of the Rangers and relayed the details of his meeting. "He wants that report I gave you."

"That report doesn't say anything."

"That's true. And that's a problem. It looks like obstruction of justice. Gilcrest should have done at least a little investigating, if just for show. But worse, you see, he told me something else that's not in that report."

"What's that," Ray asked. The sheriff had his attention.

"On Friday, after word got around about the cows, Gilcrest's cousin, one of them Jordan boys, called him and said he had seen your nephew, Todd, cross the highway on an orange ATV that day. The thing that got his attention was, Todd had a deer rifle with a scope in the gun rack. Well, it ain't deer season. Besides Todd's got a lot of places to shoot on their side of the highway. Don't have no reason to go down between those high priced houses and the Longley's place to be shooting."

Ray Gott looked startled. "You sure it was Todd?"

"Didn't seem like there was any doubt." There was silence for several seconds; the D.A. wore a blank expression. The sheriff didn't know if he should elaborate on the sighting, so he waited.

Ray wagged a finger. "Keep this quiet. I have to talk to Rod about this. But for now, make sure that cousin, you said a Jordan, keeps his mouth shut. Better yet, let's get him out of town. Whatever it costs, get him moved up to Dallas or some place. Same with that deputy. Don't care what the cost. Get them out of here – permanently. Make sure they know not to let any friends or family know where they're moving to."

"Well, the money is one thing and will help, but I don't know if they'll both jump at the offer," Bell said. "All Gilcrest wants to do is fish."

"They better. You make sure they understand they don't have a choice. It's time for you to use your muscle, if you have to."

"That's what I mean. If they don't want to cooperate, how tough do we get?"

"What do you want me to say, break a leg? Okay, tell them all those things, pain, hurt. They need to know who they'd be screwing with. If they hang around here, they've got trouble, trouble from the sheriff, the D.A. and the next Texas Attorney General." It's no secret, Ray thought, just hasn't yet been announced. Rod will be running for Attorney General next year, and four years later, the governor's race will be wide open and there for the taking. "Okay, I need to call Rod," Ray said, indicating the meeting was over.

"One other thing," Bell said, "when you talk to Rod – this Ranger, you know he is from Byar? His name is Manuel Rojas."

Ray paused. "I know him. Didn't know he's a Texas Ranger." Momentarily, Ray's thoughts drifted and the conversation was in a lull.

"Anyway, he's hot on my case about this jail problem. I need the Senator to use some of his Austin influence to call that Ranger off."

Ray knew they had already decided they could not afford to use up any capital trying to save the sheriff from his own incompetence. "Don't worry about that Jimmy. Rod is up on it. Nothing is going to happen." Ray wanted to get rid of the sheriff so he could place the call to Austin. He showed him to the door.

The sheriff left Ray's, but drove only a block before he pulled over to the curve. He reached over into the front passenger seat of his sedan and switched off the recording device. He removed the transmitter bug clipped to the back of his black tie. Another of the Bodas was on tape.

***

"That stupid twit!" was the response from Rod when Ray relayed the witness report and suspicion that his son, Todd, was the one who had shot and killed the cattle at the Longleys. "I'm going to kick his ass across Texas. Damn!" He continued spewing expletives to his brother, but directed at his son. Ray thought he should be thankful he was on the phone, as opposed to reporting to Rod in person. He was also glad when the phone call ended and knew he, for certain, would not want to be Todd when Rod got to him.

Things were moving fast. County Judge Mason Griggs, County Attorney Josh Simmons, and Sheriff Jimmy Bell all received a call from the Texas Department of Public Safety in Austin. Based on the preliminary report from the Texas Rangers, the state was assuming immediate custody and oversight of the Byar County Jail. A hearing would be held in 30 days to determine when and under what conditions the state would return management responsibility to the Byar County Sheriff's Office. A Texas Department of Corrections officer would arrive within 24 hours to take charge of the jail facility. This precipitated a flurry of additional calls. The third time Bell attempted to call Ray Gott, the D.A. decided he may as well take the call. Besides, he had something to check on with the sheriff.

"This is goin' to kill my re-election," Bell said. "If this all goes through, we'll be laughed at for months."

"My understanding is that it's a done deal," Ray said.

"There's got to be something Rod can do to stop this bull. I'm feeling desperate."

Ray could not care less about Bell's begging. No sense telling him us Bodas have decided not to come to his aid. Let Bell go down in his own quicksand. That's what our mentor, James Robert Griggs would have advised. Don't sacrifice your own reputation trying to save some crooked friend, let alone as in this case, a dumb ass. Don't associate yourself with a loser. And Sheriff Bell is a loser. Anyway, change the subject to something more important.

"Did you take care of the matter with the Jordan boy and that deputy?"

Bell smiled inwardly and thought Ray doesn't realize what a fatal error he's making. He kept his face straight and said, "Yeah, I'm handling it. Just need to pick up some cash for them boys. I've already spoken to Deputy Gilcrest on the phone, and we plan to visit the Jordan cousin this evening."

"Well, come by the law office after five today and I'll have you some expense money." Ray made a mental note to himself to drop by the bank for $10,000. That should be enough, for starters, to get two guys out of town.

Jimmy Bell sat at his office desk for several minutes following the conversation with the D.A. He contemplated his actions in response to what he thought was happening. He had troubles and had asked the Gotts for help, just the use of some influence. Surely, Rod Gott has that kind of pull in Austin. What is the big deal? Nobody escaped from the jail. Nobody had even been injured. Just say everything is fixed and make the problem disappear. Sheriff Bell continued to hash over the situation.

The Gotts have problems also. Todd Gott, the Senator's son, is implicated in a felony. The Gotts asked me, the sheriff, for a favor – no, they ordered me to obstruct justice. They're going to allow me to flounder with the bad press, embarrassment and ultimately the loss of my job. And, they still expect me to save their ass. It's what I was afraid of, and it's coming true. Well I know the Bodas apparently better than they know me.

Bell opened the right hand desk drawer where he had stashed the tape recorder and Ranger Rojas's card that contained his office and his cell phone number. He fingered the business card. Think, Jimmy…gotta keep some options open.

***

The front page of the Byar County News featured a large picture of a downed Longhorn, facing straight on. There were two smaller pictures of other cattle lying on the ground. It wasn't any of Clay's photos. They were ones taken by the girl photographer that had accompanied Marcus to the scene. The headline above the large picture read, "Longleys Resist Ranch Seizure – More Troubles." A smaller, but bold sub-headline read, "Unknown Shooter Kills Prized Longhorns." Whether intended or not by the news reporter and the editor, the impression, from reading the headlines and seeing the pictures, was that the two stories were connected.

Ray and Mason met for lunch at Griggs and Gott Law Office. Ray stopped off and picked up burgers for the meeting to discuss and mull over the front-page story.

In the article, Marcus Franks had provided more background on eminent domain. He quoted Will Longley on how a Griggs and Gott attorney tried to get them to sell their Longhorn ranch, and after their refusal seemed to threaten them with condemnation of the property. Marcus recited how first the county tried to preclude the raising of livestock on the ranch that had been in Elizabeth Longley's family for over 100 years. Then Byar County Board of Commissioners voted to seize the ranch from the Longleys to, among other things, build a golf course for the country club set and out-of-towners. There was no mention of the benefits of jobs and tax revenues in the story.

Ray said, "This is irresponsible reporting. They have intentionally tied these two events together."

Mason nodded agreement. "It not only links the two stories, it creates the impression of political bullying and shenanigans." They agreed that it would have been much better if the cattle story had been buried on an interior page and printed without the photographs.

Furthermore, there was the revelation in the news item that a shell casing was found where the shooter had stood near a tree line. Leading from the scene were ATV tracks and a cut fence where the intruder had trespassed onto the Longley's ranch. The story concluded by reporting that the incident was under investigation by the Texas Rangers, who now had sent the evidence to the state crime lab.

"So much for greasing the skids with the paper." Ray was disappointed with Mason's lack of success at influencing either the reporter or his editor. He thought he could have done a better job. Ray reluctantly revealed to Mason the more damning news that Todd Gott was probably the shooter. He had been observed near the scene, riding an ATV, and had a rifle with a scope mounted across the handlebars. Now, the presence of the shell casing added to their concern. They agreed on calling Rod and reviewing the news story before taking any action, but had to wait for Rod to call back. Once on the phone, Mason read the headlines, described the front page pictures, and paraphrased most of the article, but read some parts verbatim.

"This is going to hell faster than a pedophile priest. I can't leave town three days and every damn thing falls apart." As Rod ranted, Mason realized Rod's characterization wasn't exactly true. Everything being revealed had happened when Rod was in Byar. Both Mason and Ray felt as if they were somehow being blamed for the predicament.

"Ray, go out to the house and get Todd's deer rifle. It's a Remington .308 with a scope. That damn gun is not even a year old, but make sure it disappears. Don't take any crap off of Todd. If he has anything to say, he had better talk to me. I'm not through with him yet."

By the time the call was over, Mason was totaling up the possible charges – now, obstructing justice, for sure. It was not what the Bodas were supposed to be about. The saying about power corrupting came to his mind. He had to speak up.

"Ray, we're engaging in a conspiracy to commit a crime. Everything you do to thwart this investigation constitutes obstruction of justice. I don't pretend that we have been lily white in everything we do. In fact, I have to accept my own guilt for malfeasance of office. However, enough is enough. Count me out."

"You can't just walk out. We're looking at winning the lottery here. Millions. And then, millions more over the years," Ray said. He was thinking ahead to all the possibilities.

"I've already got millions and you guys have much more. I've always thought this convention center would be good for the county and it would be, but I don't personally need it, and certainly don't want to go to jail over it."

"What are you going to tell Rod," Ray asked, as if they were still kids, and Mason having to face up to Ray's domineering brother would be too intimidating.

"You can tell Rod whatever you desire." Mason's words were harsh and he wanted to say more, but instead held close his thoughts. And, those thoughts were many and complex. There were all the legal implications of extracting himself from the Bodas. It wasn't like a club you resign from. There was the law firm, Griggs and Gott, and then a myriad of corporations and partnerships to be sorted out.

Ray, realizing Mason's resolve, stomped from the conference room and left the law office without speaking to anyone. He first had to complete his last assignment from Rod - Todd's rifle.

Mason called his County Judge office to clear his afternoon calendar for the next few hours. He looked around his law office. It represented years of successful practice, going back to his father, and great uncle Leland Griggs. It was the kind of situation the vast majority of small town lawyers could only dream about – legal work flowing in without beating the bushes or chasing ambulances, a staff of young counselors and paralegals doing all the leg work and long hours, and above all, the financial success. Griggs and Gott would be no more.

CHAPTER ELEVEN

Forest Donovan was back at the Byar County Courthouse. He filed the suit on behalf of William and Elizabeth Longley to stop the county from seizing the Longley's ranch by eminent domain. Later, at their house, he explained to the couple what had recently transpired in other cases. He offered that their best hope, and his belief, was that Texas justice was traditionally more inclined to support the land owner than was necessarily so in other parts of the country. Worst case, Forest told the Longleys, a losing legal battle could drag out for at least three years, possibly longer.

***

After stalling a day, Sheriff Bell placed a call to Ranger Rojas. Manny got the call at his Houston office only hours after receiving the lab report on the .308 shell casing. The report said the shell held a single partial print, and there was no possibility of getting a match in the FBI national database. The Ranger knew fingerprint matching looks for 12 or 13 matching characteristics. Generally, experts look for a minimum of seven characteristics to plot. With that, other characteristics must also match. The latent partial had only three points. Comparison with a fingerprint card of a known individual could possibly include someone in or out of a suspect group, but would not be positive identification. Manny Rojas thought, as he picked up the line and discovered it was Bell, Well now – this adds some intrigue.

"There was a witness who saw someone that day. Can you get back up here to Byar to talk this over?" Sheriff Bell said.

"What did your witness actually see?"

"He can identify a person riding a four-wheel ATV with a deer rifle. I'd rather not go any further 'til you get here." Jimmy Bell knew he could not give an exact name of the witness at that time. He and Deputy Gilcrest had not followed up on the visit as the sheriff had told Ray Gott he would do. The witness was one of the Jordans, and he hadn't bothered to ask which one. It could be one of several, and while he knew of them and recognized them when he saw them, he didn't know them by first names. They were not the kind to be in habitual trouble with the law, just ole country boys working in menial blue-collar jobs. He would have to get the name from Deputy Gilcrest.

"I'll be there tomorrow – say mid morning at your office."

"Okay, Lieutenant. Tomorrow. I'll be looking for you." Sheriff Bell got off the phone and contemplated his next move. He had $10,000 cash from Ray Gott, money he was supposed to hand out to have the incriminating witnesses skip town. The money would not now be used for that. The D.A. would not publicly admit he had provided money to the sheriff to buy off witnesses. The sheriff thought, maybe I'll just keep the cash for myself. I may be the one that needs to get out of town.

Sheriff Bell learned from Deputy Gilcrest that it was Hubert Jordan, the one everyone called Hubbie, who had seen Todd Gott crossing the highway with the deer rifle mounted across the handlebars. Hubbie worked for a small-time pulp wood contractor cutting pines, loading, and driving a truck.

***

Rod Gott hastily returned to Byar upon receiving another call from Ray. Meanwhile, the rifle had been taken care of on a quick boat ride from the marina to the deepest water of the lake, along the old river channel. At the law office, it was evident that Mason had cleared out personal effects from his office.

"Good riddance," Rod stood in Mason's former office, hands on hips, just gazing at the blank wall behind the big desk. "We don't need that wimp. He'll find out he's nothing without us. What kind of files did he take?"

"Rebecca says he didn't take anything, just a box of personal junk from his office," Ray said.

"Yeah, but Mason is going to want to split up the place. Put out the word that he retired. Say he has health problems. We'll pay him off. If he makes any trouble, we'll squash the S.O.B. Damn, I can't believe that little bastard would do this now."

"That prick, Donovan, filed to stop the condemnation of the Longley place." Ray felt he had to stoop to the same demeaning verbal level as Rod.

"Get Josh Simmons over here. Just in case he has any doubts, he needs to know he answers to me, not Mason Griggs," Rod said. While sitting on Mason's desk, Rod wondered out loud, "You think Mason will back out on his personal commitment to the convention center plan? Sure, we have some personal differences over this Todd problem, but killing the whole development idea will be a detriment to the citizens of Byar County. That wouldn't be like Mason. Still, it would be prudent to think about getting Mason out of the County Judge office."

Ray didn't respond.

***

It is hard to understand what goes through an adolescent's mind when someone they dearly admire and love appears to turn on them. That is what happened when Rod finally confronted Todd in person. Todd already knew he was in trouble, from the comments previously made about how stupid it was for someone to be shooting the Longley's cattle at a most inopportune time. When his Uncle Ray showed up at his house and took his new rifle, he knew his father, or someone, had made the connection.

It was as bad as he had anticipated. Todd was about the same height as his father, but 100 pounds lighter. The slap against the side of his head took him off his feet and he collapsed beside his bed.

"I'm sorry. I'm sorry. I was trying to help. I thought it would help make them move." The tears Todd shed were far more from the anguish he felt than the pain of the physical punishment. He felt he deserved the slap even though it was the first time his father had hit him since he was ten or eleven years old. The last time had been with a belt for lying to his father.

"Don't you learn anything from being around me? Stupid! Do shit like that and then let somebody see you?" Rod had the urge to smack his son again, but restrained himself. It was the first time he had ever struck Todd in anger, so unlike the disciplinary spankings given years before. He continued his scolding. "There are too damn many people who will know about this, and if this gets out there is no telling what it'll cost us. I don't know what to do with you." Rod turned and left, with Todd still on the floor.

The last words were the ones that hurt the most. The doubt of his worth expressed by his father was devastating to Todd. Why doesn't Dad forgive me and love me still? He sat on the floor beside his bed for the next half hour. Nothing matters anymore. Whatever I do it won't be good enough for my father.

***

Rod and Ray were at the law office early and huddled in Rod's office.

"It's the damn Longleys," Rod said in exasperation. "Why the hell don't those idiots think of what's best for somebody besides themselves? They think those damn cows are more important than what this project will do for the whole county. I want those Longleys to think they have died and gone to Hell," Rod said.

"Anything else happen to those old folks and it just looks like we're out to get them," Ray said.

"Well, there's Clayton. It has to be personal. Don't want to get into a pissin' contest with Consolidated. We can put some pressure on him."

"Yeah." Ray paused in thought. He had resented and felt bitterness toward Clay for years. It was about Claire, his wife. He had lost his girlfriend to Clay Longley and when he got her back as his wife, she was "spoiled," as they say. Ray always knew that Clay, not him, had been Claire's first. This would be easy. Ray's thoughts immediately jumped to women. Clay was single. What was he doing about female company these days? Anyone at work he's screwing? Then the pieces fell into place.

"I got it," Ray said with a snap of his fingers. "Eugene Ferguson, we indicted him a couple months back for grand theft auto. He's been chopping up cars in his body shop. That cute little wife of his works at Consolidated. What if she came out and said Clay Longley made inappropriate sexual advances at work?"

Rod nodded with a wicked gleam on his face. "Sexual demands. Demands in exchange for keeping her job. I like it. Get him in trouble with the company. And the D.A.'s Office has the carrot to make her do it. First, she files a complaint with the company and then it leaks out and becomes public knowledge. About the time that gets out, another gal comes forward and says the same thing happened to her. Makes it sound believable, and looks like a pattern. Get that asshole fired. Yeah." Rod dug into his desk drawer for a small notebook.

"What are you doing?" Ray looked puzzled.

"I'm calling Ollie Harrell," Rod said, as he flipped through some pages. Finding what he needed, he picked up the phone and punched in Ollie Harrell's number. Oliver Harrell, the previous Byar County Sheriff, was in his mid sixties, and needed to supplement his retirement income. On occasion, Griggs and Gott used his services for a variety of tasks, mostly tracking down leads and coming up with witnesses. Though he had been forced to resign as Sheriff, he had managed to avoid serving any time, having escaped with a fine and probation. Since then, he had worked at a number of different jobs in nearby Huntsville, but always had a sideline that could best be described as an unlicensed private investigator.

"Ollie, this is Rodney Gott. We have a little job we need to get you on. You want to get together for lunch?" There was a brief lull. "Yeah, today, noon at the Marina Restaurant." Another pause. "See you there." Rod hung up the phone and grinned at Ray, obviously pleased with what was to come. "Get me a copy of that Ferguson file. Ollie will put the screws to Ferguson and his wife. If they want to get out of their mess, they'll go along."

"I'll bring it right back. Want me to go along?"

"No. I'll take care of getting Ollie to work. Just get me the file. Unless you got a second broad at Consolidated who we can use, we'll have to get Ollie to dig one up."

"No, that's the only one I can think of," Ray said. "Maybe some guys. Hey, if this doesn't work, we can paint him with the fag brush," Ray said, laughing; and he also got a laugh from Rod. It was the first piece of humor they had experienced in days.

CHAPTER TWELVE

Marvin MacDonald stood in the open doorway of Clay's office. He held a manila folder, and the look on his face indicated trouble. Clay was on the phone, and waived him in, pointing to one of the armchairs. He was concluding the call, and noted Marvin closed the door behind him before he settled into the chair. He never closes the door. Must be something serious, he thought.

"What do you have, Marvin?"

"Clay, this is kind of a personal item. H.R. brought this to me a few minutes ago. We have a female employee who has filed a sexual harassment complaint against you." Marvin paused.

"You're kidding," Clay said, but he knew from Marvin's expression it was no joke.

"This comes from Jeanie Ferguson. She works in Receiving. Do you know who she is?"

"Right off, I don't recognize the name," Clay said. With the division office, plus several plant locations in Byar, Consolidated Industries had several receiving sites and nearly a thousand employees. It could be any of them that Marvin was referring to.

"Me either. Says here she is married, 28 years old, one child, been with the company 18 months. Here is her file photo from Human Resources." Marvin handed Clay one page from the manila folder.

Clay studied the form. It contained a mug shot photograph of Jeanie Ferguson pasted in the upper right hand corner. She was attractive, at least in the photograph. The rest of the form contained personal information and emergency contact information. He shook his head in the negative and followed with, "Don't recognize her." Clay looked up at Marvin, and asked, "What are the details of the accusation." I wonder if I have encountered the young lady and somehow made her uncomfortable, he thought.

"Serious, Clay. Her specific complaint is that you made her sexual submission a condition of her continued employment."

Clay spit air. "That is preposterous." It dawned on him. This is no longer any mystery. This is not from something I've inadvertently done: a look, a smile, a comment mistaken for an advance. I am completely innocent of this trumped up charge. He shook his head again.

"What's next, Marvin," Clay asked, but he knew well the company policy. This matter had to be forwarded to the home office. It would be assigned to a Human Resources Employee Relations Specialist who would be sent down to investigate the complaint. If the complaint had merit, it would be grounds for discharge. Being in his position, Clay would be permitted to resign.

"Clay, you need to draft a statement to attach to the complaint. It will be forwarded together. All your statement has to say is that you do not know the employee personally, do not have any regular contact with her, and categorically deny the charge." From a personal standpoint, Marvin felt the complaint was not valid. It would appear to be totally out of character for the man he had come to know. Marvin and his wife had been to social functions and out to dinner with Clay on several occasions; a couple of times Clay had brought along a date, and his conduct was always gentlemanly. Even Clay's comments in all-male gatherings had never revealed a tendency toward sexual aggressiveness. At work, where Marvin had the greatest exposure to Clay, he had never observed conduct detrimental to the work environment.

Clay turned to his credenza where a PC sat. He brought up the word processing program, and pounded out his statement while Marvin continued to mull the situation in his mind. Clay read over his statement on the monitor, made a correction and sent it to his printer. "Done," Clay said, as he signed a single piece of paper and handed it to Marvin.

No sooner had Marvin left Clay's office than Millie walked into his office, and barely above a whisper said, "There is a constable here to see you."

Clay looked at her, somewhat puzzled. He paused a couple of seconds, wondering what a constable would need to see him about.

"Show him in."

"It's a her," was all Millie said, and returned to her desk. A moment later she was back followed by a young lady in a police-looking uniform of dark blue shirt and gray slacks.

"Mr. Clayton Longley?" she said.

"Yes I am."

"Mr. Longley, I am Deputy Constable Gill. You are being served," the constable said, and handed Clay two envelopes. As Clay instinctively reached for the offered envelopes, he realized his mouth was open and suddenly felt very dry. "Would you please sign my receipt to acknowledge the service" It was more a statement than a question as the constable presented two more pieces of paper.

Clay laid the envelopes on the desk and accepted the additional sheets. "What is this about?"

"Mr. Longley, one service is for you personally and the other is for you as agent for Consolidated Industries. You are each being named in a lawsuit. That is all I can tell you. I just serve the paper."

Clay scribbled his signature on the receipts and handed them back to the lady constable without a word. The only thing he had ever been served before were divorce papers and those came by registered mail. The deputy constable took the receipts, thanked him and left. Clay didn't know what to do next, except call Marvin back to his office. He had ripped open the envelope with his name on the outside and was about to remove the contents when Marvin walked back in.

After opening the envelope for Consolidated, Marvin scanned it and said, "It's the Jeanie Ferguson thing. Looks like she has already gone to a lawyer. They are filing for damages." He didn't look surprised and dropped the paper on the desk. Clay had also looked at his, and then handed it to Marvin.

"Going after the company and you individually." Marvin handed Clay's summons back. "I'll have to take care of this one, and Clay, you ought to think about getting representation for this matter. Beyond saying that, I really should not be providing you any advice on the personal matter."

"Yeah, guess I will," Clay said with resignation. He was puzzled. What was this all about? Why would this Jeanie Ferguson be making such a claim? Clay thought about how some people falsely claim some type of injury in hopes of getting a financial settlement from a large company. He dismissed that possibility. No, a back injury, or something on the job, would be easier. It has to be personal, but why? Yes, I'll need to hire an attorney to handle this. How about Forest Donovan? He's the only lawyer I'm working with on a personal matter, but this would not be in the area of his specialty. Besides, it would be best to keep the issues separate.

"As a friend, I'll help you find good counsel for this. Don't treat it lightly. They are asking $250,000 actual damages and ten times that in punitive damages on each suit. That's a ridiculous chunk of change. But, more importantly, to you personally, this is your reputation and your future at stake."

"Thanks, Marvin. I appreciate your support."

***

As Marvin had said he would, Clay received the call from an attorney in Houston. He was a specialist, meaning he was going to be expensive. Clay spoke to him on the phone, and explained that he did not know or recognize the photo of the plaintiff, Jeanie Ferguson. While he had been through her work area, and perhaps had seen and spoken to her before, he could not recall any specific such incident. Clay faxed the summons to the Houston office to be answered, and agreed to meet with the attorney later.

Clay had relayed to Marcus Franks the problems with the complaint and suit, so it was no surprise when Marcus called to tell him the suits would appear in the legal notices section of the Byar County News. When Clay received his weekly newspaper at work, he immediately opened to legal notices, and there it was, "Jeanie Ferguson v Clayton James Longley – sexual harassment," and "Jeanie Ferguson v Consolidated Forest Products Industries, Inc. – sexual harassment."

Clay had also revealed the problems to his parents. The legal notices in the paper would be no surprise to them. He thought about how others might react to the news. What about the couple of women he had dated since being back in Byar? What about Claire? What would she think? Would she believe it was true, and why was he worrying about how Claire Gott would react?

Clay resolved to not consume himself with the problem. It is something that comes with the territory of management.

The next day, Marvin was at Clay's door again with another manila folder. "I don't know what is going on here, Clay. We have another sexual harassment complaint." While Marvin had relied more upon his personal assessment of Clay's integrity in the first incident, a second and similar employee complaint, was enough to create doubt. The first accusation had not yet been resolved – the employee relations specialist from Atlanta, Georgia headquarters was due to be in Byar soon – and now this.

"Oh, damn!" Clay slammed his fist on the desk, startling Marvin, who rarely witnessed such emotion from his boss.

Again, Marvin handed the single sheet of paper to Clay. It had a photo of the complainant, Marie Carlisle. Clay looked at the picture for several seconds without speaking. "No, don't recognize her either. Who is she?"

"She works in Plant Security. Records show she is single, 36 years old, three children, been working here for four years," Marvin read from other material still in the folder.

"Well, is it the same as the other complaint?"

"Exactly." When Marvin said that, it was as if someone had struck the gong, at least for him. It's just like the other complaint. If I believed the first was untrue, and I did, then this is too much of the same. Something's going on, but what? Will there be another lawsuit filed? I expect there will be. There was a tinge of excitement in Marvin's voice. "Exactly, Clay."

Clay looked up at Marvin who had started to pace. He thought, Marvin looks delighted. Why? I feel nothing but anguish.

Marvin looked straight at Clay. "This is too much coincidence. I'll bet we get served again, and I'll bet Marie Carlisle has the same attorney as

Jeanie Ferguson. And, you can bet there is some connection between the two. Don't know what it is, but there is something."

Marvin's small measure of excitement made Clay feel somewhat relieved. It was good that he had someone believing in him, but that was someone who knew him and would accept his word. What about people who don't know me - what will they be likely to believe?

CHAPTER THIRTEEN

When Ranger Rojas met Sheriff Bell at the Byar County Sheriff Office, his expectation was that the sheriff would only reveal the name of the prospective witness. This person supposedly saw an individual who could possibly be the one who shot and killed the Longley's cattle.

"It will probably be late today before we can talk to the witness. His name is Hubbie Jordan. He drives a pulp wood truck, and is in the woods or on the road most of the day." Sheriff Bell was intent on establishing an impression of complete cooperation with the Texas Ranger. "Now, I haven't talked to him myself, but he is a cousin to Deputy Gilcrest, who was the investigating officer out at the Longley's. Hubbie told Gilcrest that he saw Todd Gott, you know, the son of State Senator Rodney Gott. Said he was on a four-wheeler, came across the highway from where the Longley's place is, and had a deer rifle in the gun rack."

Criminy, was the thought that came to Manny. What a revelation! Was this all part of a feud starting between the Gotts and the Longleys?' He tried not to show any visual evidence of the thoughts running rampant through his mind.

The sheriff, aware that Ranger Lieutenant Manuel Rojas was originally from Byar, proceeded, "You familiar with the Longley's place?"

"Yes, I know the Longleys, and I have been to their home," Manny said.

"Well, if you don't know, Rod Gott lives just down the highway on the other side. Big place. House sits way back from the highway. Anyway, Hubbie must have thought it unusual that Todd Gott would be out with a deer rifle, across the highway, this long after deer season. When he heard about the Longley's cows being shot, he called Gilcrest and told him what he saw. You know, the Longleys are fairly good old people, don't bother nobody, so guess Hubbie felt for them. Besides, guess he don't figure he owes the Gotts anything."

"How about you, Sheriff? Do you owe the Gotts anything?" Manny asked, but thought he already knew. He had made it a point to catch up on Byar County politics from some contacts, and was aware that Griggs and Gott essentially ran everything political in the county. It was a little surprising that the sheriff was voluntarily coming forward with this information. Something was at play.

"Truth is, yeah – I do. I like this job. I really like it, but I may not be able to keep it. When I got out of the Navy, I got on as a Deputy Constable and then got elected Constable when ... you probably remember Gibson. He was constable all those years you were growing up here – tall skinny guy, always wore a big cowboy hat. Well, when Gibson retired, I ran for Constable and got elected. Only me and a black guy were running. Then Ollie Harrell was sheriff and had to resign over some trouble. It was Griggs and Gott that helped me get elected sheriff. James Robert Griggs himself came and talked to me about running. He paid for everything." Sheriff Bell took a break and had a sip from the coffee mug on his desk.

Manny did remember Constable Gibson, and he also remembered Sheriff Harrell. He had only recently learned about Harrell's problems with the jail, and thought it ironic that small Byar County would have two sheriffs in a row get into trouble over the operation of the County Jail. Both were in trouble, but the first was criminal, and the current problem was more in the category of mismanagement.

"So, yeah, I owe the Gotts. I imagine they could have had me beat in any of the elections if they had put somebody up against me. I'd like to keep this job, but, depending on what happens ...." The sheriff's words trailed off. He thought about two different things. The issue with operation of the jail. The negative publicity over that could cause me difficulty. But even more serious – going against the Gotts.

"Sheriff, I understand how influential Senator Gott is, and also having his brother as the D.A. increases their political clout. However, having a witness come forward with information would be something beyond your control." Manny was hedging a little, but wanted to keep the sheriff talking.

"You ain't heard it all yet." Sheriff Bell reached down, opened one of his desk drawers and retrieved the tape recorder. It was unhooked from the receiver, and was just the recorder/player. He sat it in the middle of the desk between the Ranger and himself. Bell instinctively knew there was no need to hold anything back and attempt to negotiate with the Ranger. He would not try to deal for some mitigation of his problems with the jail security.

"When I got word about the Jordan boy being a witness, I went to see the D.A., Raymond Gott, at his house. Call it professional courtesy. Now, I'm getting ahead of myself. First, what happened is the D.A. had already gotten Deputy Gilcrest's report, and then he told me to get Gilcrest out of town. Didn't want anybody talkin' to him about the investigation or what had happened out at the Longleys. So I told Gilcrest to take a week vacation. Didn't seem like a big deal at the time. You know, just keeping him away from the news media folks. Anyway, when I call the D.A. and tell him I need to see him, I'm a little concerned about covering my own ass. I wired myself, and I got the whole conversation on tape here." Sheriff Bell punched the play button and the recording started with the sheriff's comments for record before leaving his patrol car.

Manny Rojas listened carefully to what turned out to be a more than adequate quality recording of the conversation. The taped conversation lasted through Ray Gott saying he had to contact his brother. Then it came to an odd, quick stop. The abrupt ending of the recording raised the Ranger's suspicion.

"Is that the complete conversation between you and the D.A?" Manny said.

"Yeah, that's all that was pertinent."

"Well, Sheriff, I want the original tape. All of it, right up until you turned the recorder off." Manny knew that from an evidence standpoint, a partial recording would be hard to get admitted.

"I got it here," the sheriff said with a slight sigh, indicating the desk drawer. This damn ranger is thorough. Wanted to keep my own plea to the Gotts confidential, but guess I'm gonna have to give it up. "I'll go ahead and tell you what's on it." The sheriff paused a couple of seconds and then opened the drawer. "I asked the Gotts for help on this jail thing. Thought maybe they could get it quashed." Sheriff Bell handed a cassette tape to Manny, knowing that his future now rested in the hands of the Texas Rangers.

"Let me sign a receipt for this," Manny said.

While Sheriff Bell dug in his desk for a receipt pad he said, "You know I'm dead meat if this thing blows up on us." Jimmy Bell did not know of anyone who had been physically eliminated, murdered, or what have you, as a result of crossing the Gotts, but that possibility always existed. After all, no one had ever done something like this to the most powerful figures in the several surrounding counties. He did not know what Ray and Rodney Gott might do.

"One other thing, Sheriff Bell," Manny said. "Word has gotten out that a .308 shell casing was found at the Longley's place. Do you know if the Gotts might own a .308?"

"Never asked them. If they do, and they are buying ammo for it around here, it would be from either Wal-Mart or Fuller Sporting Goods. Might ask them."

"Okay. I've got a little checking to do. What is a good time to get back with you to interview Hubbie Jordan?"

"Meet me back here at six. I'll have Deputy Gilcrest, and we'll all ride out to see him."

Ranger Rojas left the Sheriff's Office after getting directions to Fuller Sporting Goods. He knew the location of the Wal-Mart store, since he had seen it out on the highway. It was one of the many changes that had occurred in Byar since Manny had left. He visited Fuller's first. Instinct told him that the wealthier the people are, the less likely they are to be seen shopping at Wal-Mart.

A Texas Ranger, even a former local boy, walking into the small town sporting goods store was the next best thing to having a celebrity visit. Cooperation was eagerly offered. Manny first asked the store owner if he knew if the .308 was a popular rifle in the area. Mr. Fuller indicated that in the five years they had been in business, he had not sold more than half a dozen .308 caliber rifles. He quickly retrieved his Acquisition Deposition Log that is required to be maintained by all federally licensed firearms dealers. The log includes a listing of where and when the firearm was purchased, manufacturer, model, caliber, and who the gun was sold to. He started with the most recent entries and worked back. It didn't take long.

The last .308 sold was the previous November, and the buyer was Rodney Gott. The Ranger copied down the data on the Gott purchase. To avoid raising any suspicion, Manny let Mr. Fuller continue reviewing his log until he had found four more .308 rifle purchases over the time he had held the Federal Firearms License. Manny also recorded those details as they were found. The Ranger left the store explaining to Mr. Fuller that, due to an on-going investigation, he could not discuss any details.

Manny was back at the Sheriff Office early. He didn't want to waste time, since he planned to drive back to Houston that night. They found Hubert Jordan at his double-wide trailer home waiting for them. Hubbie Jordan was 22 years old, an eleventh grade dropout, and married, with one child. Only a few years older than Todd Gott, and though not friends, he knew Todd on sight. The handwritten account that Manny obtained from Hubbie was in complete agreement with the sheriff's story.

On his drive back to Houston, Manny mulled his next move. He felt with the .308 shell casing, the record of the purchase, plus the witness report, he had more than adequate justification for a search warrant for the rifle in question. He did not think that either Sheriff Bell or Deputy Sheriff Gilcrest would be inclined to forewarn the Gotts of the impending search. His plan was to return to Byar County with the warrant in hand, obtain a court signature, and immediately execute the search. This would be a sensitive issue, but cut-and-dried. He goes where the evidence leads.

The apparent conspiracy to obstruct justice by the D.A. – now that was a different issue. That was a big one. Charging a currently elected District Attorney with a felony would have to go up the chain, probably to Headquarters – maybe the Texas Attorney General. It was not that Manny expected anyone in his chain of command of fearing confrontation with the politically powerful. He did not. Again, it would be where the evidence led, but you don't want to catch your bosses blindsided.

Manny thought about what Sam Collins, the Byar County News editor had said, "All hell is about to break loose."

CHAPTER FOURTEEN

As Marvin had predicted, Clay and the company were served with another lawsuit. Just as before, the plaintiff claimed sexual harassment. In fact, everything was the same except the second plaintiff had a different name. Marvin had notified Consolidated Headquarters Legal Office of the suit and had personally filed Consolidated Industries' response with the Byar County Clerk or Court. He had to do the same on the suit by Marie Carlisle.

Marvin confirmed the upcoming visit of the company Employee Relations, who would interview both complainants. The representative would also interview Clay Longley. Corporate policy precluded a wide scale investigation that would likely make public knowledge of the claim, and potentially damage the reputation of any innocent party. Marvin was well aware of this, but being a company legal representative, he still had a responsibility to protect the firm from spurious legal claims. He felt the complainants, whatever their game was, made a tactical error in also filing a legal action. He now had a responsibility to investigate the claims with whomever were in a position to have knowledge of the possible transgressions.

The place to start was with the Warehousing Manager. It was mostly to let the department head know he would be talking to employees on a legal matter. Next was the head of Material Receiving, Jeanie Ferguson's supervisor. Her name was Ella Young, and she sat in a glassed-in office overlooking a warehouse floor. Marvin knocked on her door without calling ahead.

"Mrs. Young, I'm Marvin MacDonald from the Legal Department. Don't believe we have ever met," Marvin said as he extended a hand.

"Pleased to meet you, Marvin. Everyone calls me Ellie," she said with a friendly smile and firm handshake. She motioned to a chair, offering Marvin to sit. "What can we do for you in Receiving? Hope we're not in that much trouble."

"No, Ellie, just something I have to check up on. You have a little time to talk?"

"Now is as good a time as any."

Marvin detected a hint of nervousness in her voice. "It concerns one of our employees. What can you tell me about Jeanie Ferguson?" He intentionally left it wide open to see what kind of response he would get.

"Oh, Jeanie. Well, I would rate her as satisfactory. Nothing really outstanding. She does her job. She is on the quiet side – kind of reserved – gets along well with her co-workers. Anything in particular you're interested in?"

"Well, what about her personal life? Any boyfriend problems or things like that?"

"No, she's married. I don't believe there is anything like that going on here. Now, at home – I don't know if you are aware, but her husband was arrested for auto theft. I don't know how common a knowledge that is, but she told me about it. She said she may be needing to take some time off from work. I guess he is going to trial soon."

"No, Ellie, I wasn't aware of that." Marvin wrote on his note pad, *husband arrested,* and followed that with, *need $???* He looked back up at Ellie. "Anything else you can add?"

"From my conversation with Jeanie, I formed the impression that she believes he is guilty. She never once claimed to me that he wasn't. I would think that if she thought he was innocent, she would have said so. Her husband runs some kind of a garage."

"Is all of her work right here in the warehouse?" Marvin asked, waiving his hand toward the area outside the windows.

"Yes, right here on the floor or maybe sometimes just outside the doors to speak with drivers. Mostly, right here where I can see her, but she is not here today. She called in sick this morning."

"Would you happen to know if she is a friend of Marie Carlisle. She's a security guard."

"No. I don't know her, either. She isn't someone who works around here."

"Ellie, I appreciate your time. Sorry, I can't tell you what this is all about at this time. Maybe before long, though." Marvin got up to leave, and acted as if it were an after thought with his next question. "Oh, Ellie, have you met our new Vice President, Clayton Longley? He is originally from Byar."

"Yes. He is very nice. My husband knew him. They went to school together. My husband was a year younger and I was four years younger than him, so I didn't know Mr. Longley before."

"He seems to get out a lot. Has he been through here?" Marvin hoped he had sufficiently camouflaged the most important question.

"A couple of times he has come by with the Warehouse Manager. They just ask how things are going – that's about it."

Marvin figured he had what he had come for. If it ever got to that point, Ella Young may have to give a deposition. That could wait.

Marvin's next stop was the Security Department. The Department Head referred him to Marie Carlisle's Shift Supervisor. They worked straight days, Marie because she had children and could not work the rotating shift available to other security guards, even though it paid a salary premium. Her supervisor was Jim Morgan, a retired Air Force

NCO. Jim looked like he was near retirement age, but still hung on to a regular job. After introductions, Marvin got down to basically the same questions he had asked about Jeanie Ferguson. With the question about boyfriend problems, he got a completely different answer.

"Marie's always gonna have boyfriend problems," Jim said with a chuckle. "Every swinging dick between fifteen and fifty can be a boyfriend. Not me. I stay away from that trouble."

Interesting, Marvin thought, let's explore this line further. "Would you imagine someone might threaten to get her fired from her job if she didn't submit?"

"Hell, no! If anybody said that, I can tell you it ain't true. If a guy even hinted that he wanted to dip his wick, she'd be shuckin' that uniform faster than a two dollar whore."

Marvin wondered how the colorful speech of Jim would look if he had to give a deposition. He chuckled at the whore quip and said, "And her location? Where she works?"

"She's on the back gate. Checks all the trucks coming and going. Only comes up here to clock in and clock out. Course, I swing by all the posts several times a day to keep a check on my troops."

"Would you know if Marie is friends with Jeanie Ferguson in Material Receiving?"

"I know who she is. Cute as a spotted pup under a red wagon. Nah. They ain't nothin' alike."

"Thanks a lot, Jim. Appreciate talking with you. By the way, have you met our new Vice President, Clayton Longley?"

"Seen him several times up around the main building. Ain't shook his hand, but he spoke to me. Hear good things about him."

"Well, Jim, I'll tell him he needs to meet you. You take care, and thanks again."

Marvin returned to his office to add to his notes while the memory was fresh. He had previously thought there was no merit to the complaints; now he was convinced. It wasn't likely Clay, in the months that he had been there, had ever been in close personal contact with either woman. One, Jeanie Ferguson, may be motivated by a need for money. That may have precipitated her claim. The other, Marie Carlisle, wasn't the type a man would have to work on to get sexual favors. They didn't seem to have anything in common, except the same lawyer who filed the same lawsuit. Something or someone brought them together.

Since this internal investigation related to an external lawsuit, and since Clay was the division executive, Marvin felt compelled to share with him his initial findings. Had it been only an internal employee complaint, the information he had gathered on the employees would have been treated as personal. Privately, he hoped it was something Clay could provide to his personal attorney and perhaps use to his advantage.

***

Except for the divorce lawyer Clay had used in Georgia, he had not previously needed legal representation. Now he was working with a number of lawyers. There was Marvin at work, Forest Donovan with his parents' case, and Felix Christman, his personal attorney in Houston. Clay had sent copies to Christman, and spoken to him a couple of times on the phone, but had not yet met with him in his office. He had thought and wished the sexual harassment suits were something Forest could handle. Clay and Forest had struck up a natural friendship, and Clay felt more comfortable confiding in Forest. It was not surprising that Clay related to Forest during a phone call the problems he was experiencing.

"Clay, please don't take this as criticism, but I think you're being naïve." Forest took Clay's description of the events at face value, and Clay had told him everything - including what Marvin had found out about the two plaintiffs. In his experience with Clay, Forest had found no reason to think there could possibly be any truth to the claims. "You are treating this like it's something totally unrelated to your parents' problems, because you don't see the connection. Me, I'm just the opposite. I look at it as related, until someone demonstrates to me that it's totally unrelated."

"You mean you think Griggs and Gott are behind this?"

"Call me a suspicious, sinister-minded bastard, as I'm sure some people do, but I wouldn't put it past them. Just look at what's going on."

"What would they have to gain? They aren't even the legal representatives for the women. They sure as heck don't expect Consolidated or me to hire them to defend the suits."

"Simple. It's harassment. Make life miserable for you. Cost you money and ruin your reputation. Generally, keep you busy. Maybe even get you fired."

"Well, I don't believe it'll get me fired. I've spoken several times to our president. There appears to be no one who believes these complaints."

"They don't have to get you fired. Just get you moved out of Byar. There goes your close support to your parents. See what I mean?"

"Yeah. Don't screw with the Bodas. I told you about the Bodas, didn't I?

"Yes, you did. You know, there are power hungry cliques like that all over. They don't call themselves by cutesy names like The Bodas, but they work the same."

"If your suspicions are true, we need a way to trace this back to Griggs and Gott."

"You had said before that the Sheriff is a political crony, so that appears to be out. Let your guy in Houston take care of answering the lawsuits. Consolidated will answer their suits, and I've got an idea I'm going to pursue," Forest said.

Forest got off the phone with Clay and immediately placed a call to the Houston office of Ranger Lieutenant Rojas. Forest gave Manny his version of how the events in Byar were connected.

"I'm going to call Clay and try to see him. I'll be in Byar in a couple of days," Manny said after hearing the details.

"I wouldn't be calling you to discuss this, but our feeling is that we would receive no satisfaction taking this matter to the Byar County Sheriff."

"I suspect I may be able to get a little more cooperation out of Sheriff Bell than you can. But I do understand. Thank you for bringing this to our attention." Manny accepted Forest's input as he would any such report from a concerned citizen. From what he knew about Byar County local politics and the players, he thought Forest's suspicions were reasonable. He wanted more details before he jumped into what was on the outside a personal matter.

Manny called Clay's office, but didn't get him. The secretary told him he was on a plant tour and could be reached on his cell phone. He tried that.

"Hello, Clay. This is Manny Rojas. Can you speak now?"

"Manny, good to hear from you. Yeah, I'm just on my way back to the office. What's up?"

"I'm going to try to be in Byar tomorrow. I wanted to see if I could drop by for a few minutes."

"Sure. I've got an eight o'clock meeting in the morning and I think I'm free after that."

"It will be ten before I can get there. I spoke to Forest Donovan. He believes there is a connection between things happening in Byar. I know some of these things are personal and you don't have to discuss them with law enforcement, but it might help if I can get some details."

"I'll make you a copy of everything I have. I don't mind sharing it with you. I'll see you tomorrow morning, then." Clay ended his cell call and thought, as he walked between buildings back to his office, I've wondered about how to dig into the lawsuits. How can someone determine if in fact the women have been put up to filing these complaints? So, this is what Forest had in mind. Get the Texas Rangers involved.

CHAPTER FIFTEEN

Ranger Rojas met with Clay as planned. Clay was ready with copies of the suits against him. Also as planned, Clay called Marvin in, and he provided copies of the suits against the company. Marvin also produced copies of his notes on his interviews with the women's supervisors.

Manny studied the copies. It was one more item to discuss when he went to see Sheriff Bell. Leaving Clay, Manny drove to the Byar County Sheriff's Office for that meeting.

"Welcome back, Ranger." Sheriff Bell knew he needed friends, and this Ranger certainly had to be one of them.

"Sheriff, we have a couple of items to cover today."

"Okay. I guess I want to get things done. I been lying to the D.A. about sending those boys out of town. This has been like an ax hanging over my head."

"I've got an appointment with a judge at one o'clock. All he knows is that I'm asking for a search warrant. It's for Rodney Gott's house, and I expect you to accompany me," Manny said.

"Guess I got to do that. Boy, they gonna be some pissed." Manny well understood the 'they' Sheriff Bell referred to were the Gotts, Rod and Ray. The Ranger would be obtaining a warrant to search the home of a state senator, the brother of the D.A., and the most prominent citizen of the county.

"We'll also need a couple of deputies standing by to help execute the search. We go immediately from the judge's chambers to Gott's home." Manny told the sheriff what was about to happen, and then planned to stick close by the sheriff throughout the warrant request and search.

Sheriff Bell picked up his phone and punched in a couple of numbers. It was to his chief deputy down the hall. "Chip, I need two deputies for a search this afternoon." There was a pause, and then the sheriff continued. "No. You hang around here. How about Gloria and one of the guys?" The sheriff wanted at least one female present at the search of the Gott home. If someone had to deal with an irate Mrs. Gott, a female deputy might do better. He didn't expect it, but if the search involved going through women's clothes and such, it was always preferable to have another woman do it. "Have them at the front of the courthouse at one."

"Good," Manny said when the sheriff hung up. "Next item of business. Who do the Gotts get to do their dirty work?" Manny had decided to investigate this head-on instead of starting with the women, and working back. He also knew that the term "dirty work" might have a wide range of interpretations. He was curious what it meant to the sheriff. It didn't take long, and didn't seem the sheriff had to think about it.

"That would be my predecessor, Sheriff Harrell. Yep. Ollie Harrell. He's getting on now, but still goes running whenever they call. Never made it a practice to find out what all he does for them. I've always made it a point not to cross swords with him."

"I guess I should have suspected that," Manny said. An ex-sheriff would be a good one to have on the payroll for some lawyers who wanted to run roughshod over the local legal system. He would know plenty of shady characters, and have a considerable amount of experience at squeezing the weaker members of society to gain whatever cooperation he needed. "What about a local attorney named Robert Ward?"

"Divorce lawyer. Must do more than divorces, but I don't know what else. Never seen him in Criminal Court. Divorce seems to be big enough business around here."

"Do you know a Jeanie Ferguson?" Manny intended to get a rundown of Clay's adversaries, before exposing his hand to the sheriff.

"Yeah. We know her husband. Grand theft auto. He runs a paint and body shop. She got him out on bail. Other than that, don't know anything about her."

"One more. Marie Carlisle?"

"Marie. Can't seem to hang on to a man. Had plenty of chances. Her mother and my mother are first cousins, so we're kin, whatever cousin that makes us. I'm older than her, so I've known her since she was born. She's got problems with her oldest boy. He's only 16, but they got him for selling meth crystals in Lufkin. Put him in Juvenile Detention. You know, methamphetamines, the stimulant drug that-"

Manny silenced him with a sudden glare of disdain. The ignorant audacity of a small town sheriff supposing he needed to explain to a Texas Ranger what "meth" was. In his line of duty climbing up through the ranks of law enforcement he'd raided many a makeshift laboratory that produced the cheaply manufactured stuff. He cleared his throat. "Sheriff Bell, can we stay on point?"

Bell stuck his hands in his pockets and fell silent as Manny considered. The pattern was obvious. There are two women, each with a family member having legal problems. That was the connection between the two, besides working at Consolidated. There was also an ex-lawman who might influence them, and who, just so happens, does the dirty work for who Manny was now viewing as the suspects. Now he had to tie them all together.

"What's the deal with all these folks?" Sheriff Bell said.

"Oh, that's something else I'm working on. You know where this lawyer, Robert Ward, has his office?" Manny read the address to the sheriff.

"What say we go over and visit him before lunch?" Manny intended to keep the sheriff with him, even if he had to buy his lunch.

"Sure," Sheriff Bell said, rising from his desk. He and Manny left the office and walked down a short hall. The sheriff stopped to tell the lady at the front that he would be out of the office until mid afternoon. They took Manny's unmarked car for the few blocks to the law office of Robert Ward.

Manny's intent was to surprise and shake the small town lawyer. It wasn't often that a Texas Ranger and the local sheriff walked into a one-lawyer office at the same time. In fact, it was the first time any law enforcement officer, who wasn't a client for a divorce, had ever set foot in Ward's office. It was also well known to lawyer Ward that the Texas Rangers work on high profile cases, usually those involving major crime. It meant serious business when a Ranger knocked on your door.

It was a small office with one large outer reception room for one secretary, and it looked like there was Ward's office plus another smaller office to the side, maybe a small conference room. The lawyer's door was open and Manny knew he would be heard when he introduced himself. He removed his hat and held it in his left hand.

"Good morning, Ma'am. I'm Ranger Lieutenant Rojas, and you probably know Sheriff Bell. We are here to see Mr. Ward." Manny could see the awe on the secretary's face. He also could see in his peripheral vision the lawyer rise, round his desk, and come forward. Manny looked at him. He looked a few years younger than Manny. He wore a long sleeve white shirt; his tie knot was loosened; he was thin and white and his pants appeared baggy. He didn't have the look of success.

"Ranger Rojas, you said? Robert Ward," the lawyer said, as he shook hands with Manny. "Hello, Sheriff," he added as he also shook hands with Bell. "What is the nature of this visit?" He retreated to his office, motioning for the ranger and sheriff to join him in his office. "Can I get you gentlemen anything to drink?" Both shook their heads no. and he proceeded to close his office door without saying anything to his opened-mouthed secretary. He returned her puzzled look with one of his own.

Manny started the conversation. "Mr. Ward we have some questions for you concerning a couple of your clients."

"Well, first let me remind you about attorney client confidentiality." Ward almost regretted his statement. He wondered if it was too blunt. Would they think he was going to be uncooperative in what must be something of grave importance? And that something, he could not at the moment imagine.

"We are not intending to go into details on your relationship with these clients, so I don't feel you will have the necessity to invoke that privilege." Manny stared intently at the lawyer. Ward broke eye contact with the ranger and looked to the sheriff who nodded his agreement, and was just as stone faced, taking his lead from Manny.

"Okay. What do you need?" Ward made a small, barely detectable gulp as he spoke. It was enough for Manny to notice. The ranger felt he had his prey and, thankfully, the sheriff wasn't blowing it.

"Mrs. Jeanie Ferguson and Mrs. Marie Carlisle." Manny didn't say anything else. He waited.

"Yes. Yes, they are my clients." Ward unconsciously cut his eyes toward the file cabinet in the corner. Manny knew what that meant. "I represent both of those ladies in pending actions." He didn't know what else to say.

"We know about these women. This investigation relates to how you came to represent these two clients." Manny had emphasized the word "investigation." This was a lawyer. Manny didn't have to say anything about knowingly making a false statement in an investigation.

"They, aah, my clients were referred by a friend of theirs." Ward paused and looked at Ranger Rojas. Manny didn't respond. That non-response let Ward know he was expected to continue. "First, Mrs. Ferguson was brought to me, and then Ms. Carlisle."

"Brought to you by who?" Manny continued his stern and serious expression.

Ward looked at Sheriff Bell. Obviously, he was reluctant to say. The sheriff nodded a yes to Ward and pursed his lips as if to say, "tell him."

It was Oliver Harrell, Ward thought. It's okay to tell them. Harrell had not said anything about keeping it quiet. This must be something bigger than Harrell. Probably something I shouldn't get involved in.

"You said Harrell brought them to you. How did he do that? Did he actually walk them in here?"

"Yes." Ward shook his head in the affirmative. "He came in with Mrs. Ferguson. She wanted him to sit in with her."

"She told you she wanted him to sit in with her?"

Ward thought a moment to recall the actual meeting. "Harrell said she was very nervous and wanted him to stay, and I think she agreed."

"Without going into specifics on her complaint, tell me about her request for legal representation and legal action." Got him talking, Manny thought, I'm getting the cooperation needed.

"She was unsure exactly what needed to be done. She didn't know what legal remedies were available to her. Harrell helped out. As I recall, my thoughts were to file against the company. It was Harrell who suggested also filing against the individual, and she agreed." Ward remained as perplexed in appearance as he was inside. Why do I have the Byar

County Sheriff and an officer of the Texas Rangers in my office investigating a sexual harassment case?

"How did it go with Marie Carlisle?"

"When she learned that someone else had a similar experience, she decided to come forward with a complaint."

"Ms. Carlisle told you that?" He suspected not. Or if she did, the words were put in her mouth by someone else. Manny kept his face straight.

Ward wrinkled his forehead, remembering. "Harrell said that. Guess she heard about it from him, because she told me she did not know Mrs. Ferguson."

Manny wondered how strong the women were. It appeared that Jeanie Ferguson had been reticent, and Harrell had orchestrated the meeting with the lawyer. "Did Oliver Harrell escort Ms. Carlisle to your office or did she come in on her own?"

"Harrell came in with her." Ward paused as a realization sunk in. I've been snookered. I saw dollar signs when Jeanie Ferguson appeared with what looked like a potential windfall. A lawsuit against a deep pocket corporation and one of their executives could earn me more in fees than a years' worth of divorce work. Then a second client. Too good to be true, but a second victim reinforces the first. Finally, my big chance to get out of the depressing business of representing mostly hostile divorce clients. Whether it's the husband or wife I represent, the damn thing always degenerates into a cat fight. Ward scowled. Too good to be true, all right. Hoodwinked.

"How did that meeting progress?" Manny's question snapped Ward out of his melancholy muse.

"Harrell sat in again, if that is what you mean." Yes, the lawyer thought to himself. Ollie Harrell played me like a fiddle. I want both of those women back in my office and I want them here alone. "My recollection is that Ms. Carlisle was more forthcoming. Of course she is more aah ... mature than Mrs. Ferguson, so understandably is perhaps more comfortable in this situation."

"Would you say that Ms. Carlisle came into your office with specific legal remedies in mind?"

"I would say she had prior knowledge concerning the other plaintiff. So yes, she wanted the same thing."

"How about Oliver Harrell? What was your prior relationship with him?

"I took a deposition from him once before on a different kind of case," Ward said.

"Mr. Ward, are you representing any other family member of either of these clients in perhaps some other legal matters?"

He shook his head negative. "This was the first time I had met either of them. And, no. I do not, to my knowledge, know any of their families."

Manny wanted to ask Ward if he had any indication that either of the women may have been coerced into filing the complaints, but he felt that would be a bad question. It would put the lawyer on the spot where he could only answer in the negative. Any other answer would essentially be an admission that he was part of the conspiracy to file a malicious and false claim. At this point the Ranger was satisfied that the former sheriff, Oliver Harrell, had put the women up to filing the lawsuits. Proving that would be less difficult if the lawyer was neutralized. A direct question to him would unnecessarily require the attorney to go on the defensive. He might even require Ward's assistance in the future. Manny turned to Sheriff Bell.

"Sheriff, knowing what you know about these two clients, the other legal problems we previously discussed, as well as the background and reputation of Oliver Harrell, do you think it possible that these two clients of Mr. Ward may have been subject to some form of intimidation, manipulation, or coercion?" Manny looked back at Ward to determine his reaction.

"It is beginning to look a lot like that to me," the sheriff responded with what he felt was the answer the Ranger wanted. Even though Bell concluded the same, he wondered about the question. Why would the ranger ask me instead of directing the question to Ward?

The lawyer was becoming more nervous. He wanted to get up and retrieve the two files and show the law enforcement officers that he had nothing to hide. He mulled over the situation. These men know far more about this than I do. Are they laying a trap for me? There would be two witnesses against me for anything I say. Two experienced witnesses. I would rather be with them than against them. Besides, I think Harrell lied in that deposition last year. That old bastard. I'd better speak up. "Gentlemen, let me assure you, I would never be a party to a conspiracy to extort money via a false claim."

Mission accomplished, Manny thought. The lawyer now believes the claims to be possibly false. More than that, he thinks it is about the money. And, if he thinks it is about the money that the women may collect in a successful suit, he is not part of a conspiracy involving Harrell and the Gotts. "Then, Mr. Ward, would it be correct to say that Oliver Harrell did not in any way suggest to you that he expected to share in any monetary windfall?"

"Of course I have no knowledge of what may have been discussed between Mr. Harrell and the women outside my presence. I can say for a certainty there was no mention by Harrell of expecting me to pay him anything."

Manny noticed Ward had previously used the term "my clients", and now referred to them as "the women." Not sure if that means anything. "Mr. Ward, thank you for your time. Let me leave you my card," Manny said, as he rose from his chair and handed him the card. "I would appreciate it if you would contact me if you learn anything I should know concerning these two clients." Manny purposely left it vague as to what the lawyer should call him about.

After leaving the law office, Manny followed Sheriff Bell's suggestion and pulled into a small restaurant for lunch. The conversation invariably got back to the meeting with Ward.

"I might be a little more help on this if you let me in on what it is you're going after," Bell said.

"I'll do that. But first, just from what you do know, tell me what you think."

"Well, I didn't tell you this earlier, but I know Marie filed against her company and Longley. I gather Jeanie Ferguson did too. Guess I missed that in the legal notices. These two gals are suing for a bunch of money. Harrell put them up to it. Both got a family member in trouble with the law, and probably need the money. Now, Ollie Harrell takes 'em to Ward, who he probably barely knows. That's peculiar, because Ollie has been the legman for Griggs and Gott for years. Why didn't he take 'em to the big law firm instead of that second rate divorce lawyer?"

"We're on the same page, Sheriff. Let's assume Harrell is still working for the Gotts. They have Harrell take the women to someone else because they don't want to be involved."

"Yep. Everybody knows Griggs & Gott already has a fight going on with the old Longleys, so they want this to look like something else."

"Additionally, I don't believe it's about the money," Manny said. "Frankly, I don't believe the claims the women are making are true. Harrell knows they aren't true and never expects that these lawsuits will result in a big settlement."

"If it ain't money, it's favors. If there is anybody who can help Ferguson and Marie's boy get out of their troubles, it's Griggs and Gott. They got the influence."

"And if it were the money, it could be several years before they could collect, and that would be too late to help them." Manny valued having someone from the area to bounce ideas around with. He knew Sheriff Bell had valuable knowledge concerning the locals. It was too bad he had not paid enough attention to the operation of his jail. "I think you're right. I believe Harrell squeezed the women to file the complaints. Each of them filed the identical complaint against Clayton Longley at Consolidated, and then the identical lawsuits."

"You mind if I take a shot at Marie? I think if she was forced into this, she'll tell me," the sheriff offered.

"I was kind of hoping you would do that. Sounds like Jeanie Ferguson might be a little weak. I plan to talk to her. If we can get one or both of them to cave, we might be able to convince Harrell to spill on whatever or whoever is behind this."

"I expect that will be the hardest part. Ollie's been around a long time, and is pretty tough. He ain't likely to voluntarily give up anything or anyone, especially the Gotts. But I see where this is all going."

"Sheriff, I once had a captain that always said, 'It is easier to prove something you already know is true than it is to just keep digging until you uncover the truth.' He also cautioned that you don't ignore the facts. Let's just be sure we don't make up the facts and impose our version on the…and at this point, I have to call them perpetrators."

CHAPTER SIXTEEN

"I wouldn't be surprised if the judge isn't on the phone right now with Rodney Gott, warning him about this search warrant," Sheriff Bell told Manny as they were leaving the courthouse.

"We'll find out soon enough," the ranger said. Manny did not expect Rod Gott to be home at the time. The state legislature was not in session, so he expected the Senator to be in town, but most likely in his office. He did expect to find Mrs. Gott there, and figured Todd Gott to be in school, probably his senior year of high school.

The drive from the courthouse in town out to the Gott home took Manny and the sheriff 15 minutes, with the two deputy patrol cars following. They passed by the Longley place on the right, and a little further down the highway turned left into what was a half-mile long driveway, leading to the Gott house. For several hundred yards along the highway, the Gott property was easily identified by the white three-rail fence.

At the entrance to the ranch, stood high gateposts constructed of white stone. Stretching across the top between the posts was a decorative wrought iron header containing the stylized initials, *R. G.* Past the entrance was more of the white fence stretching another quarter of a mile or more. At the road level, in the open gateway, the cars bumped across a cattle guard, there to keep the numerous horses kept by the Gotts within the confines of the ranch. The gateposts supported a wrought iron gate that was swung open. Manny figured it was closed at night and left open during the day. It was probably remotely controlled from their cars and from the house. The roadway leading to the house was concrete, and wide enough for two vehicles to pass. It was straight and level, and ran along the crest of the hill with the pasture on each side dropping off to lower elevation.

Manny had looked at the house from the highway earlier. He knew it was large. Up close, at least for Byar County, it was massive. It was two stories and a good 150 feet across the front. Manny thought the style would be called Greek something or other. He didn't know. There was a front porch with a balcony above it supported by heavy stone columns, the same material as the gatepost on the highway. The porch he estimated at fifty feet across, and the front facade of the house was again the same white stone, the rest looking like stucco or plaster with more stone accents around windows. Manny noticed the house was not as deep as it was wide, and the drive way curved around the right side of the house and led to a detached four car garage.

Further to the right and back was the horse stable and riding pens. If it had not been the home of Rodney Gott, Manny certainly would have been overwhelmed. It was by far the most elaborate place he had ever visited to serve a search warrant. The porch was up two steps from the ground level and 15 to 20 feet deep to the front door. Manny noted the pale granite tiles that he, Sheriff Bell, and the two deputies stood on waiting for someone to answer the chime he could hear after pushing the button.

Shortly, a middle aged Hispanic woman opened the door. She smiled and nodded when she saw Manny. "Mister Gott is not at home," she said, assuming these policemen were there to see the Senator.

"Is Mrs. Gott here," Manny asked.

"Please come in. I will get her." The woman left the guests standing in the foyer. Manny had removed his hat and the others followed suit. Within a minute, Margarette Gott came to the foyer from the rear of the house.

"What is this about?" Despite being in the States for more than 25 years, she still had a distinct French accent. She was pretty, blonde, trim, and impeccably attired. Manny could tell whatever she had been doing in the rear of the house, it certainly wasn't working.

"Mrs. Gott, I am Lieutenant Rojas of the Texas Rangers. I suppose you know Sheriff Bell." She looked at the sheriff without saying anything, and then returned her glare to the Ranger.

"And, why are you here?" She put her hands on her hips.

"Ma'am, we have a warrant to search the property," Manny said as he handed the paper to Mrs. Gott.

"Search? Do you know whose home this is?" She turned on the sheriff. "How dare you bring this man here. I will not permit this until Rodney is here." She did not look at the warrant.

"I'm sorry, Mrs. Gott. We really don't have any choices. If you will just show us where the gun cabinets are, we shouldn't take long," Sheriff Bell said.

"I am going to call my husband and the District Attorney," Margarette Gott said, as she stormed away.

Manny said, "Sheriff, we need to treat this like any other search. We do not wait for permission."

The sheriff summoned the deputies. "We are looking for a Remington rifle. The caliber will be .308. Probably have a scope on it. Don't need to look any place that would not hold a deer rifle."

The housekeeper was standing in the doorway at the back of the foyer. The sheriff asked her where the den or game room was, or where guns might be kept. Everyone followed her as she left the room, also heading toward the back of the house. She led them through a large family room with windows across the back, looking out onto a patio and pool area. They made their way to the right rear corner of the house into what was essentially a library. Noticeably, along one wall there were no books. It contained a glassed-front gun case.

All four of the law officers were astonished at the extent of the collection. "Damn," the deputy sheriff said. The wood cabinet had half a dozen glass doors providing access to the firearms. To the left were rifles, many with scopes, and in the center, the long guns were evidently shot guns. The right, one-third of the case was taken up by handguns displayed on pegs. The deputy tried one of the doors in front of the rifles, and found it was not locked.

"Be careful there," the sheriff said to his deputies as they started individually examining each of the rifles. He turned to Manny. "Looks like a lot of money tied up in this assortment. Must be 30 rifles and shotguns in there, and 25 or more handguns." Manny grunted, more preoccupied with the return of Mrs. Gott. It didn't take long.

"What the hell is going on here, Bell?" It was Rod Gott followed by Margarette Gott. He had gotten to the house only a few minutes after the warrant servers.

Manny and the sheriff had the same thought simultaneously. The judge called him.

"Rojas, you are going to regret the day you came back snooping around here." Rod Gott had the warrant in his hand shaking it in front of the ranger's face. He had not bothered to look at the warrant; he knew what it was about.

Manny noted the smell of alcohol on Rod's breath. Must have had a liquid lunch. His natural instinct was to strike back at the verbal assault. Instead, his years of training told him to be calm, reserved, and professional.

"There is no .308 Remington here." It was the deputy sheriff.

Manny did allow himself the luxury of addressing Gott by his first name rather than mister or Senator. After all, they had attended school together as kids. "Rodney, we have a warrant to search the premises for a rifle that you purchased last November from Fuller Sporting Goods."

"You're wasting your time. That gun was stolen right after I bought it."

Manny raised an eyebrow. "Did you file a police report?"

"Never got around to it." Gott was turning crimson.

Manny fingered the side of his nose and pursed his lips. "How about an insurance claim?"

Rodney folded his arms and widened his stance. "No. I don't have time to worry about peanuts." He wagged a finger in Manny's face. "I want your ass out of here, and right now."

Manny stared him down, unimpressed, cool. "Where else do you keep firearms on the property?"

"Nowhere." Gott sneered, turned his head to the side and spit air.

"Rodney, you are making this more difficult." Manny looked at Sheriff Bell. "Have your deputies search the remainder of the house for additional gun racks. Look in every closet and under every bed. And check again with the housekeeper. See if she knows of any other places guns are kept." Manny returned his eyes to Rodney. He looked at him much like he did common criminals. At this point, that is how he viewed Senator Rodney Gott. The two locked eyes for a long test of mettle. Gott broke the optical battle off when the sheriff came back after speaking to the housekeeper outside the doorway.

"Bell, if you think we'll let this slide, you're mistaken. You better start cleaning out your desk."

"Just trying to do my job, Senator." Bell motioned to Manny. "Lieutenant, can I speak to you in private?"

"Certainly," Manny said and accompanied Bell out of the foyer.

Once the sheriff was alone with Manny in the huge family room he said, "The housekeeper. She says Ray Gott came and took a rifle out of the house several days ago. Todd put up a little stink because it was his gun. All she knows about it."

"Good, Sheriff. Let your folks search a little longer and then call them off. I don't want Gott to think he can chase us off with threats. And, get the name and address of the housekeeper."

Manny wandered out onto the rear patio. He marveled at the expanse of luxury. This ranch must be a whole section, 640 acres - one square mile. What a place. Green pastures, manicured lawn, huge mansion – it must take a number of hired hands just to maintain the estate on a daily basis. How do some people acquire something like this while the rest of us work for a salary? Manny knew well the psychological danger of being a law enforcement officer, always dealing with the criminal element. Eventually, the lawman may start viewing everyone with whom they come in contact, as a criminal. He questioned himself. Am I giving Rodney Gott the benefit of the doubt? Am I thinking of him being innocent until proven guilty? No, but I am going where the evidence takes me.

CHAPTER SEVENTEEN

Not having a local District Attorney to work with presented a handicap to a ranger building a case. Normally, the D. A. would be collecting statements, assembling other evidence, and presenting it all to a Grand Jury to obtain indictments. Since the Byar County District Attorney was one of the targets, Manny would have to pursue an alternative.

It did appear that Sheriff Bell was giving full cooperation. Sheriff Bell personally took a statement from the Gott's housekeeper stating that Ray Gott removed Todd Gott's rifle from his brother's house.

The sheriff also reported to Manny that Marie Carlisle finally admitted to him that the former sheriff, Oliver Harrell, had convinced her to file a complaint against Clay Longley, and file the lawsuits. According to Marie, Harrell told her if she would make the sexual harassment charges, the District Attorney would get her son transferred to Byar County, and then the D.A. would have him released to her.

Harrell had also told her that she might wind up getting some money out of the deal if Consolidated wanted to settle out of court. Harrell made a strong hint that if she did not go along with it, he and the D.A. would see that the boy was transferred to the adult prison with hardened criminals and sexual predators. Sheriff Bell had Marie sign a statement detailing the facts.

The apparent crimes were stacking up, and they all had one thing in common – the Gotts. The State would follow the Local Government Code of Texas that provides a means for removal from office of county officials, including the District Attorney. The General Grounds for Removal identifies "official misconduct" as one of the justifications for removal. Manny felt he had sufficient evidence to have Ray Gott so removed.

The process started with a resident of the county filing a petition with the District Judge. Since the obstruction of justice by the D.A. dealt with the shooting of the Longley's cattle, the Ranger thought it appropriate that he give them an opportunity to be informed, even though his plan did not include their participation. Manny called Clay to set up a meeting in Byar, telling him only that it dealt with his parents' Longhorns, and he wanted to bring them up to date on the investigation. Clay arranged for the meeting to be at the Longley's ranch. He immediately placed a call to Forest, who wanted to attend.

***

Manny brought Sheriff Bell along for the meeting. He cautioned the attendees on the confidentiality of the information he was about to give them until after it became public record.

"The shell case that you recovered, a .308, contained only a partial finger print. It's of little use. One of the local owners of a .308 rifle is Rodney Gott. He purchased a rifle this past year, evidently for his son Todd," Manny explained to an attentive audience.

"Then it was the Gott boy that shot our stock." Will said, jumping ahead.

"There's more. The Sheriff's Office has also identified a witness who observed Todd Gott riding an orange-colored ATV across the highway with a rifle, the day your cattle were slain. We have a statement from that witness. Sheriff Bell advised District Attorney Raymond Gott of the existence of the witness, and the D.A. directed him to make the witness unavailable. We executed a search warrant of the Gott home and didn't find the firearm in question. We do have a witness statement that a rifle belonging to Todd Gott was previously taken from the home by Raymond Gott. The Gotts have two orange-colored ATVs, each outfitted with a gun rack for hunting. We believe there is sufficient testimony to charge the District Attorney with obstruction of justice." The Ranger thought it best to leave out some details - like the identity of witnesses and the existence of the tape recording.

"I've had this feeling all along that the Gotts were behind this," Will Longley said.

"I have too," Forest said. "This has always looked like more than, and I'll use the term *simple,* malicious vandalism." Everyone was nodding their head in agreement.

"Where do we go from here?" Clay said.

"Texas Statutes, under Local Code – that is the part of the law that defines the operation of county governments – provides procedures for having a county official, including a district attorney, removed from office." Manny addressed his explanation to the Longleys, assuming the Sheriff and Forest were at least somewhat familiar with what he was saying. "The Code requires addressing a petition to the district judge detailing the case against the county official. This petition must be filed by a six-month or more resident of the county. Sheriff Bell will file the petition." Manny had already confirmed with the sheriff the planned process.

"What about having Will and Elizabeth file the petition," Forest asked. He was thinking about being sure the condemnation of the Longley property was tied, at least in the eyes of the public, to illegal activity by the Gotts.

"Being long time residents of the county, they certainly have a right to file a petition, but I think in this instance Sheriff Bell should be the petitioner. Of course, the sheriff will be supported by the Texas Rangers and the Texas Attorney General if necessary."

"Well, we sure aren't afraid of the Gotts," Will said.

"No, sir. I'm sure you're not, but the sheriff has first hand knowledge, and frankly is the more qualified to file the petition."

"I agree," said Clay. "No point in you being involved."

"We're the ones that are out thousands of dollars. I want to nail whoever shot our cattle. If it's that kid, he is plenty old enough to know better." Will was more agitated than normal.

Sheriff Bell entered the discussion for the first time. "In a situation like this, meaning there is a financial loss due to criminal activity, we ask the victims what they would rather have. Would you rather get your money for the value of the lost cattle or would you rather see someone go to jail."

"The money is substantial. Of course we would rather get the money," Elizabeth Longley answered without seeking consent from her husband. Will nodded. There was no disagreement between them.

"Most times folks tend to say they want to get their money."

Forest gave his view to Will and Elizabeth, also intended for Clay. "If you have a decent case against Todd Gott, and it sounds like you do, it should be easy to get the Gotts to cover the loss. They certainly can afford it. You could pursue a civil case, a lawsuit for damages, and that may take a year or so. I think what the sheriff is saying is, agree not to go for criminal charges against Todd Gott in exchange for immediate restitution from Rodney Gott. Now, this doesn't have anything to do with the petition or the case against the D.A."

"That's pretty much what I was thinking," the sheriff said.

"You might want to hold off for just a while on any action against Todd Gott. Give us a chance to pursue the petition to remove Raymond Gott from the D.A. Office," Manny said.

"Of course," Forest said for the Longleys. He understood that if the Longleys needed the threat of criminal action against Todd to get Rodney Gott to agree to a settlement, it would be better if Rod's brother were not the D.A. "But this is not something that I can do. It's a violation of ethics to threaten criminal action to force a civil settlement."

Manny said, explaining due process under Texas law, "Part of what Sheriff Bell does when he files the petition is, he applies for a citation to be issued against the D.A. A certified copy of the petition and citation will be served to Ray Gott. The citation will require the D.A. to appear in court five days after service to answer the petition. If the District Judge finds merit in the charges, the case is set for trial. The judge may also immediately suspend the D.A. from office and appoint a temporary replacement. We will ask for immediate suspension."

"Just to be sure the judge doesn't get cold feet having to deal with the Gotts, Ranger Rojas will be accompanying me before the judge."

"We'll also have a representative from the Texas Attorney General's Office. It'll get out fast that we are loaded for bear," Manny said, displaying his confidence that the District Judge would not try to short circuit the process.

***

Word finally got around that the largest law firm in Byar County was breaking up. Marcus Franks contacted Mason Griggs at the County Judge Office and obtained an interview. Mason provided background on the origin of the firm, starting with his great uncle, Leland Griggs, in the 1920s. followed by his father, James Robert Griggs. Marcus wrote the story for the paper much the way Mason told it. Except for the "no comment" when asked why the firm was dissolving after such a long history, Marcus thought the judge was far more relaxed and open than he had been the previous time they had met.

Mason made it a point to state that he continued to strongly support the development of the Byar County Convention Center, and that he hoped equitable agreements could be reached for the acquisition of the property that was required. Marcus also asked what Mason's plans were for the future, and agreed the answer could be off the record. Mason confided that he intended to complete his elected term as County Judge, not seek re-election, and then to open a small private practice in Byar. He promised to contact Marcus as soon as he was ready to make the announcement, probably within a couple of months.

Marvin MacDonald convinced Consolidated Human Resources that the complaints by the two women were more a legal issue than a personnel concern. The postponed visit by the corporate employee relations specialist was cancelled. Marvin would be working through the plaintiffs' attorney, Robert Ward, to take a deposition from each woman, but since the Texas Rangers were investigating the possible extortion conspiracy, Marvin would wait.

Manny contacted Jeanie Ferguson at her home one evening after she got off work. Her husband was not home, but she invited him to sit in the family room.

"Mrs. Ferguson, our investigation has led us to believe there is a conspiracy to extort money from Consolidated Industries, and from Mr. Clayton Longley. We have found no evidence to indicate Mr. Longley is guilty of the claims that you and another employee of Consolidated made against him." She sat passively on her sofa while Manny spoke. "I will also tell you that the other woman has admitted that her charge is not true. Before you possibly dig yourself deeper, let me tell you, if your complaint and your lawsuit are not true, this is a crime."

"I really need to speak to my husband. Today at work I received a call from my lawyer, Mr. Ward. I have to go see him about this tomorrow at his office."

"Mr. Ward is your attorney for these lawsuits. Are you saying you want to talk to Mr. Ward to represent you for the possible commission of a crime?"

"No."

"Do you know Mr. Oliver Harrell?"

"Yes. I know him." Jeanie fidgeted in her chair, biting a nail.

Manny tugged on his cheek, regarding her for a second. "The other woman who made the same complaint as you have made, has admitted that Oliver Harrell coerced her into filing the complaint and lawsuit. She made the complaint in exchange for a promise that District Attorney Raymond Gott would get her son out of some legal problems."

Jeanie looked down. "I was only trying to help my husband."

She's about to give in, Manny thought sure. "Please tell me in your own words exactly what happened,"

"Mr. Harrell came here at night and talked to Gene and me. Gene is my husband, Eugene. Gene was arrested for stealing cars and using parts in his paint and body shop. He hasn't had a trial yet. Mr. Harrell said that Gene was going to prison for many years. He told us he could get the charges dropped if we would file this complaint. He said the District Attorney would do that. He said we needed to see this lawyer and file a lawsuit too. It would make it look more ...." She searched for the word "...legitimate. He said we may even collect some money if my company wanted to settle it."

"Mr. Ferguson also agreed to this scheme?"

"We didn't do it for the money. Mr. Harrell said we had to ask for the money. It was to keep Gene from going to prison. Mr. Harrell said that if we didn't do it, the District Attorney would send Gene to prison for as long as possible, maybe 10 or 15 years."

"Did either you or your husband know Mr. Harrell before he came to the house that night?"

Jeanie was wringing her hands. "No, sir, we didn't. We have a little girl. She wouldn't have a father if Gene is sent to jail."

Manny had to press on, even though the pleading tone of her voice indicated she might fall apart any second now. "Who decided on the amount of damages you asked for in the lawsuit?"

She sighed in resignation. "Mr. Harrell told the lawyer how much. He said it was to make them know we were serious. He told me everything to say." She leaned forward, buried her face in her hands and let out a sob.

"One final question, Mrs. Ferguson, then I'm through, promise. Is there any truth to your complaint against Mr. Longley?" Many felt he had to have a definitive answer. There could be no surprises later.

Jeanie's sobbing intensified. Her face still in her hands, she said, "No, sir. It's not true. The only thing Mr. Longley has ever said to me is 'Hello.' I'm sorry I did this. Mr. Harrell didn't give us much of a choice." She lifted her face, daring a look.

Manny clucked his tongue, produced a pad of paper and pen, and handed them to her. "I know this is hard, but I do need a written statement from you. Please start at the beginning, and tell in your own words what happened and, to the best of your recollection, the things that were said."

She held the pen to the paper, pausing. Her eyes bespoke her intense fears as she braved the question, "How much trouble am I in."

Manny sat back in his chair and brought two fingers to his lips for a moment, thinking how best to answer. I feel sorry for this woman. From Robert Ward's description of Jeanie Ferguson and my own questioning, I can tell she's a timid soul - easily manipulated by the likes of an Oliver Harrell. I'll not pursue her as a conspirator. There are far more guilty people to prosecute.

He huffed, brought his hands together in a clap, leaned forward and rested his chin on his clasped hands, elbows on knees. "Mrs. Ferguson, there are two things I'm trying to determine in my investigation." He sat upright and held up a forefinger. "First, is your claim true? You have indicated that it is not." A second finger popped up. "Secondly, were you forced into making a false claim? If what you've told me is accurate, I would expect that you would not be in much trouble."

Jeanie managed a small smile. As she started writing, Manny mulled the other participants. Oliver Harrell was one of them. There was no question about that. The real question in his mind was whether the scheme could be tracked back to Griggs and Gott, or at least to the Gotts. Manny had heard that Griggs and the Gotts were splitting the blanket. What about Mason Griggs? Something made him quit the law practice with the Gotts. Lifelong friends?

CHAPTER EIGHTEEN

Sheriff Bell had made arrangements with the District Judge's clerk to appear before him as the final item of business for the day. The courtroom would be empty except for the judge, the court recorder, and the clerk. The sheriff, accompanied by Ranger Rojas and a prosecutor from the Attorney General's Office, appeared as scheduled. The sheriff presented his petition, describing the evidence to support the charge of official misconduct on the part of the District Attorney.

Manny took the opportunity to speak, and assured the judge the Texas Department of Public Safety, Division of the Texas Rangers was part of the investigation. The Attorney General prosecutor also advised the judge that his office was coordinating with the Texas Rangers. He informed him also that pre-coordination had been made with the adjoining county to prosecute the case, since this is what the Texas Local Code provides for if the removal case is against the District Attorney. The prosecutor also stated for the record that if Byar County failed to respond to the charges, the Attorney General's Office was prepared to assume prosecution responsibilities.

Jimmy Bell knew he was well past the point of no return. He had gone over to the other side to be at odds with the political elite of the county. He felt certain that had he appeared alone before the judge his petition would have been summarily rejected.

The non-verbal feedback from the old magistrate was obvious disapproval of what he was forced to do. Here, in probably his last year on the bench, he was not interested in getting entangled with the Gotts' problems, and for sure did not want any help from the Attorney General's Office on how to run his courtroom. He didn't want a fight with those damn Republicans. The judge accepted the petition, and ruled that a citation would be issued to District Attorney Raymond Gott to appear in court the following week.

***

Ranger Rojas still had other business in Byar before returning to Houston. It was 5:00 p.m. when Manny arrived at the modest red brick home. He found Oliver Harrell's Jeep wagon parked in the driveway, so he knocked on his door. Sheriff Bell said that Harrell was a tough old bird. Manny wondered how tough.

"Mister Harrell, I'm Ranger Lieutenant Rojas," he said when the man opened the door. He was greeted with a frown. They had said Harrell was in his mid-sixties, and he looked it, but he also looked physically fit.

He had a full head of white hair and clear hazel eyes that could be seen behind his wireframe glasses. He had a thick neck, barrel chest and trim waist. Manny figured this was someone who could still hold his own in a tussle.

"What can I do for you, Ranger?" There was no warmth in the question.

"I am investigating a case of extortion. May I come in?"

"Sure." Harrell stepped back, holding the door wide open. When Manny was inside, the older man led the Ranger through the living room, the dining room, and into a den. He pointed to the vinyl-covered sofa for Manny to sit, all without speaking. No one else was present so Manny assumed Harrell lived in the house alone. It had that look about it.

"What's this about extortion," Harrell asked.

"Mr. Harrell, do you know Mrs. Jeanie Ferguson and Ms. Marie Carlisle?"

"Yeah, I know them." There was no point in lying about that. It wasn't the first time he had been questioned by law enforcement in the last 20 years of doing odd jobs for Griggs and Gott. There was also no question of why the Ranger was at his house.

"Please tell me how you came to know them."

"I think somebody told me about Ferguson, don't remember who. Said she needed some help on a problem she had at work. Just went by to see what I could do. Marie, I've known her for years. I think when she heard about the other gal's problems she called me to see what she could do about her own problem."

"We're getting different stories here. In both instances, the women have given statements that you contacted them. Also, in their statements, they've admitted that their claims were false, and that you had coerced them by threats to make those claims."

"Not true." It was all Harrell would say.

"Mr. Harrell, what is your connection to Griggs and Gott, Attorneys at Law?" Manny realized that Harrell would not be volunteering any answers. He only responded to the question asked, nothing more.

"Don't have any connection."

"Are you saying you do not perform any services for that law firm?"

"Oh, I've probably done some work for some of their clients."

Manny thought to himself that he should have already gone after Harrell's banking records. Harrell is denying what I'm betting will be obvious once I get around to subpoenaing his bank accounts. He's had years of receiving checks from the lawyers, and it's likely they are so smug, overconfident and arrogant they all took it for granted that it needn't be a cash under-the-table business. He would get right on that.

"These two women in question - both indicate that you promised District Attorney Raymond Gott would use his office to alleviate legal problems of family members. Are you familiar with the nature of those legal problems?"

"Wasn't an item of discussion. We just talked about that Longley guy hitting on them at work and demanding sexual favors."

"What about your reference to the D.A.?" He thought sure mentioning the D.A. would get some type of response or emotion from him. But nothing. Not so much as a squirm.

"Again, not true," Harrell said with flat voice.

"Frankly, Mr. Harrell, I'm inclined to believe the statements of the women. This investigation will continue. It would be unfortunate for someone like you to spend his final days in prison for doing someone else's dirty work. You can expect to see me again." Manny rose and headed for the front door with a silent Harrell following.

***

A smiling Marvin appeared in Clay's open doorway. "Just received a phone call from Mr. Robert Ward, attorney for Jeanie Ferguson and Marie Carlisle. He advised Consolidated that he is filing today to withdraw the lawsuits by his clients against Consolidated."

"That's good news. Wonder about mine," Clay said.

"I expect he'll be contacting your attorney also. He said that further investigation has convinced him that the claims have no merit. He actually apologized. Imagine that."

"You mean you lawyers normally don't do that when you screw up?" Clay said in jest.

"Yeah. We're a lot like engineers in that respect." Marvin had grown more comfortable with Clay, and enjoyed the light-hearted sparring.

Millie stuck her head in around Marvin, who was still in the doorway. "Clay, Mr. Robert Ward on line two for you."

"Hey, there he is," Marvin said.

Clay answered the phone with his normal salutation. "Clay Longley, may I help you?"

"Mr. Longley, this is Robert Ward. I represent Mrs. Jeanie Ferguson and Ms. Marie Carlisle in these lawsuits. I apologize for disturbing you. I would normally be contacting your attorney; however I do not yet know who you have engaged. But, anyway, while I have you, I would like you to know that the lawsuits will be withdrawn."

"I thank you for calling, Mr. Ward. That news helps make my day."

Clay nodded to Marvin and Millie who were anticipating the official news. Clay gave him his attorney's name and phone number in Houston. After he was off the phone, Clay said to Marvin, "I want you to know how much I appreciate your support in this. It would have been easy for you to believe otherwise, but you believed me, so thank you."

"You're welcome, but I still don't know what this was all about. Why would they do it?"

"Forest Donovan thinks it's connected to the problems with my parents. His theory is that it's part of the harassment by the Gotts to get the ranch." Clay had come to believe Forest's view of the situation was accurate, and now didn't mind sharing that with Marvin.

"Well, I've got to consult with Human Resources about the two women. They both filed sexual harassment complaints through the company, and if their claims are false, they will be terminated."

"Someone convinced them to, or made them do it," Clay said.

"In my superficial internal investigation, I found out Mrs. Ferguson has a husband who is going to trial for car theft. I'm sure she'll be in need of some extra money. That could be her motivation. Don't know about Ms. Carlisle."

"Let's not be too hasty. I think the Gotts are behind it."

"You may be right. Both of the women concerned are considered good employees."

"Just hold off everything until we know the full story."

***

Rod Gott was in his Senator's office when he received the phone call from the old judge. Of course, the District Judge was not supposed to be calling, no more so than when he had warned Rod about the search warrant, but he thought it would be one last favor. He told Rod everything – the sheriff, the Texas Rangers and the Attorney General, all ganged up on his brother. He told Rod the petition was to remove the D.A. from office for misconduct, that is, obstruction of justice. The District Judge would have to order a jury trial, and the evidence would be convincing. The sheriff had Ray on tape ordering him to intimidate and hide witnesses. There would also be testimony that Ray disposed of evidence. Ray had taken Todd's rifle from the house. The trial would also convict Todd, at least in the public's eye, of killing the cattle at the Longley Ranch.

What the hell is happening, Rod thought when he was off the phone. These pricks – Jimmy Bell and Manny Rojas. That unappreciative bastard Bell. He owes me and he does this shit. And that damn Mexican. How the hell did he get to his position to cause this much trouble. He never made better than a C in school. Ray was due back to the Law Office soon, so Rod waited. He assailed Ray without regard to the presence of several young associates working late in the office complex. It got loud.

"I can't believe you could let yourself be outsmarted by that dimwit Jimmy Bell. For Christ sakes, you let him record you!"

"I can't imagine what I said that would...." Ray was cut off.

"You told Bell to make those witnesses get out of town. You gave them money. Damn."

Ray recalled, approximately, what he had told the sheriff. Things like 'Get rough,' 'use some muscle,' and 'break a leg' were in there somewhere. That would be damning evidence. Rod paced around Ray's office cursing and muttering while Ray dropped silently into his executive style desk chair.

"If things weren't screwed up enough, this does it. There goes the statewide race. Hell, I may not even be able to get re-elected to the Senate." Rod was talking to himself as much as to Ray. His comments weren't lost on Ray.

"Remember, what I did was for Todd and for you. If they had gotten their hands on that rifle, you know there wouldn't be any doubt. Instead of sending him off to college, you would be seeing him on visiting day at Huntsville." Ray exaggerated a little, using the colloquial term 'Huntsville' to mean the state prison. As D.A., he could have determined what evidence was valid and, given all the circumstances, Todd would not even have gone to trial. No, it ultimately wasn't about keeping Todd out of the state prison in Huntsville or even the county jail, it was protecting the Gott name. The Gotts were politically powerful and they wanted to stay that way, albeit big fish in a little pond.

Rod stopped pacing long enough to give Ray a condemning "how dare you" stare that included "you stupid ass."

Ray struck back. "I'm the one that's in trouble, and you are thinking how it affects you. You're worried about a damn election. I'm worried about going to jail." It was just words to Rod, but Ray's own words were like being hit by a train. He rose from his chair, leaned forward with his hands on the desk and repeated them one by one for emphasis. "Going. To. Jail."

"I didn't tell you to be stupid," were Rod's last words as he stormed from Ray's office. He jerked the door closed hard and loud, leaving Ray standing at his desk.

Approach it as a legal problem, Ray told himself. Witnesses? It was a Jordan fellow, and it had to be someone at Rod's house. Yeah, it had to be the Mexican housekeeper. It wouldn't matter if they disappeared or were unable to testify – they had sworn statements.

Ray had recently reviewed the Local Code in contemplation of using it to remove the sheriff from office. When he had read over it he never dreamed it was about to be applied to himself. It wasn't a trial just to remove him from office, although it would surely do that; it would be a conviction. The penalty would be imprisonment. Ray didn't think about guilt or innocence. He knew the answer to that. This is why Mason walked out on us. We have gone too far past the line, that fuzzy line that the Bodas always pushed back and forth to suit our purposes.

Ray knew there was likely to be no legal maneuver or gimmick that could materially affect the situation. He would be convicted. He would be incarcerated, and would share a world with some of the most despicable vermin he had had the duty to put away – to protect society. Yes, I will know some of my new associates. A D.A. in prison will be worse than an ex-cop in prison. I will be subjected to the most gruesome treatment other prisoners can inflict on a fellow inmate. Rape, beatings…murder?

Ray didn't have the wherewithal to do any work, so, thoughtlessly, left his office to drive home. He was driving his dark blue BMW, a benefit provided by the law firm. His mind wandered to his wife Claire. There was also his and Rod's mother, who Ray and Claire continued to live with. What will I tell them? This will devastate them. And yes, it will end Rod's political career, which until now, seemed so bright. It was too much to contemplate alone. Mason was gone and Rod had deserted him.

The Beamer was traveling at the 60 mile per hour speed limit. Ray punched the accelerator as he approached the bridge overpass. The speedometer passed 90. He took aim and at the last second Ray dropped his hand and unfastened his seat belt.

CHAPTER NINETEEN

"The D.A. was killed in a car wreck. It happened about an hour ago," Marcus Franks excitedly reported to Clay on the phone. It was the first Clay had heard. He had left work, stopped at his parents to share the good news on the lawsuits being dropped, and had headed over to the airport to piddle with his aircraft.

"What happened?" was all Clay could think to say.

"Single car accident. His car left the road and ran into the bridge overpass concrete pilings. Dead at the scene. I got out here just as they got him out of the wreck."

"Was he alone?" God I hope Claire wasn't in the car, was Clay's silent thought.

"Yeah. Guess he was on the way home."

"Claire, his wife, she isn't out there, is she?"

"No. Rod was here, but left. Guess he's going to break it to their mother and Ray's wife. He smelled like he had a few, but didn't act intoxicated. The DPS didn't stop him."

Clay wanted to go to Claire. He wanted to console her for the loss of her husband. Despite the current hard feelings between him and the Gotts, Clay thought he did not remember when it was he didn't know Ray and Rod, and felt some measure of personal sorrow. At times like this, personal adversity should be put aside. He washed his hands and left for Pecan Estates.

Clay knew where Ray and Claire lived, although he had never been in the home where Rod and Ray were raised. He had also never been invited into Mason's home, next door. He found the driveway full of cars. When he knocked, it was Mason who opened the door.

"Hello, Mason. I just heard, and wanted to come over."

"Yeah, Clay, come in." When he was inside, Mason introduced Clay to his wife, whom he had never met. Clay found Claire sitting in the den at the rear of the house. There were already a number of visitors offering condolences and whatever assistance they could.

"Claire, I'm so sorry to hear," Clay said as Claire rose to greet him. Clay held out a hand, but as Claire got closer, his natural inclination was to hug her tightly, which he did. He felt her hugging back, and had to resist the temptation to kiss her on the cheek. It wasn't the time or place.

"Thank you for coming, Clay." Claire's eyes were wet, any makeup long ago wiped away.

"Is there anything that I can do for you?" Clay said.

"No. No. I don't know. I guess Rod will take care of everything. The doctor is here. He's taking care of Mama Gott, in her room. It's really bad for her. I can only imagine what it is like to lose a child, even one as old as we are. You remember my parents, don't you?" Claire said, as she pulled Clay's arm toward the end of the sofa where the Brooks were seated. Clay exchanged greetings with the couple, whom he had not seen since he and Claire had broken up, during college.

Others were arriving to console the family. One of the new arrivals was a black lady who came directly to Claire. She was their housekeeper, who had left for the day, but upon learning of Ray's accident, had returned to the house to work for as long as needed. Claire greeted new arrivals as Clay made small talk with the Brooks. Some of those who came in brought food items, as is the custom throughout the South.

Rod Gott came into the den from a hallway that led to the bedrooms. He immediately spotted Clay and came toward him. "What are you doing here, Longley? My brother isn't even cold and you're here trying to...." Rod let his words trail off, not completing the charge. There were plenty of guests close enough to hear Rod, and probably most of them assumed Rod meant Clay was there to hit on the newly widowed Claire. "We would rather you not be here," Rod said.

"I'm truly sorry to hear about Ray," Clay said, even though he didn't believe it would be accepted with the sincerity he felt. He was sorry, true. Most of the sorrow he felt was for Claire.

Rod's voice was more like a hissing viper than a growling dog. "You damn Longleys are the reason this happened."

Clay looked at Claire. She was staring at Rod with a disapproving frown. Without saying anything further, Clay started for the door. Rod followed him out, ranting over Clay's shoulder as he walked.

"Wish to hell you had never come back here. I ought to just have you Longleys disappear. I know people who can do that. Think I'll just do it myself." No one but Clay was close enough to hear Rod's threat.

Clay stopped on the walkway. He turned and looked up at Rod. His instinct was to be on alert and ready to fight - fortunately so. Clay leaned back to avoid a wild and wide right hook. He countered with a left - caught Rod square on the jaw before he regained his balance. Clay hadn't hit him as hard he should have. He was ready to follow with a right jab. Not necessary. Rod stumbled a step to his left and went down on all fours. Out of shape, fat and drunk...those factors did him in.

"What was that all about?" Clay addressed the question to Mason, who had followed shortly behind them.

Mason looked at Rod who was still on his hands and knees. Rod slowly struggled to his feet without speaking. He staggered toward a silver SUV parked in the driveway. He opened the door, but stopped to deliver one last threat.

"You Longleys better watch your back. This isn't over."

"I don't know that I've ever seen him so stressed," Mason said.

"I'd call that gone mad. I think he just threatened to kill me and my family." Clay had felt his heart racing, but began to relax once Rod drove away.

"It's this convention center project and the property disagreement. I think he sees his political career going down the drain ... and now Ray's death," Mason said. He thought about the issue with Todd shooting the Longleys' cattle, but didn't mention it. He didn't deny that Rod had made a threat.

"I don't know why he thinks the Longleys are the source of all his problems. Y'all are the ones trying to take our property," Clay said, his tone and expression including Mason in the accusation. "Then Rod's kid shot Dad's cattle. Who are the trouble makers?"

"Clay, I had nothing to do with that and in Rod's defense, he didn't either. That is something the kid did, on his own."

Clay considered that statement. He had no proof otherwise, but had his suspicions. "Well, he sure tried to cover it up, and that's something that's not over with." Clay had calmed now, and was able to speak at a normal conversational level. "I can't believe he really thinks it's anyone else's fault for Ray's accident. What could he have meant by that?"

Mason's voice trembled. "There was no apparent cause for the accident, or should I just say, the crash." He was visibly shaken, having lost his best friend for his entire life. "Rod thinks Ray drove his car into the bridge." Mason immediately wondered if he was saying more than he should have. He had been around enough people under stress to recognize they often speak too freely. Clay had not considered the possibility, but he knew what Mason was saying. From his last meeting with Manny Rojas and Sheriff Bell, he appreciated the legal problems presented to the D.A. Clay understood what the motivation would have been to cause Ray to take his own life. Yes, the conflict with the Longleys could very well be a cause, but not the root cause. It was not from what the Longleys had done, it was what the Gotts had done to the Longleys.

"Intentionally?" Clay said.

"Word gets out fast. Sheriff Bell and Manny Rojas from the Rangers went to court today and petitioned to have Ray removed from office for misconduct."

Clay looked at Mason. He's unaware I already know these details, he thought.

Mason said, "I didn't know Ray's psyche was that fragile. I suppose you know I left the law firm. We were in a period of disagreement, but we've been friends and neighbors for so long, I figured we'd get past it and still have some contact."

"I read that in the paper. It didn't say why you left, though." Clay thought this a good opportunity to fish for an explanation. Byar needed to know everything.

"Actually, I should keep this all confidential. I would appreciate it if you wouldn't repeat anything I've said. It can only hurt Claire and Mama Gott." Mason clammed up after that statement.

Clay understood and agreed. He would not do anything that was likely to cause anguish to Claire. Clay also realized Rod's insinuation and unspoken characterization of him as an opportunist concerning the new widow was correct. He loved Claire and now she was available.

***

The Byar County News front page headline read, "D.A. Gott Dies in Auto Crash" and was accompanied with a photo of the smashed and unrecognizable BMW. The article reported that the investigating officer from DPS estimated the vehicle was traveling at 100 miles an hour when it hit the bridge. Marcus had three different articles in the paper. He had heard rumors and declined to refer to it as an auto accident, but he did not write that it was a possible suicide. The headline article reported the details of the crash, the seventh auto fatality in the county for the year.

Another front-page article covered the life and achievements of Ray. On page three was the story about Sheriff Bell's petition for removal from office, an action that was now moot. Readers could draw their own conclusions.

Clay had sent flowers, and also a sympathy card, to Claire with a handwritten note. He didn't indicate his intentions, but he knew in his heart that he intended to stay in touch with Claire. There were no other women in his life. He had already committed himself to Claire, but he could not rush it. Claire deserved a period of mourning and adjustment.

Meanwhile, Marvin had Consolidated HR contact the two women who had filed complaints against Clay, and, in each instance, the women retracted their assertion of sexual harassment. Clay's record was clean when Manny came calling the next time.

"That was a shocker about Ray," Manny said.

"Yes. It was something I never expected. The county turned out for the funeral. I went, but stayed in the background. No point in getting Rod turned on again. He threw me out of Ray's house."

"Word around Austin is that he's a big time intimidator. You know, that's the way he treated everyone in high school. Anyway, the reason I came by is to give you an update on the investigation. I'm confident that

Jeanie Ferguson and Marie Carlisle were forced into making complaints against you. Their lawyer called and said the suits have been dropped."

"Yeah, I heard the same thing from him and my lawyer," Clay said.

"Ferguson has a husband going to trial for grand theft auto, and they were threatened that if they didn't cooperate, the D.A. was going to bury him. If she goes along, the D.A. drops the case. Carlisle has a son in county jail in Lufkin. Same kind of threat. If she cooperates, the D.A. gets the kid out and sends him home. Otherwise, they feed him to the perverts."

"I knew it had to be something."

"Oliver Harrell, the old sheriff, was the D.A.'s muscle. He dragged them both in to see that lawyer, and ramroded the whole deal."

"Now with Ray gone, does that pretty much end the investigation on the cattle?" Clay said.

"As far as a criminal case, I don't believe we have sufficient evidence. I could get prints from Todd Gott, and maybe include him as a suspect, but remember I told you I doubt we can get the shell casing admitted as evidence. Also, Rod claims the rifle in question was stolen. They could admit Todd crossed the highway with a rifle, but it was one of the other rifles. I saw them. They have plenty of other rifles it could have been."

"Forest mentioned something about a civil case," Clay said.

"Probably your best bet. Who knows, Rod may want to settle that out of court."

"I'll talk to my parents. It's not in his normal practice, but maybe Forest will help with that. Maybe he can get some of Rod's money." Clay chuckled to himself at his own quip with the 'Forest' part.

Manny said, "I spoke to Harrell. Nothing yet from him, but I'm going to make another run at him. Without his man in the D.A. Office, he might change his attitude."

"What happens to the D.A. office? Who fills the vacancy?" Clay asked.

"The Byar County Board of Commissioners appoints someone to serve until the next general election. For the most part, I understand the Board is mostly Griggs and Gott cronies. I suppose we'll wait and see who they appoint."

"One thing I also wanted to ask. What about the Texas concealed handgun law? I've been thinking about getting a license." The change in Texas law had occurred while Clay was living in Georgia, and he had read something about it, but did not know the details. He thought the Ranger would be a good person to ask.

"Any reason why you're considering it?"

"Rod Gott took a swing at me, and threatened the lives of all the Longleys."

Manny's eyelids raised. "Any witnesses to the threat?"

Clay bunched his lips, shook his head and scratched his chin. "No. And maybe it was nothing, but I figure, why not?"

Manny nodded. "If you want to carry a handgun, either concealed on your person or in your vehicle, you must have the permit. To get that, you have to take the course and exam, demonstrate proficiency with the weapon, and be photographed and fingerprinted for the application. I'm sure you can find someone local who is teaching the course, and they'll provide you the request for the application."

"I think I'll do it."

Manny dropped his professional Ranger demeanor and spoke to Clay as an old friend. "I'm sure being in the infantry, you're comfortable with firearms. Do you have a pistol?"

"I've got a 1911 Service Model, .45 ACP."

"One of my favorites," Manny said. "Kind of big for a carry weapon, though." Manny was very familiar with the old Colt model that had for years been the standard military sidearm.

"Yeah. I'll probably just leave it in my car. If need be, I may get something smaller."

"Still carry a .45 myself," Manny said, patting his stainless sidearm holstered at his waistband. "This is a Smith & Wesson, double action. But I loved the old Service Model."

"While I was on active duty the Army converted to the Beretta 9 millimeter as the standard sidearm. Lots of the old hands weren't happy about that. They never thought the 9 millimeter had enough punch," Clay said.

"Same thing in the Air Force. We carried the 9s. As far as the license, I discourage it for some people and endorse it for others. Just don't let that .45 get you in trouble."

CHAPTER TWENTY

Once Clay broached the idea of Forest handling the civil suit against Rod Gott for the Longleys' loss, Forest agreed to take it on. He relished the idea of getting the Senator in court. He filed the suit in Byar County as William and Elizabeth Longley vs. Rodney Burnette Gott *et al.* The total value of the lost Longhorns was documented to be $27,000, and Forest suggested asking punitive damages of ten times that amount, plus fees. He cautioned the Longleys to not get excited about the prospect of winning the punitive damages, but a jury might award something.

Clay was pleased when he received a phone call from Mason Griggs alerting him that the Byar County Board of Commissioners were going to hold a special meeting to address the appointment of an interim District Attorney. He in turn called Manny, and the Ranger agreed to attend the Board meeting with Clay.

The norm was for the Board to meet twice monthly in regular meetings held on Wednesday nights at the courthouse. A special meeting was typically called for emergency actions or for topics outside the mundane finances and county road maintenance issues that consumed most regular meetings. Anticipating an unusually large attendance, Mason moved the special meeting into the larger of the two courtrooms.

It was somewhat of a surprise when Manny appeared, accompanied by the representative from the Texas Attorney General Office. Manny introduced the lawyer to Mason before the meeting started, and Clay, Manny, and the prosecutor, took seats in the front row. The pending appointment attracted a number of resumes from Byar County attorneys. Mason's call had the effect he desired. State Senator Rodney Gott would not be the dominating influence on the actions of the Board. Surely, Rod had his own candidate, one he had previously introduced to the three commissioners that he considered to be in his pocket. All of the attorneys who had submitted resumes to demonstrate their interest in the appointment were present and prepared to address the Commissioners if given the opportunity.

After calling the meeting to order, Mason addressed the assembly.

"Thank all of you for attending this very important Byar County Board of Commissioners Meeting. I say this is important, because what we do here tonight will have a long lasting influence on the future of the City of Byar and Byar County. Recently Byar County has been the scene of an investigation by the Office of the Texas Rangers, as noted by the attendance of Ranger Lieutenant Manuel Rojas." Mason motioned to Manny to please stand up. "Ranger Rojas is originally from Byar, and many of you may remember him. Thanks for being here tonight," Mason said as

Manny took his seat.

"The investigation I mentioned has also attracted the attention of the Texas Attorney General's Office, who has a prosecutor here this evening. Mr. Tanner, would you please stand." Mason paused briefly to allow the prosecutor to be recognized, hoping the gravity of State oversight would have an influence on the Board of Commissioners. "Thank you, sir," the judge addressed the Attorney General's representative, and continued his introductory remarks.

"It is appropriate that these gentlemen be here tonight because, as I'm sure you all know, the investigation I mentioned dealt directly with the Byar County District Attorney. Over the past two weeks, my office has received a number of resumes of Byar County attorneys exhibiting interest in the appointment of an interim District Attorney. On behalf of the Board, and the citizens of Byar County, I thank you for your desire to serve your community in public office."

Mason continued. "The appointment that the Board of Commissioners will make tonight will be to fill the remaining seventeen months of Mr. Gotts' term – essentially until the next general election. A portfolio of all resumes has been provided each Commissioner. One resume in your folder is that of Nathan Kirkland. Mr. Kirkland, would you please stand?" Again, Mason paused while a gray-headed man seated up front stood and faced first the Board, and then turned and faced the courtroom of citizens. He smiled and gave a friendly wave to the audience.

"Thank you, Mr. Kirkland. Gentlemen, Mr. Kirkland recently retired from the Harris County District Attorney Office where he served as Assistant District Attorney for the previous 12 years. He has a total of 32 years of legal experience and has recently moved to Byar County where he has built a retirement home on Lake Byar. I particularly sought out Mr. Kirkland, and asked him to consider this interim appointment. I assured Mr. Kirkland, that should he be appointed, the workload would be nothing like what he has known in Houston. Mr. Kirkland, should he receive this appointment, commits to not seek elected office next year - his appointment would be only interim. It would serve to provide our cadre of Byar County attorneys a level playing field to seek election by the voters next November. The floor is now open for discussion or consideration."

Rodney Gott stood up. "Judge, let me say something before you try to cram this appointment down the throats of the Commissioners." He walked to the front of the courtroom. "We appreciate you gents from the State being here, but frankly we don't need the help."

Mason, who had been seated at the center of the conference table, facing the courtroom, pushed his chair back and stood. "Senator, let me remind you that by Texas law, it is the responsibility of the elected Board of Commissioners to fill this vacancy, and the appointment will be made by the Board."

Rod eyed the commissioners as he spoke. "Since you're pushing your outsider candidate, I'll endorse our local candidate. Josh Simmons has been our County Attorney for the last three years, and is the natural choice to fill this un-expired term. We all know Josh, and he knows us, and he knows the problems of Byar County." He made quick eye contact with the contractor, the real estate broker, and the lawyer. He wanted to make sure the three votes he felt he controlled had no doubt about what he expected of them.

Mason was still standing, not to be intimidated. He delivered his next words in a voice more stern than he had ever spoken to Rod. "Thank you, Senator. Now, if you will please take your seat, we will continue with the business at hand." Rod shot him a mean look, obvious to the members of the Board and those sitting near the front. But Mason was in a position where Rod could not hurt him. He had decided he wasn't seeking re-election.

"Cool it, Mason. I'm speaking as a citizen, and you're not as big as you think. I think you just want a place holder in the D.A. Office so you can run, yourself, next year."

Mason raised his right hand. "I pledge to the Board and to the citizens of Byar County, I will not seek election to the Office of District Attorney next year…or at any time in the future." He had a thought of how to expand on his promise of not seeking the D.A. position, just to be sure it was believable. "I think we have a number of potential candidates who will make an excellent D.A.," he said, tapping on a folder of resumes.

Rod was near fuming. "And Josh Simmons is the most qualified of all, so get on with appointing him." The members of the board appeared antsy. A couple of them squirmed in their seats.

Clay had enough. He was also a citizen, and as such felt compelled to speak up. He stood and addressed Rod. "Why don't you sit down and stop trying to bully the Commissioners?"

"Well, Longley, you're someone to talk about bullying." Rod turned to face the courtroom. "You all know the Longleys – descendants of Wild Bill Longley, the Texas murderer." He added a chuckle for the benefit of his audience. The accuracy of his statement was unimportant to him; it was merely a put-down. He figured the public would hold it against Clay for the sins of another Longley more than a hundred years ago. He was wrong. While the Wild Bill legacy was not something the Longleys honored, they never denied it either. Everyone knew that. "What are you going to do, Clayton, try to blind side me again?"

Clay felt the blood surge to his face and neck. The Wild Bill comment he knew was harmless. The accusation of 'blind siding' made his heart race, even though he doubted any other person, other than Mason, knew specifically of what Rod was speaking. Clay had to consciously make sure he didn't clench his fist, his natural impulse.

"No, Rod. You're doing yourself in." Clay spoke in as calm a voice as he could muster, and sat down. He had learned long ago that no one else can make a fool of you. Only you can make a fool of yourself. Clay felt Manny's hand as the Ranger had reached over and gave his forearm two pats, as if to say, "You did the right thing by not going any further."

Meanwhile, Manny was thinking if Rod did not sit and permit the Board to proceed, he, as a law enforcement officer, would have to step in. Rod shuffled around a few steps and sat down. He realized Clay was right – he was going too far.

"Members of the Board, the floor is open for discussion," Mason said, trying to get the meeting back on track.

"I support Judge Griggs' recommendation that we appoint Mr. Kirkland. It is an opportunity to fill the vacancy with a person of great experience, while also leaving the field wide open for whomever wants to run in the next election. It doesn't give anyone an unfair advantage. It is the best thing for Byar County." The comments came from Commissioner Pender, the physician assistant.

"I'm in favor of Josh Simmons." It was the contractor.

"I suspect everybody has decided on their choice. Let's vote," said the real estate broker. He was greeted by a positive nod of the head from each of the other Board members.

Mason held up the white, paper coffee cup that had been sitting before him. "Okay, gentlemen. Here is the procedure. Each of you, and I, have one vote. It will take three votes to determine the choice of the appointment to fill the office of District Attorney. To be fair, I have created slips of paper with each name from the resumes that are in your folders. The names are in this cup, and I will draw them out one at a time."

"Any person who receives one or more votes will go into a runoff if no one is selected. In the event we have a tie with two nominees each receiving two votes, the nominee with only one vote will be dropped out and we'll vote again on the choice between the remaining two. The first candidate to receive three or more votes is the selection. Are there any questions on the procedure?" Everyone agreed they understood.

Counting Simmons and Kirkland, there were seven names in the cup. Mason drew the first paper slip, unfolded it and read the name. "Arnold Bronson. Gentlemen, what is your pleasure? All of those voting for Mr. Bronson indicate by raising your right hand." No one voted for Bronson, nor did they vote for the next name that Mason read. The third slip of paper that Mason withdrew was for Nathan Kirkland. "Nathan Kirkland. All of those voting for Mr. Kirkland indicate by raising your right hand." Mason and Pender raised their hands, as did the Commissioner, who was a lawyer, and who looked intently at Mason to avoid giving a glance in the direction of Rod Gott.

Mason got the vote he had hoped for. He had anticipated correctly that the lawyer serving on the Board of Commissioners was himself interested in pursuing the Office of the D.A. Had he gone along and cast his vote for Rod's man, he would have insured himself a steep uphill campaign the next year. Given the choice, he would rather have the more level field. Besides, with all the bad publicity, and the rumors going around, it looked like Rod Gott's influence over all things in Byar County would be on the decline.

"Miss Secretary, please record that Mr. Nathan Kirkland received three votes and is selected by the Byar County Board of Commissioners to fill the vacant office of District Attorney," Mason said to the Commissioner's Clerk, but also said it for the benefit of all attendees.

"Stupid asses," Rod said, and followed that with more mumbling profanities. His words were barely audible, but heard by a few seated close by as he shot from his seat and hustled to the back of the courtroom to the exit. From his body language, the rest of the attendees who were unable to hear his response had no question concerning his displeasure. For a few moments, all eyes were on Rod to catch any further display. Those wanting to see more fireworks were disappointed.

Rod left the meeting knowing that control was slipping away. Just a short time before, everything was going his way. The Bodas ruled. His irrational, high and mighty, arrogant thoughts, overwhelmed him.

Everyone is turning against me. Before, Mason would have been a team player and we would have put Simmons in as D.A. Hell, we wouldn't have been doing this at all. Ray would not have killed himself, and he'd still be the D.A. if that chicken-livered Bell hadn't rolled over on us. That damn Longley brought in that prick Donovan; he brought in the Ranger and then the Attorney General. And that little asshole Franks from the News was sitting there scribbling down everything said. No telling what he's going to write. Can't even get three votes out of the friggin' Commissioners. Screw it! Damn those Longleys.

CHAPTER TWENTY-ONE

Clay located a handgun instructor in Byar. He taught the standardized course in either two evening classes or one all-day Saturday class. Clay opted for the two evenings. Classes were held in his small shop; there were only two other people in attendance. After passing the written exam, they had to return on Saturday morning for the handgun firing test at the instructor's outdoor range, set up behind his shop. Clay used his .45 ACP while the other two used smaller weapons. The man had a 9 millimeter Ruger, and the lady used a .32 revolver. Compared to the other two guns, Clay's .45 sounded like a cannon.

The holes punched in the man-shaped target were also far more impressive and not just because of Clay's superior marksmanship. It was a pass-fail shooting proficiency test, and they all qualified. With the certificate from the instructor, Clay sent off for a license application. He had to, in turn, obtain fingerprint cards and mug shot photographs to submit to the State. He was warned that it would take several months to receive his permit.

Meanwhile, Forest called to report on the progress of the civil action against Rod Gott. He said he had gotten a call from Gott. "I laid the case out for him. Just as I suspected, he first tried to bully me. I guess that's just his normal mode of operation. Anyway, as we suspected, he really doesn't want to air it out in public. He offered a low-ball settlement, ten thousand. I told him I had to present it to your parents, but told him it was unlikely they would accept. He withdrew the offer, and wants to meet."

"Let's meet. Do the folks have to be there?

"Not really. Probably you shouldn't either. Besides, he wants to meet here in Austin this afternoon. Said he's in town for a couple of days. I think I can represent them. He cussed about the value of cattle and about us dragging a kid into court. Got the impression he really doesn't want his son to be put on the stand."

"Money shouldn't be an issue, except the Gotts don't give money away, but always buy the things they want." Clay was thinking back to when they were kids, and Junior Gott contributed to the baseball league as long as his sons were playing. Rumor was that they would also buy votes at election time, and things like that.

"For now, I think we should stick to our guns on this. My gut feel is that we can get actual damages, a reasonable fee, and anywhere from zero up to ten percent of punitive damages. I'm looking at this as easy money."

"Go ahead, Forest. I'll let my parents know you called." Clay got off the phone and placed a call to his parents. There was no answer. Normally he would wait and tell them when he dropped by the house after work. Today he would not be visiting. He was meeting Marcus Franks at the airport, and they were going to make a twilight flight in Clay's homebuilt. Clay tried again later and there was still no answer. He tried their cell phone; still no answer. Finally, near five o'clock, when he would be leaving the office, he called Marcus and canceled their flight.

When Clay pulled up in front of his parents' house he assumed they had just gotten home. Will's extended cab Chevrolet pickup truck was there, and the passenger side and rear doors were open. As he walked by, he noticed grocery bags on the back floorboard. He took the three remaining Wal-Mart bags and proceeded to the front door. He opened the door and yelled a hello to be sure he didn't startle them. There was no response. Clay then saw sacks of groceries spilled on the floor as he crossed the foyer into the center kitchen.

Something is wrong.

Another step and he saw what. Will and Elizabeth Longley, both sprawled on the floor, face down. Blood pooled around and under each of them.

"No! Dad! - Mom!" No response. Clay didn't expect any. They're dead. What happened? Clay set the bags on the floor away from them to check his mother for a pulse, and then his father. Nothing. There was a lot of blood on the floor. It wasn't bright red; it was a dark crimson and drying. The bodies were so close together the puddles of blood had flowed together.

Clay tried to rise from his squatted position, but felt weak and nauseous. He pushed off the floor with his hands to get on his feet. His knees were quivering and he thought he was about to fall, but finally got his legs to move and he backed away.

Call 911. It's a crime scene. Don't touch anything. How is it I can think rationally? Cell phone. Use the cell phone.

"My name is Clayton Longley. My parents have been killed." He thought "shot." but did not say so. He gave their address and provided specific directions to the Longley home. He had to stay on the phone several minutes providing other information, such as identity of his parents, his own address. Finally, he was told that assistance was on the way. The 911 Operator was trying to keep him on the line, but he wanted to hang up. Finally, he told her he had to go, and cut her off. Immediately his cell phone rang, but he would not answer it. It stopped ringing and Clay called Forest. He had the urge to talk to someone, and Forest seemed the right person to call.

Clay heard the sounds of sirens getting closer. He walked outside while still talking to Forest. Two sheriff department cars coming from Byar pulled off the highway 100 yards away and came down the drive or, "The Lane" as Elizabeth liked to call it. The last thing Forest told Clay was that he wished he was there with him, and that he was calling Manny Rojas. They had not spoken of murder, but that is what each was thinking.

The second car to pull up was Sheriff Jimmy Bell; closely after, a Texas Department of Public Safety patrol car appeared from the other direction and also turned into the drive. All the cars left their emergency lights flashing. Sheriff Bell held the deputy back from entering the house.

"Are you sure there is no one else in the house?" Sheriff Bell asked.

"No. I mean yes, I mean ..." Clay looked skyward, shook his head and sighed. Collect yourself, Clay. He looked back at Bell and spoke with an even voice. "They lived here alone. I was in there maybe ten minutes before you drove up."

"Didn't see anyone leaving?"

"No. I'd been trying to call them for several hours and got no answer. I normally come by most evenings about this time. It looked like they had just gotten back from grocery shopping. The truck door was open, and I took some bags in and found them."

The DPS patrolman introduced himself to Clay. He and the sheriff knew each other. Clay led the two into the house while the deputy stayed outside to look around. The trooper again checked the pulses of Will and Elizabeth, as a formality.

"We don't do anything until the coroner gets here," the sheriff said.

"Looks like gunshot wounds," the DPS officer said, kneeling over the bodies, being careful not to disturb them further. "Don't mess with anything. I need to get some photos." While he went to his car, Sheriff Bell led Clay out of the kitchen back into the foyer.

"Let's just get out of his way. When was the last time you saw or talked to your parents?"

"Last night. I had dinner with them. Here," Clay said, pointing a fore-finger down.

"You know if they kept a lot of cash or valuables here at the house, you know, something people would hear about?" The sheriff was just covering the possibility of a robbery. It wasn't what he was thinking.

"No. They did everything with checks. They don't even use a debit card. I would say they probably wrote a check for these groceries." Clay knew his parents didn't use a computer, and were slow to accept most forms of electronic banking. They had only recently discovered the advantage of having an ATM card to make cash withdrawals. The DPS officer returned with a camera and took numerous pictures.

Sheriff Bell peeked inside a couple of the plastic grocery bags Clay had set on the floor. He retrieved a cash register receipt from one, and held it up before examining it closer. "Checked out at Wal-Mart at 10:50 A.M." One of the spilled bags on the floor exposed a roast. Sheriff Bell reached down and touched it with the backside of a finger. "About room temperature, I'd say. It has to have been six to seven hours since your folks left the super market."

"They would have come straight home from shopping. It must have happened around 11:15 or 11:30." The impact of the situation was beginning to weigh on Clay. At the age of his parents, it would not be unusual for one of them to die, even suddenly. Both at once, was more distressing. But murdered, and him being the one to find them. He winced and closed his eyes tight to stem imminent tears. Not now. Hold on.

Clay turned away, not wanting to look at the scene any longer. He wondered if he would ever get the image out of his mind. Every time I think of my parents in the future, will this be the picture that flashes before me? No, I won't allow that. Too scary. I'll think of something else – a pleasant time.

Clay was at the front door when two more cars came down the drive. The first he recognized as the red Mazda Miata belonging to Marcus Franks. He walked out to meet him.

"I heard it on my police scanner," Marcus said as he exited his sports car. "What is it?" Marcus thought he already knew. The radio traffic he had intercepted on his scanner had said there were two bodies. He suspected the worst.

"My parents. They were shot."

"Man, I am so sorry to hear that." Marcus skipped the handshake and hugged Clay. For the first time, tears flowed from Clay's eyes. He was choked, and unable to respond for a few moments.

The man getting out of the other car was elderly. He greeted Marcus by name and introduced himself to Clay as Dr. Hughes. He said that he was the Byar County Coroner. The doctor went into the house leaving Clay and Marcus out front.

Marcus retreated to his car and produced a small camera. The last time he was at a crime scene at the Longleys' home he had a photographer with him. This time he would have to rely on pictures that he took himself, with his good, but not professional-grade camera. Marcus backed up and took several shots of the house with the police cars in front. He asked Clay if he could go inside for some pictures. Clay agreed, not seeing any harm, and believing Marcus would be discreet.

The DPS Officer came out to talk to Clay. "Can we get you to look around inside and tell us if there is anything missing?

"Sure," Clay said, and went back into the house. The coroner was bent over the bodies on the floor. He was taking body temperatures while Sheriff Bell was talking to him – telling the coroner what he suspected, Clay thought. He walked through the kitchen into the den. Everything looked normal.

"They have any money, jewelry, guns, or things that someone may steal?" the DPS Officer said.

"A coin jar," Clay said and pointed toward the master bedroom. "No expensive jewelry, I think. A couple of shotguns."

Clay led the way into the bedroom. He pointed out the five-gallon water bottle that sat on the floor beside the dresser. Clay remembered the clear plastic water jug from childhood. His father had dumped loose change into that bottle for years. About once a year they emptied the bottle, rolled the coins, and took them to the bank in Byar. The cash was then used for something frivolous. Several times they went to Galveston for a weekend mini-vacation, and stayed in a hotel across the seawall from the beach. A couple of times they went to Houston for an Astros baseball, or an Oiler football game, and once they spent the weekend in San Antonio. The water bottle was still there, and held a couple of inches of coins. Clay hadn't thought about the money bottle in years, and wondered what they had been doing with their "mad money" since he had been gone.

He opened the door to the walk-in closet. All the way in the back was the Winchester pump 12-gauge shotgun. He picked it up and showed it to the officer. Also standing in the corner was the 12-gauge Browning semi-auto that Clay had received on his twelfth birthday. It was too much gun for a twelve-year old boy, but his father had told Clay he would grow into it. It was a much finer firearm than the old pump his father used. Even after Clay was in college, he and his father would quail and dove hunt. Will had kept a bird dog back then. In more recent years, his father had complained that there were few birds left to hunt, and when old Duke had died, he did not get another bird dog.

He showed the officer his mother's mahogany jewelry box. Opening it revealed a number of pieces of jewelry. "Her wedding rings were probably the most valuable pieces of jewelry she had," Clay said, running his finger through the miscellaneous items. "She wasn't much on things like this."

"She is still wearing her rings," the officer said. "Your father also has his wedding band and watch on, but his wallet is missing. Except for that, it doesn't look like robbery."

Clay looked directly into his eyes for emphasis. "No. It wasn't robbery."

"Do you have any idea who would have done something like this?"

"Yes. Yes, I have an idea. Everyone in Byar County will have an idea." Clay's grief at the loss of his parents suddenly gave way to the greater emotion of anger. He stuck out his chin, narrowed his eyes, placed his hands on his hips, and shot a look of high intensity at the officer. "Rodney Gott did this."

"You mean Senator Gott?" The officer was incredulous, taking a step back.

Clay stepped forward. "The same. He threatened me and my family. His son slaughtered my father's Longhorns. I don't have any doubt."

"This investigation will no doubt be turned over to the Rangers. I'm calling it in as a double homicide. I'm sure they'll need a statement from you."

"Lieutenant Manuel Rojas is familiar with the situation here. A friend of mine is already calling him."

"Rojas is a good man, one of the best. Here is my card if I can do anything for you." The state trooper handed Clay a business card. "The sheriff and coroner will handle everything here. Please don't disturb anything around here until they finish whatever investigation they'll be doing."

As the DPS Officer was leaving, Clay's cell phone rang. It was Manny. "I'm in Beaumont now. I'm on my way."

CHAPTER TWENTY-TWO

It was comforting to Clay to have the support of friends like Forest, Marcus, and Manny. Within a matter of hours all three were at Clay's home in Lake Byar Estates. Each, in their way, was trying to do something for him. At times, all three were on their individual cell phones talking to someone or screening calls on Clay's home telephone. In the course of the evening Clay's secretary, Millie, and her husband, showed up at the house with a bucket of chicken and side orders. Marvin also came by, as did Sam Collins, Marcus's editor from the Byar County News. Sam brought pizzas.

The news of a double murder in Byar County traveled fast. Clay had to return to his parents' home to dig out addresses and phone numbers of Longley cousins in Lee County. There was a Sheriff's Office car still there, and the yellow police tape was strung everywhere. Inside was a deputy dusting for prints. Clay identified himself and told the deputy why he was there.

The bodies had been removed, but the dried blood remained. Clay knew that he would eventually have to clean it up. There were so many things that he would have to do. He didn't yet know what it took to close out the affairs of someone whose life ended suddenly and unexpectedly. One thing he did realize while thinking about what relatives he needed to contact to inform them of the deaths was; now he was alone. Yes, he had friends that he was thankful for, but no family. No parents, siblings, spouse, children. He had no one.

When Clay returned to his home with his mother's address book, he found an additional car in the drive and Claire waiting for him. He had not seen her since Ray's funeral, some three weeks previously. Clay had wanted to call her, but knew it was much too soon. Claire was seated on the big leather sofa in the den. She stood as Clay came in.

"Hello, Claire," Clay said as he extended his hand to her; but she ignored it and reached around to hug him with both arms. She hugged tightly and Clay returned it. He wanted to kiss her, at least on the cheek, but thought better of it with Forest, Manny, and Marcus in the room. He thought how ironic it was that after all these years they had now hugged twice, each time as a result of a family death.

"I was so sorry to hear," Claire said. "Mason asked me to give you their condolences. He's the one who came over and told me, about an hour ago. We all just can't believe this has happened." Claire still held on and relaxed her hug. She drew back a little.

"Thank you. And thank you for coming over. Have you met everyone?" Clay said, nodding to the others.

Claire smiled at the small group and said, "Yes, we met. I'm glad you have someone here. I was afraid you were alone." Her comment told Clay something. Claire is here for the same reason as the others. They don't have to be here. They don't owe me anything. They could have called and express condolences, sent flowers and maybe a sympathy card, and attend the funeral. That would have been the easier thing to do. For most people it isn't comfortable to face the mourner. No, these are friends. They're here because they care about me.

Claire and Clay drifted off to the kitchen while the other men talked quietly in the den. The kitchen was large and open, with all the modern conveniences. There was room for the white oak table and four chairs where Clay normally ate his meals, that is, if he bothered to make a meal. From the table he could see the largescreen television in the den, so there was no need to sit in front of the screen to catch the news or an occasional ball game.

Clay offered Claire something to drink. She offered to make hot tea if Clay would show her where everything was. He pointed out the tea bags and cups.

"Normally don't drink hot tea, but I think I'll try some too," he said. Clay sat at the kitchen table while Claire busied herself with the chore. It took only a couple of minutes before each were sipping tea. The thought of it made Clay smile.

"I think this is the only time we've been alone…since college." Since we broke up, he thought, but avoided saying those words.

"Yes." Claire seemed distant for a while. "I'm enjoying remembering what it was like."

"We've each come a long way since then." It took Clay a few moments to mentally stumble through years of work, and the Army, to get back to the same page Claire was obviously on. Then he smiled.

Claire said, "It makes you wonder, do we still know each other? Are we the same people we were then?"

"You mean the 'you can't go home' thing?"

"Kind of like that." She smiled and lifted her cup.

Clay shrugged. "I guess that means we, that is, everybody…changes, and things change, places change."

"Is that change always bad?" Claire said. She took a sip and set her cup down. "Can it be for the better?"

"Can't see some things being for the better," Clay said, rubbing a hand across the top of his head to call attention to his thinning hair. "But you are as beautiful as I ever remember." Clay thought, god I'm terrible at gushy words. I hope she took that as a sincere compliment – the way I meant it.

"Oh, I didn't mean those things." Claire looked at him and asked the question she had wanted to ask for the last twenty plus years. "What really happened to us?"

It wasn't as if Clay hadn't thought about that the past six months. He had and he knew the answer. Yes, he had rationalized what he thought best back then, but now he knew better. Clay reached across the tabletop and grasped one of Claire's hands that were resting on each side of her hot cup. She didn't pull back.

He looked down and let out a slow audible breath. "I know I was stupid back in college. I've known that a long time. I thought I had reasons back then." He lifted his face slowly, and hunched one shoulder.

Claire gave a small nod and pursed her lips. "I know. And, I should have never let you get away with foolishness. I would have waited, or gone with you."

"Yeah. But the way I was then, today you would probably have an ex named Clay."

"I always have had," Claire said.

Clay squeezed her hand a little tighter. "If you will forgive me, I promise not to be stupid any more."

While not flowery, and on the surface certainly not romantic, to Claire those words sounded beautiful. She smiled, put her free hand on top of Clay's, and caressed it. Without another spoken word, they were in agreement. Claire's blue eyes were wet and glassy.

"I know it's too soon, but I want to tell you." Clay paused to avoid stumbling over his words. "I think I have always loved you."

Claire blushed, lowered her face, and then raised it again to gaze in his eyes. "I've always loved you. I never stopped thinking about you." Clay was struck with the memory that in matters like this, she was always more positive and direct.

"It is too soon, though," Claire said. She loosened her hold on Clay's hand and withdrew her own hand to her lap.

"I don't want to push it," Clay said, and then tried to clarify his statement. "I don't want you to feel like I'm ..." He stopped and shook his head. Darn, just can't ever think of the right words at the right time.

That was fine with Claire. She knew Clay, it was so like him. She giggled and wagged a hand in the air. "Somehow, my mother knows. I haven't said anything, but she told me to stay away from you for three months." Claire had a little smile, almost a chuckle.

"That was probably given as good advice. But I want to see you. Guess I can wait until the three months are up." Clay got up, walked over to the side of the refrigerator and pulled off the small magnetic calendar. He took the pen from his shirt pocket and circled a Saturday date some two months later. He handed it to Claire. "Keep this. Here is our first date. Will you join me for dinner?"

"Call me?" Claire said as she clutched the little calendar. Clay took it to mean that since they would not be seeing each other they could talk on the phone. "I really should go," she said, standing and taking her cup to the sink. Clay followed suit and followed her to the den. She told his friends it was nice to meet them, and said goodbyes.

Clay followed her out the front door to her car parked in the street along the curb. After opening her door, Claire turned to Clay. He hugged her again and this time did kiss her on the cheek. He stood there as she drove away. On this, the darkest day of his life, Claire had just made it brighter.

If any of the three had notions of what was transpiring between Clay and the widow Gott, they didn't say anything. Clay asked Forest and Manny if they would spend the night at his house, telling them he had three extra bedrooms. Forest said he planned to stay. Manny said he had anticipated going to a motel, but hadn't taken time to call one yet. He had called his wife when leaving Beaumont and told her he would not be home as planned. He agreed to stay.

Manny's decision was based on two things, the first being the conveniences of not having to look for a room and secondly, it looked like someone was out to kill the Longleys. Protection of a citizen may be required. He also had things to cover with Clay, so waited until Marcus had left.

"I've spoken to the coroner, the sheriff, and the DPS officer," Manny said as Clay returned to the den. "If you feel up to it, I'll give you a rundown."

"Sure, why not," Clay said with a heavy sigh, while thinking, It's too late to start making phone calls to relatives, and I'm not ready for bed. When I do retire I want to be 'dog-tired' so I can fall asleep immediately.

Manny nodded, knowingly. "Other than the back door being forced open, there is no physical evidence. The sheriff believes the perpetrator was in the house when your parents returned from town. The time was about 11:00 a.m."

"That excludes Rod Gott as the trigger man. He definitely was in Austin at the time," Forest said.

Manny and Clay both acknowledged Forest's comment before Manny continued. "The DPS officer told me that you two had looked around, and so far, the only thing missing is your father's wallet. His conclusion is that it wasn't a burglary or robbery. I want to take a look around myself in the morning, but so far, from what I've learned, I agree. The sheriff says about the same thing. The coroner said the murder weapon was a .22 caliber." Manny paused, regarding Clay and how he was taking in this information. He looks a bit squeamish. Better ask. "Clay. Do you want to hear this?"

Clay looked to the side, and with a slow nod said, "Yeah. Go ahead."

"Twenty-two long rifle hollow points. Each shot twice, once in the back of the head and once in the temple. They didn't suffer. It was instant. Probably he had them get down on the floor and then shot them from behind. Then shot each one again to make sure they were dead. There were no empty cartridges, so the weapon was probably a revolver. The bullets were recovered and it may or may not be possible to match up to anything in the future. Frankly, it has the appearance of a professional hit."

"You mean someone was hired to kill them," Clay asked.

"That's the consensus."

"Rod Gott," Forest added his thought to the conversation. No one contradicted him. "That's why he was in Austin. Setting up his alibi. He wanted to get together at noon, and came by the office and then apologized for not being able to stay. Said he had something come up but he wanted to resolve the suit. He never intended to get anything accomplished. I'll bet you can't find any other reason he happened to be in Austin today."

"It'll be a couple of days before we can find out about the fingerprints at the house. Tell the truth, I don't expect anything to come of it. If it were a pro job, he would not leave any prints. Again, if it was a paid job, it's unlikely to be a local, and he won't still be in the area. Without someone talking, these are the most difficult murders to solve."

"Get Gotts' bank records and see if he pulled out cash," Forest said.

"That may be a good indication with the average guy, but someone like Rod Gott could have cashed a check for ten, twenty or even fifty thousand and said he went to the casinos in Louisiana and lost it. Doesn't mean we won't look at it. We will." Manny's comment satisfied Forest that the Ranger considered Rod a suspect and would be investigating.

"Clay, I notice you don't have a home security system here." Manny motioned to indicate the house.

"Guess I never thought I needed one. This isn't exactly a high-crime area. Lake Byar Estates is a gated community with only one way in and out. We don't have a gate guard, but there are lights, sensors and digital cameras that record every vehicle coming or going."

"Good for solving a crime but doesn't prevent anything. Still, it might be a good idea to get something, installing a security system may give you some advance warning," Manny said.

"I'll do that. By the way, I took the concealed weapons course and have my application in for a permit."

"You're talking like you believe Clay is next on the list," Forest piped in with what had the effect of a question.

"Just cautious," Manny said. "You going to be packin' that .45?"

"I haven't gotten anything else yet." Clay had been thinking about getting another, smaller pistol, and had looked up a few on the computer. He figured he had plenty of time. Now, he planned to step up his research on what he wanted. He liked the looks of Manny's sidearm. Maybe one of those? He did want a double action, which the older .45 Service Model was not. "I might carry it until I get something else." Clay thought, but did not say, yeah – like tomorrow. I'm not waiting on the permit.

"Be safe." The Ranger hoped he had said enough for Clay to get the message he should start carrying the weapon now, without telling him to violate the law. Manny excused himself and left the room for another cup of coffee.

"Clay, let me change the subject." While Clay and Manny were talking guns, Forest was thinking ahead. "Do you want to raise Longhorns?"

It caught Clay by surprise. He gave Forest a puzzled look. Then it struck him. The whole confrontation with the Bodas surrounded the Longhorn cattle hobby, or semi-business, favored by the elder Longleys. They were gone. If Clay wasn't interested in taking over the ranch and tending the cattle, then, only if he insisted on continuing to own that particular property, was there a legal issue between him and Byar County.

"Forest, I have never given it any thought, but right off, no. I don't have any interest in keeping the herd."

"Okay. The most expedient thing for Byar County to do is to negotiate with you. If you are dead, there are major probate and succession problems that can stretch for years. Alive, you are no threat to Gott.

"Thanks, Forest. But you're wrong on that. I believe Rod is motivated by vengeance." Clay knew that love and hate were the two strongest emotions. Rod was the type of person that would let his anger override otherwise good sense and logical thought. One thing Clay was positive about from his life experience, not the least of which was his training as an infantry officer, the best defense is a good offense. You take the fight to the enemy. Don't wait to let them execute their battle plan. Yes, he planned to take every step necessary to defend himself against any assault launched by Rodney Gott or some hireling, but he also started thinking about how to go on the offensive. "If things are like I suspect, I'm the biggest threat Rod Gott has ever faced in his life."

CHAPTER TWENTY-THREE

Sociologists tell us the ancient tradition of funerals, where we mourn the deceased, is of more importance to the living than the departed. It signifies grieving and marks the event of saying good-bye. It has become fashionable to refer to funerals as a "celebration of the life" of the lost loved one. Regardless of how it is viewed, it is a dreaded and joyless ceremony. And it was so for Clay, who had to contact relatives, make arrangements, and then accept sympathies and condolences. It was his task alone. He had no one to share his burden. Returning home from the cemetery was a relief from the grueling three days since he had found his parents murdered.

A double funeral is an unusual event, especially in a small community. The Longleys were widely known in Byar County, and equally liked and respected. They had friends from their old neighborhood, his work with the paper mill, her work at the hospital, their church, and in latter years their acquaintances resulting from the Longhorns they raised. Relatives were scarce, but friends plentiful.

Clay's friends, old and new, also attended. Clay saw Claire and her parents, the Brooks. Mason Griggs was there as was Sheriff Bell. Many people from Clay's company were present, including the president of Consolidated Forest Products who arrived by corporate jet with a small entourage. His state senator, Rod Gott, did not acknowledge the event, either by sent condolences or attendance.

Forest had come and remained at Clay's, assisting with any detail or menial task. Marcus was in and out and helped Clay compile the newspaper obituaries for his parents. Manny had to return to Houston, but returned with his family for the funeral. He brought his wife Caye, and their daughter Brittany Joelle. Brittany was a twelve-year old version of her beautiful mother. Manny had told them about the Longhorns and asked Clay if it would be okay to go by the Longley Ranch to see the cattle before returning to Houston. He also told Clay he would be back in Byar within a few days.

***

Manny called Clay with an update on the investigations. He said he had met with the new District Attorney. Since the Longleys had filed a civil action against the Gotts for the shooting of the cattle, the D.A. was reluctant to go to the grand jury with the evidence available. The D.A. did agree to keep the investigation open and would ask the Sheriff to bring Todd Gott in for fingerprinting and questioning.

Manny said, "The D.A. is preparing a case to take to the grand jury for an indictment of Oliver Harrell for extortion. He has bank records to show that Rod Gott had paid Harrell $2,000 that corresponded to the time the false lawsuits were filed. The connection to Gott is weak, but the indictment might motivate Harrell to talk."

What Manny was thinking, but not telling, was that if Gott had hired someone to kill the Longleys, he likely would have gone through his dirty deeds connection, Ollie Harrell. Likely the senator would not have been in direct contact with such an unsavory character as a professional hit man. So far there was no evidence, only suspicions.

Clay thought about contacting the Perry brothers at the cattle auction barn to take care of selling the remaining Longhorn herd. He located all the registration paperwork on the cows and then started having second thoughts. Instead, he called them to find someone to care for the cattle on a daily basis while the herd stayed on the Longley Ranch. The Perry's put Clay in touch with a young couple they thought would be available and interested.

Clay called and then met Freddie and Carla Roberts at the ranch. Freddie was raised locally on a farm, where his father ran a small herd of beef cattle, and the family was well known by the Perry brothers. Freddie was working days in a tire shop and Carla was a receptionist for a dentist. Looking after the remaining Longhorns required only a couple hours a day, and Freddie jumped at the chance to earn an extra two hundred a week until something permanent was decided.

Clay ultimately thought about his parents and what they would have wanted. True, he wasn't interested in keeping or building a herd of registered Texas Longhorns, but he was considering the perceived injustice of the county taking the farm. His parents had repeatedly said, 'it isn't right.' And to Clay, it wasn't right – to Forest, it wasn't right. Even Manny had weighed in with his opinion on the eminent domain seizure of the ranch. No – it wasn't right. Maybe that kind of thing would sound legit to some Washington liberal, but in Texas – it wasn't right. Who would not defend the property rights of an elderly couple against a government entity that wanted to turn their little home place into a golf course and maybe home sites for the affluent? Clay had to fight it out – for Will and Elizabeth.

This skirmish, in the bigger battle of American jurisprudence, had probably cost the elder Longleys their lives. Winning this one would be their legacy. Forest had warned that a court may decide in favor of the county, but in Clay's gut, they had to fight. He also considered that by fighting, if Gott had mellowed in his hatred, his own persistence would certainly reverse that trend. There would be no reason Rod would not have him in his sights. Clay called Forest to learn what had to be done to continue the suit against Byar County.

Instead of hiring someone to clean the kitchen floor, Clay felt he had to do that himself. It was a sad and lonely chore that he accomplished the day after the funeral. Then he was left with the task of going through his parents' personal possessions. What was he to do with the things Will and Elizabeth had valued enough to keep for so many years? Clay had always known his father to carry a Case XX pocket knife. He was surprised to find in his father's sock drawer no fewer than twenty Case knives, all worn from carrying and use. Will preferred the Stockman model, but there were also a variety of other models, including a couple of much smaller penknives for Sunday wear.

These kinds of things that were personal Clay would keep; clothes he bundled for donation to charity. Home furnishings would also go to charity. Clay decided to keep his mother's set of silverware and china that she brought out for special occasions and Sunday dinner with guests. He decided not to do anything else with the house and ranch for the time being.

Clay had seen the advertisements for the gun shows in Houston. It seemed there was a gun and knife show almost every weekend somewhere in the area. He made plans to attend, believing it would be the best place to examine a number of the semi-automatic pistols that he thought he would be interested in buying. He could order one locally, but wanted to see and feel it first. Besides, the gun show would be a good outing, with a chance to also see a number of antique and collectable weapons. He also had something else in mind, so he would go alone.

It was Saturday afternoon before Clay arrived at the convention center where the Texas Gun Dealers Association sponsored gun show was held. He first wanted to look at pistols. Most current models were on display by one of the many vendors. Clay had in mind a Smith & Wesson, and wanted to also look at a Colt model he had read about. He found those and examined each, but continued looking. Finally, he picked up a semi-auto pistol about which he had read little. He tried it out for feel and weight. It was the Glock Model G36. It was double action, .45 caliber, and lighter than other pistols he had held. The Glock was also thinner, a little more than one inch thick. It was designed as a concealed carry weapon. He liked it immediately, selected it, and completed the considerable paperwork for his purchase.

Clay continued looking, and found a vendor who dealt in new and used gun parts. There were plenty of used parts for the 1911 Service Model. He picked up a used barrel. It was a well used standard five inch with a paper tag price of $18.00. Clay went for a new extractor and a new firing pin. He also picked up a new, but cheaply made .45 magazine. He paid the merchant the total of $72.98, including tax, with no records – no questions asked.

A little further down the line, Clay found a booth specializing in reloading equipment and supplies. The booth also sold reloaded ammunition. Clay picked up a bag of copper jacketed .45 ACP reloads, 50 rounds in a plastic kitchen baggie. They were cheap at $12.00. He returned to Byar satisfied with the success of his mission.

Clay stopped at his hangar at the airport. He had moved most of his tools, including his bench vice, from his home garage to the hangar. He removed his .45 Service Model from under the seat of his truck and took it with his new purchases into the hangar. He put the used .45 barrel in his vice and gently tightened down. He carefully placed the sharp corner of a small cold chisel into the breech of the barrel and tapped it with a hammer. Despite the hardness of the metal, he was able to dig a scar large enough to be visible to the naked eye.

Next, Clay placed the new magazine in the vice. He dinged the top edge of the magazine and surprised himself by how much softer the metal of the magazine was compared to the barrel. The dent was too big, so he used a set of pliers to straighten the lip enough to not obstruct the use. All the better to make a distinctive mark on an ejected cartridge, he thought.

There were far more rounds in the baggie than Clay figured he would need. Most would go for target practice. He dumped some of the reloads onto the workbench. He field-stripped his 1911 to remove the original barrel, then reassembled it using the barrel he had bought. He loaded several rounds of reloads into the clip and inserted the clip into the butt of the pistol. Clay held the gun up with his right hand, pulled the slide back with his left hand, and let it go. The .45 slammed shut, stripping the top round from the magazine and pushing it forward into the firing chamber. The hammer was cocked back, with the grip safety depressed, and the safety off. The gun was ready to fire.

Clay was careful to keep his finger clear of the trigger. He repeated the cocking exercise, and the round in the chamber ejected and fell on the hangar floor. He continued cocking and ejecting until the slide stayed in the open position, indicating the clip was empty. He picked up the four rounds from the hangar floor and held them under the shop light for examination. Each of the cartridge cases was well and similarly marked with scratches.

Clay loaded the clip to full with seven rounds he had wiped clean with a shop rag. He wanted to ensure that neither his, nor anyone else's, prints were on the cartridges. He field stripped the pistol again, replaced the scarred barrel with his original, and inserted his original clip. He wrapped the extra barrel and clip in a shop towel and placed them in a workbench drawer. He placed the new firing pin and extractor in his handkerchief, and then in his pocket for assembly into the gun at a later time. That part of his plan was ready. He just did not know "when" and "how."

A few days later, Manny called. He said Sheriff Bell had contacted the Gotts and asked them to bring Todd in for questioning. The sheriff had said that his extension of courtesy to the Gotts was met by a mendacious tirade by the Senator. Manny chuckled and said, "I wasn't aware the sheriff knew those kinds of words."

"Yeah, Byar is full of surprises these days." It was humorous to Clay also.

"Anyway, it looks like Mrs. Gott and Todd are gone. Sheriff Bell and a deputy went to the house to get a statement and fingerprints after Gott said he wasn't bringing the boy in. The housekeeper said they had packed, and were on a trip."

"Isn't the kid in school?" Clay didn't know for sure, but school was in session and the son was near graduation.

"He was. The sheriff caught up with Rod and was told that Mrs. Gott took Todd to France to complete school. They fled the country. Can you believe that?"

"No, I can't. Just to keep from paying for the cattle he shot?" Clay said, thinking as he spoke. That was the reason Rod would suffer the separation of his family for the rest of the school year. Obtaining a matching fingerprint or an admission by Todd would assure the success of the suit for damages.

"You never know what some people will do," said Manny.

When he was off the phone with Manny, Clay called Forest to tell him.

"Sounds like the Senator is trying to salvage his political career," Forest said.

"Do you think he believes he has a future?"

"Look at it from Rod's point. Ray is dead, and any scandal associated with Ray is moot. Todd is out of the country. He's going to get a continuance on the damage suit until after the next election. Nothing is going to happen on that even if you try to force it."

"The D.A. is going after Harrell. Maybe he'll break if they have a good case against him and Rod putting him up to threatening the women."

"From what I hear, it won't be that easy to get Oliver Harrell to squeal. It might take a year or more to get him to trial, and then if he gets any incarceration, it'll be a couple years. He might serve six months or a year. Gott can just pay him for that time. I think Rod actually believes he's got it all under control."

Forest's summation was discouraging. The S.O.B. gets away with everything, even murder, Clay thought. By the time he was ready to leave his office, he had in mind the "where" of his plan. He had to stop by the airport.

At daylight the next day, Clay was sitting in his pickup opposite the entrance to Rod Gott's home. The wrought iron gate was closed. It didn't matter for what Clay was doing. He held the GPS receiver from his aircraft and set in a waypoint for his exact position. The display indicated it had an accuracy of three meters, a little over nine feet, based on the number of satellites being received at that time.

The instrument also showed an altitude of 170 feet MSL, or mean sea level. Clay knew the altitude reading was in the ballpark, but not as accurate as the position. He next took a handheld compass, the commercial version of the military compass he had used as an infantry officer. He took a sighting down the straight driveway to Rod's house. It read 188 degrees magnetic. Clay noted the boulders, each about three feet high. They had been hauled in, and lined the driveway. The big granite rocks were spaced every twenty yards or so. It only took a minute and Clay was on his way.

A half hour latter, Clay had made his way through the woods to the east edge of the Gott property. He figured he was some 200 yards off the highway. He took a latitude and longitude reading with the GPS for that exact position. He picked out the fifth boulder from the gate along the driveway and took a compass sighting on it. It took another 45 minutes before he had worked his way up to the west side of the Gott place. He again took his current position and a compass sighting on the fifth boulder.

Back at his house that night, Clay transferred the position information he had recorded with the GPS to a hand made chart on the backside of an old E size engineering drawing. From each position he plotted the compass bearing he had taken to the fifth boulder. Where the three bearing lines crossed, He calculated the latitude and longitude of what he thought would be the center of the driveway, and manually entered that position into his GPS. The measurement confirmed that point to be 140 yards from the position where he had sat in the truck on the highway. He felt the position on the driveway was accurate to within at least twenty feet. Close enough, he hoped.

CHAPTER TWENTY-FOUR

While Clay enjoyed having someone else fly with him, and Marcus was always available and eager, he was now at the Byar County Airport alone. It was early dawn, and there was no activity on the field. On foot, Clay carried the GPS receiver out to the runway to the touchdown point on the runway, and entered that position, or what aerial navigation and GPS call a waypoint. He stepped off toward the approach end of the runway a distance that he counted to be 140 steps of one yard each. He entered another waypoint on the GPS for that position. The two points held the same relationship to each other as the two points he had plotted at the Gott driveway, just a different magnetic heading. He headed back to the hangar.

Clay slipped the device back into its mount, located above the glare shield of his aircraft. He had time before he planned to be at his office, so decided to give it a try. He rolled the plane out of the hangar, fired up the engine, taxied out to the runway, performed his engine checks and took off. He turned downwind and flew well past the point he would have normally started his turn for a landing approach.

Finally, he banked to the left and held the turn until the runway was dead ahead. He slowed the aircraft to the minimum approach airspeed of 48 knots and held the attitude. He eased off power to continue the approach down the glide path toward his waypoint off the end of the runway. When he hit the waypoint, Clay punched the button and the GPS went to the next waypoint. He checked his altitude at 300 feet above the ground. He closed the throttle so the engine produced no thrust, and intended to hold his airspeed on down to touchdown.

He passed through the next waypoint, the one that represented the planned touchdown point, with still 100 feet of altitude. He needed to be lower at the first waypoint, by a hundred feet.

Clay added power and waved off the approach without touching down. The next time around the landing pattern he set up further out from the first waypoint he had named B2 in the GPS. He maintained runway heading at 48 knots as he approached B2. He hit B2, closed the throttle and noted 250 feet of altitude above the ground. Still a little high, so Clay held down on the right rudder with his right foot while banking the aircraft to the left. He knew the cross control put the aircraft into a slip, or unbalanced flight, the benefit being the aircraft descended faster. Clay held it until only a couple feet off the runway, and the plane touched down as the GPS showed B1. He completed the landing, satisfied with what he had done. He taxied to his hangar with plans to get back to the airport to practice his approach at night time. He still needed more work on the execution of his idea.

That evening, Clay was back at the airport. He had decided to add another waypoint to his GPS approach. He took off, flew around the area for an hour or so, including flying over the Longley and Gott ranches. On the GPS, he selected the position he had named G2. He maneuvered to cross north of G2. When G2 was bearing 188 degrees magnetic, it was six tenths of a mile from his position. Out the left side of the aircraft, he looked at the Gott place. The long driveway looked like a narrow runway, but with a huge obstruction at the far end – the Gott mansion. Clay was too high to get an approach perspective of the makeshift landing strip, and didn't want to hang around looking suspicious. His homebuilt aircraft, with the pusher engine and propeller was unique around Byar Airport, and easily distinguishable from the common front engine general aviation singles in the area.

By the time Clay was back at Byar County, it was getting near dark. He determined over the Unicom radio frequency there were no aircraft in the landing pattern. Clay set up for a long straight-in approach to the runway. He noted his altitude when one mile from B2, and continued his descent. He had to slip the aircraft to be at 200 feet altitude as he passed over B2. He continued his 48 knot landing approach and touched down exactly at B1. Clay added power and lifted off. Another long approach at a lower altitude gave him the opportunity to enter the waypoint six tenths of a mile out from B2. He would later identify it as B3. His altitude estimate was good. He held his 48 knots of airspeed with the engine at idle, passed B2 at 200 feet above the ground, and touched down at B1. It worked out well, but then again it was only barely dark, and he had his landing light on, as well as runway lights.

That evening, Clay, using his handmade chart, plotted a position he then manually entered on the GPS as G3. It was similar to B3, the initial position for starting an approach. He then went to his back patio and burned his handiwork chart on the propane gas grill.

On Friday evening, Clay made it a point to drop by the Marina Restaurant and peek into the lounge. Sure enough, he found Rod there holding court with some local hangers-on and wannabes.

Clay returned home and made what had become an almost nightly phone call to Claire. They always found something to talk about. Claire, who had essentially managed Ray's property investments, was still involved in occasionally buying and selling some small pieces of property, and handling rentals on a few pieces of commercial real estate. She also worked with a local architect, and a number of sub-contractors for Gott Custom Homes. Some years before, Ray had obtained full ownership of Gott Custom Homes and turned the business operation over to

Claire.

As they talked about what Claire did, Clay was impressed with her knowledge of housing trends, design, construction and general business savvy. Several times the conversation had hit on the subject of the proposed convention center project. Claire repeated that she believed Byar County needed the project, and that it would be of substantial benefit. They were both cautious to avoid disagreement.

Sometimes the subject of Ray would come up. She had said a couple of times that she had loved Ray. She knew it was possible to love more than one man, no matter what some people would say. Clay was careful not to disparage the memory. It was also obvious from Claire's comments that Rod was not one of her favorites. She didn't like the way Rod had treated Ray and Mason or even his own mother. Often Claire mentioned that Mama Gott was suffering from depression, as well as mild dementia.

Clay waited until 10:00 p.m. and made a swing back by the Marina Restaurant. Rod's silver SUV was still parked in the same spot. He wanted to get a look, so decided to peek into the lounge again. Unfortunately, Clay met Rod at the front door being escorted by one of the bartenders. It was too late to avoid the confrontation. Rod was visibly drunk, being held steady by a firm grip under one arm, but stumbling along on his own power.

"Look. It's Bad-Ass Longley." Rod directed his slurred comment to Clay, who did not respond. Instead, Clay stood aside to allow plenty of room for the two. "Go get a drink and tell him to put it on my tab. It may be your last."

"Is he going to drive like that," Clay asked the young man holding Rod's arm.

"Nah. I'll drive him home and drop him off. Got to be a regular part of my job."

"Let me go! Don't need any help. I'll drive myself," Rod said, as he struggled to free himself from the helping hand. The bartender released his arm and stepped back. Rod continued to stumble forward until he reached the big Dodge. He leaned against the door with his left hand and turned to his right to face the doorway where Clay remained. He raised his right hand and managed to extend his fat middle finger for Clay's benefit, as he pulled the door open. Rod turned back to the vehicle and climbed inside, slamming the door.

"He's always asleep before he gets home. I have to drag him out of the truck and push him in the front door. I don't know what happens to him after that. Don't care," the young bartender said, as he turned and went back into the restaurant. Clay was left standing alone as Rod backed the Dodge out of the parking spot marked, "Reserved – Club Management."

Rod gunned it and squealed the tires as he zigged a couple of times out of the parking lot.

Clay waited until the SUV was out of sight and then got into his own truck to follow. As far as he was concerned, Rod had just made reference to his intent to end Clay's life. Since he was drunk, and even with a witness, the threat would be given no credibility. Think I'll follow him. Maybe he'll do himself in.

Clay was far enough behind Rod that he could not tell how badly the Dodge was weaving. Fortunately for Rod, his home was close, and there was no other traffic. Clay saw Rod turn right and stop at the gate to his home. Clay slowed to a crawl and then saw the lights from Rod's vehicle start moving again on down the driveway. When he eased on past the entrance gate, Clay could see that Rod had closed the electric powered gate behind him.

***

Events were progressing much as Forest and Manny had predicted. Ollie Harrell was indicted, but wasn't talking, and Gott was delaying Clay's damage suit on the Longhorns. Clay felt it was only a matter of time before Gott initiated something to take him out of the picture. He had no fear of Rod in a face-to-face confrontation, but he recognized that he was developing paranoia, thinking at any time he would be struck down from behind, or by someone lurking in the dark. Clay questioned his own rationality. He never fully satisfied himself whether he was considering self-preservation, vengeance, or justice. He finally concluded that it would be irrational to believe Gott would do nothing. He had to act first. Clay knew and had planned what he believed he had to do and how he would do it. He pinpointed the "when."

CHAPTER TWENTY-FIVE

Clay arranged for a Friday visit with the manager of one of the paper mills in his division. This particular manager, Clay knew to be an avid golfer. Though he was only an occasional weekend duffer himself, Clay did play without embarrassing himself too much. He suggested that he stay over on Friday night and host the manager and his wife for dinner that evening. They could then go out for a round of golf on Saturday morning. The mill manager lapped up the chance to socialize with, and to have a friendly competition with, his boss in an environment where he was certain to shine.

The selected out of town mill was located in southern Arkansas, and Clay told them he would be arriving at the small local airport in his own plane. He asked that a company car be checked out to him during his visit. Clay had Millie make a hotel reservation.

He had also selected this particular plant because it was approximately 210 miles from Byar, and located in a small city with an unmanned airport, much like Byar County Airport. Clay's plane would cruise at 100 knots while burning about five gallons of fuel per hour. Since aeronautical charts are formatted in nautical miles, Clay, being a purist, opted to use an airspeed indicator calibrated in knots, or nautical miles per hour, rather than the MPH gauges civilian aircraft are typically outfitted with. While it made a small plane sound faster to say its cruise speed in MPH rather than knots, since a nautical mile is 15% longer than a statute mile, it also required a continuous conversion when manually flight planning or navigating, which Clay preferred to avoid.

It was a two hour trip one way, give or take a few minutes. With the plane's 20-gallon fuel tank, it would mean refueling at the destination airport for a round trip. For obvious reasons, flight planning always includes more than adequate fuel to complete the flight.

Clay loaded his clubs and overnight bag on his aircraft. Before putting his 1911 .45 service model pistol in the plane, he took the shop towel containing the extra .45 barrel and loaded magazine. He field stripped the .45 and installed the old scarred barrel and the newly acquired cheaply made magazine. The original barrel and magazine then went into the towel, and everything went into the passenger seat. The new extractor and firing pin were still wrapped in the handkerchief and in his luggage. The remaining .45 reloaded shells that were not loaded into the magazine had been shot at the outdoor range where the spent bullets and shells had been mixed with thousands of others.

Clay departed Byar County Airport at mid morning after spending a couple of hours in the office. The flight took him over the piney woods of

East Texas, across the Sabine River into Louisiana, and then more piney woods on up to Arkansas.

Clay occupied himself by keeping a flight log, and navigating with the GPS. As was his practice when flying, he would play "what if?" It consisted of periodically touching the throttle and saying to himself, What if the engine suddenly died? In his mind he would go through the litany – *aviate, navigate, communicate.* First he would let the airplane slow to the best glide airspeed, while looking for the nearest suitable emergency landing site. His plane was designed to have a ten to one glide ratio. For every one thousand feet of altitude above the ground, he could glide forward about 10,000 feet, almost two miles. At his cruising altitude of 3,500 feet, a little over 3,000 feet above the ground, he could glide for roughly six miles.

It would be unfortunate if Clay really had to put the emergency plan into action, for there weren't many open fields along this route. Once over North Louisiana, the farmers' fields became more plentiful. The rest of the drill dealt with checking the engine instruments and controls, identifying his location and finally making a mayday call on the radio.

Approaching his destination, Clay called in on the Unicom radio frequency for the uncontrolled field, meaning no control tower. Clay knew that many times, when no other aircraft are in the landing pattern at that airport, no responses are received. On this occasion he received a response. There were no other planes in the landing pattern. He was told the wind direction and the runway being used. The reply had come from the FBO, or Fixed Base Operator, located on the field.

After landing, Clay taxied his plane to the only large hangar on the airport. He saw the fuel pump and parked up close. A man in a gray jumpsuit greeted him when he exited the plane.

"Hey. Welcome to Canney. First time I've seen one of these. Seen them in the magazines, but hadn't seen one that somebody built."

Clay was pleased by the admiring look he was getting from an airplane guy, and engaged him in typical aviator talk. "Yeah, guess I'm one of the few already flying. The only other one I've seen was the demonstrator that I got a hop in before buying the kit. So far it has been a great little plane."

"Where you from?"

"Down in East Texas. It'll need about ten gallons to top it off," Clay said.

The attendant gave a quick nod. "Sure thing. You the Consolidated big shot?"

"Well yes, I'm from Consolidated, but I don't lay any claim to being a big shot."

"Couple of young ladies brought that car over for you this morning," the FBO man said, waving toward a white Chevy at the edge of the parking lot. "I got the keys inside."

Clay smiled. "Great. Thank you."

"Gonna spend the night, huh." He said it as a statement rather than a question. "Tie down is free. Have to charge you if you want to put it in the hangar."

"Tie down will be fine."

When the FBO completed the fueling, Clay handed him a credit card. He wanted a receipt for the purchase, and followed the man inside.

After settling up, Clay accepted the car keys with the accompanying check out documentation. The paperwork, already filled out as he knew it would be, had the Chevy's odometer reading recorded for when it left the mill, along with his name and other information. It would be a permanent record of his use of the vehicle and how many miles it was driven from the time it was checked out to him until it was checked back in.

Clay started his plane and taxied to an empty tie-down spot on the ramp, away from other aircraft. He used his own ropes to tie down to the pad eyes spaced out in the concrete ramp. He pulled out the golf bag that had been stored behind the seat, and his other bag that had been strapped into the passenger seat on top of his pistol. He slipped the pistol under the seat so that it was out of sight, and locked the cabin doors. Clay carried his luggage to the Chevy in one trip, and tossed it into the trunk.

Having printed a map from his computer at the office, Clay was able to drive directly to the mill. Though he had met the manager a couple of times, it was his first visit to this paper mill. Eventually, he would visit all of the facilities in his division. These visits were nothing more than a formality. Clay was escorted by the manager and introduced to numerous management personnel and employees. Before leaving the mill to check into his hotel, he arranged for the manager and his wife to pick him up for dinner. That fit his plan, but he still had minor shopping to do.

Clay also knew where the nearest Wal-Mart was located. That was his first stop. It was a quick in-and-out. He purchased three 5-gallon plastic gas cans, paying cash. In the parking lot, he moved the bag to the back seat and left the clubs in the trunk with the gas cans. The next stop was at a small service station to fill the gas cans. Again Clay paid cash, not wanting any credit card records. *This isn't something I like to do,* Clay thought, concerning hauling a trunk load of gasoline. A rear end collision could end in a fiery disaster.

The hotel was one of the national chains and more than adequate. Clay used his Consolidated credit card and found his room. He did his personal chores, dressed casually, and waited for his dinner companions to come by.

The mill manager, his wife, and Clay, were of similar age. During dinner, the couple each had two glasses of wine. Clay stayed with iced tea. While the conversations stayed light, Clay's mind drifted several times. Would this man be willing to do what I'm planning? Is it a crazy idea that a rational person would reject?

Clay was dropped off at his hotel by 9:30. The plan was to meet at the clubhouse at 7:30 the next morning. He had only an hour to kill so he set his alarm and lay on the bed, hoping to get at least a few minutes of sleep. His mind would not permit it. Details raced through his head. Have I thought about everything? I can back out right up until the last moment.

CHAPTER TWENTY-SIX

It was 11:00 p.m. when Clay arrived back at the airport. As he suspected, it was deserted. He had tracked the weather forecast for several days and was confident there would be no surprises. The sky was clear and moonless – for the next five hours. Clay took one of the gas cans, placed it in the passenger seat and strapped it in. It was the only place he could put it to ensure it remained upright. Just like the gas in the trunk of the car, it was something he considered a risky practice, and was done only out of necessity. As he moved about quietly, Clay continued to scan the airport for any sign of activity.

After removing the tie-down ropes, he slid into the cockpit and went through his mental checklist – charts, flashlight, penlight, water bottle, loaded .45. Clay started the engine without letting it rev any higher than necessary to avoid making excess noise. He let off the brakes and allowed the plane roll forward without adding power, using the flashlight, held out the open hatch, to avoid turning on his much brighter landing light.

Normal operation would be to turn the aircraft position lights on, but Clay planned to leave them off for the entire flight. He also did not plan to use the radio, although he did turn it on. He turned down the parallel taxiway and continued to idle the engine, rolling slowly toward the end of the runway. Fortunately, the approach end of the runway was adjacent only to farmland, and there were no residents who might notice the late night flight operations.

Clay swung the plane to face into the light breeze and performed his engine checks. He flipped the landing light toggle switch on and then quickly off to assure he was lined up on the centerline of the runway. When in position, he pushed the throttle forward and let the light plane roll. A few clicks on the radio transmit button would have brought the runway lights on, but that was not his intention. The takeoff roll was brief and Clay flashed the landing light a couple more times before reaching lift off speed. At 45 knots, he lifted the nose and the plane flew off the runway surface as it continued to accelerate. At 70 knots and 500 feet of altitude, some 200 feet above ground, Clay eased back on the throttle. It was a beautiful night for a flight and he had approximately two hours to enjoy it.

The GPS, with the G3 waypoint selected, allowed him to track directly to his destination. All of his precautions and self-training would go for naught if he had a real emergency on this flight. It was the peril of single engine flying in the dark. Clay was reminded of the old joke about engine failure at night. Set up a glide, turn the landing light on and try to avoid hitting large obstacles. If that wasn't working out – turn the landing light off. That brought a smile and a small chuckle.

Clay still kept the flight log, and was able to back up his GPS navigation with radio navigation and visual citing of airport beacons and small towns. He always wanted to know the location of the nearest airport. He cruised along at 2,500 feet altitude for a smooth flight in the clear, dark sky. When 20 miles from his G3 location, he eased back on the throttle and descended to his selected altitude. At five miles on the GPS readout, he throttled back further and slowed the plane to 55 knots.

When the GPS clicked down to zero distance, he rolled to a shallow left bank, then steadied on a heading of 188 degrees, and squeezed off a little more power to start his decent. Clay selected G2 and held the nose up a little to get to his 48 knot approach speed. He didn't have time to look around, but could see the lights from the City of Byar off to his left in his peripheral vision. Had he looked, he would have been able to see scattered lights of Lake Byar Estates off to his right. Dead ahead it was mostly dark.

Clay concentrated on his airspeed, heading and altitude, but thought he could pick out the lights at the Gott ranch gatepost. Past that, it was dark. The G2 position came up fast. The GPS had shown Clay that he had 1.5 minutes, but it seemed to elapse in triple or quadruple time. He switched to the G1 position as he was passing through 230, feet above ground. Anxiety was so high he considered waving off the approach. He swallowed hard. Push on. This has got to be done.

It was the gatepost that was lighted. The white stone reflected light well. The driveway lay straight ahead, just past the lights, but Clay's chosen runway was no more than 20 feet wide. There were three-foot boulders on each side. If he hit one, it would destroy the plane and probably kill him. The gatepost sailed under the nose and Clay could not resist hitting the toggle switch to flash his landing light on for a moment. Lucky he did, as he was able to correct slightly to the right or he would surely have struck the left side boulders. Damn, this is crazy!

Clay flashed the landing light once more to confirm his lineup. He closed the throttles, eliminating the little bit of thrust still being produced by the engine. It was too soon. He was so slow there was no raising the nose to flare into a normal landing. The plane dropped in hard – he had misjudged his height above the ground. Clay's first thought was he had surely damaged the aircraft. He had never hit the ground so hard. He still had to get on the brakes. He pressed hard on each toe brake as he pushed the nose over hard. He managed to flash the landing light again. He was good.

The plane was on the left edge of the concrete driveway. He came to a stop with one wheel in the grass. The wing tip of the high wing design cleared the boulders on each side, but the wing strut that reached from the lower fuselage to one-third the way out to the wing tip was vulnerable. Clay scanned his engine instruments, and then pulled the fuel mixture control off to shut down the engine. Half of his fuel was used up.

Clay opened the hatch and swung his feet out. His knees were quivering. He placed a hand on each knee and waited a moment. He looked down the driveway toward the huge house. He could see the outline of the mansion, thanks to a light located somewhere behind the house, probably on one of the horse barns. The front of the house was unlighted and there appeared to be no lights on inside the house.

Clay exited the plane and with the pen light from his shirt pocket, started looking over the aircraft. Despite what he felt was a minor crash, the plane looked okay. Clay looked back toward the gate and could see that it was closed. No one would be coming through the gate unless they had a remote controller, or the gate was opened from the house. He estimated he was half way between the gate and the house. It was at least 1,000 feet back to the gate. On such a dark night, he did not think anyone could see the plane from the highway. He had landed slightly longer than planned, but was satisfied with the situation so far.

It was quiet, so Clay decided he would follow his primary option and pour the five-gallon can of auto gas into his tank. Using regular grade automotive gas did not concern him. Many owners of light aircraft with his type engine ran only auto gas without difficulty. Clay felt nervous. He unstrapped the plastic container and went about fumbling with the spout. He managed to get the gas poured into the tank, secured the cap and strapped the empty jug back into the passenger seat. Had he not been able to get the gas into the plane, it would mean a landing at some remote airport along the way back to Arkansas and risk being seen. Trying to get back on exactly the estimated en-route fuel requirement was an even greater risk.

The takeoff roll for Clay's plane would be about 400 feet with less than full fuel and only one person aboard. Since there was essentially no wind, it did not matter which direction he would use for takeoff. Even though the obstacle, the two-story mansion, was higher to the south, Clay decided to leave the plane pointed as it was. He left the plane with only his penlight and the .45, wearing the dark colored clothes he had donned for this mission.

It was 1:20 a.m. and as Clay got closer to the house he could see that Rod's Dodge Crew Cab was parked in front. He had thought about what he would do. The plan was to knock on the door, get Rod out and take care of him. Two rapid shots. It was simple. It wasn't the way it would have been done in the old West. Had it been a hundred or more years ago, with everyone suspecting the injustice brought on one family by another, Clay would have called him out, in broad daylight with many witnesses. Too bad that version of frontier justice was no longer available, he thought. Maybe I should have brought a rifle and drilled him from a distance. Same way Todd Gott shot my parents' Longhorns. Nah, not my style. Besides, I want Rod to know, even if it's only momentary, that he can't get away with murder. Justice may not come in the form of a badge and courtroom, but justice will come.

As Clay approached the dark house, he heard the yap of a small dog. There was a pet in the house and it had been alerted. Maybe it had heard the plane land. Then a light came on inside. It wasn't in a front room, but could be seen through an undraped first floor window. Clay stopped short when outside lights came on, lighting the entire front porch. He did not know if it had been turned on from inside the house or perhaps by a motion sensor he had activated.

Clay thought he might still be outside the arc of light spread from the floodlights, and be unseen from the house. The dog continued to be agitated. This is actually better, Clay thought. Walking up and banging on the door is the part of the plan I don't feel comfortable with. I want Rod to come out. Face to face. Do it, Clay, now.

Clay raised the .45 automatic and fired one shot into the air. The semi-automatic cycled, ejecting the spent cartridge into the grass. He waited about ten seconds.

"Gott!" Clay yelled. "You want me – come get me!" There was no visible movement in the house. "Hey, Rod Gott!" He wasn't coming out. What if he called the Sheriff's Office or Highway Patrol? Clay thought. He stepped back a few feet, a prelude to canceling the mission and running for his plane. "Rod Gott!" Clay said one last time.

The anxiety of the wait was terminated by what sounded like cannon shot coming from the right front corner of the house. Clay's natural instinct, or maybe it was his military training, caused him to hit the deck with the .45 between him and the direction of the deafening gunshot. He had his pistol at the ready with a two-hand grip. Then he saw Rod. First, he thought he recognized him by the physique, and then for certain, as Rod stepped up onto the end of the well-lighted porch. A mistake, Clay thought. While he did not know where Rod's shot hit, Clay assumed it came in his general direction. He also saw why that shot had created such a boom. Rod held a massive handgun. Clay figured it had to be a large frame magnum, probably a .44, with a ten-inch barrel. Rod was moving across the porch, getting closer to Clay's position.

"Longley! I know it's you! Yeah, I had those old people killed, and you're next."

Another booming shot and Clay could see fire from the end of the hand cannon. The shot wasn't close enough to cause Clay to rush his own shot. A little closer and he would drop him. His target was 50 feet away and getting closer. A thought flashed through Clay's mind. A firefight for the best man to win. This is better. This is fair.

Rod moved to his right. He knew where Clay lay in the grass. He wondered if he had gotten him with the first shot. His second shot was insurance. He planned to take cover behind the next stone column and place a well-aimed shot into the body on the ground. He thumbed back on his .44 magnum.

As he rushed forward to take cover, he stumbled.. He instinctively stretched his hands forward toward the white stone porch column to break his fall. Too late.

The long barrel of the revolver, pointed up at an angle, hit the stone and flexed his wrist further. The trigger got squeezed. Fire and lead smashed into the rock as he continued to fall toward the column.

The heavy lead bullet, compressed to a misshapen blob amidst bits of flying rock, ricocheted at an upward angle and traveled only a matter of inches before hitting Rod under the chin. The big man's head snapped back as his body continued down. The slug penetrated the fat of the neck, the esophagus, and splintered the second and third vertebrae. The stone column had stolen most of the original velocity, so the bullet lodged in the throat.

Clay held his pistol at the ready. As soon as Rod cleared the next column, he would fire. It would be two shots. Shoot – shoot – roll – look. Be ready to continue firing. The third shot from Rod's hand cannon ended the fight. Rod was down. There was no movement. He had hit the floor hard, and crumbled in an uncontrolled fall. He still wasn't moving. Clay waited a few moments and got to his feet. Somehow he knew it was over, but he held his .45 at the ready. He approached the porch wondering what had happened.

The handgun had dropped from his hand to the tile-decked porch. Blood was gushing from the gaping wound in his neck. Clay reached with his left hand and felt for a pulse on Rod's left wrist. There was none. What would I have to do if he wasn't dead? Clay backed away and lowered the hammer on his pistol.

This is what I came for. I could feel cheated, but all I feel is…relief. It is done. Clay turned and jogged toward the plane. He tossed the pistol into the passenger seat beside the empty gas can and quickly went through his pre-start check by memory. He cranked the engine and looked toward the Gott mansion. It was a quarter of a mile away.

Clay stood on the brakes and brought the power up. He hit his landing light switch. He wasn't going to risk a mishap now. The driveway ahead was lighted. He released the brakes and danced on the rudder pedals a little to keep the plane centered as he accelerated. He held the nose down until he had 50 knots, let it come up and lifted off. At 60 knots he held the attitude to climb out at a steeper than normal angle. He made a shallow bank to the left and turned off the landing light. The lights of the Gott mansion disappeared under the aircraft right wind. He easily cleared the building by two hundred feet.

Clay made a slow turn to the left. He wanted to look at the highway that ran in front of the gate. He continued the climb and the turn until he could cross the highway at a right angle. There were no vehicle headlights or taillights in site.

Chances are good I haven't been spotted. Set course for Arkansas.

CHAPTER TWENTY-SEVEN

It was a two-hour return flight, and Clay still had things to do. As soon as he leveled at 2,500 feet and was settled on the direct course, he started with the GPS. Methodically, he deleted each of the three programmed waypoints and then checked to see if he could call them back up. He certainly would not want to answer any questions about why he had Rod Gott's driveway programmed into his navigation equipment.

The next chore to take care of was the .45 semi-auto. Clay knew he could field strip the pistol blindfolded. That skill would be handy in the reduced light of the cockpit. He had the aircraft trimmed so that only an occasional nudge of the flight controls was necessary to keep him straight and level.

Clay squeezed the magazine release and dropped the loaded clip into the seat between his legs. He slowly retracted the slide and let the live round in the chamber also drop into the seat. With the slide forward, he completed the disassembly enough to remove the barrel. In reverse order, Clay took his original barrel from the shop cloth and reassembled the gun. He then jammed the original magazine in without loading a round in the chamber.

Now to get rid of the evidence, Clay thought. Since I didn't get a chance to shoot, there will be no ballistics that can be traced to this old barrel. I want to make sure that if a slug was available to match up to a gun, it would never match the original barrel. But I did leave a shell casing somewhere out in the grass. If that is ever found, it could match to the scar I made in the barrel and maybe scratches from the magazine I dinged up. The firing pin and the extractor are the only other components that could possibly be matched to the casing. Changing out those parts is not something to be done right now, with no autopilot. Those will have to be done later. The unfired rounds are also the same as the spent casing. They have to go. With one hand, Clay stripped the unfired cartridges from the clip and into his lap. He counted them. Six. All accounted for. Loaded the magazine with seven rounds, and fired only one.

Clay was over the Sabine River bottom-land and figured it was better than most places to ditch his unwanted bullets and parts. The worst thing he could do would be to casually toss something out and have it fly back into the pusher propeller. He pulled back on the power and let the plane slow to 60 knots. He cracked the hatch open enough to be able to flex his left wrist in a manner to push the barrel down far enough to ensure it cleared the prop. A few moments later the empty magazine went. Then, one at a time, he flicked the six bullets down into the darkness. All told, the parts and rounds would be scattered over at least a mile or so. Not much chance anyone will ever find any of those. Clay pushed the power back up to cruise and felt a measure of relief wash over him.

It was still a dark night. Moonrise would not occur until the time of his arrival back at the airport. There were plenty of stars in the sky on the clear night, as well as scattered lights on the ground. Clay passed 40 miles south and east of Shreveport, but was close enough to see the well-lighted city. The air was smooth and there was no other air traffic. Even if there had been other aircraft tooling around over north Louisiana at that time of the night, they would not have seen Clay without his running and strobe lights on. He also did not have the IFF on, making it more difficult for Air Traffic Control to detect and track the small plane with radar.

Finally, Clay had time to reflect. He thought about the approach and landing, essentially in the dark, on the Gott driveway.

I was lucky. It wasn't that good of a plan. I could easily have smashed into one of those boulders. That was probably beyond my skill level. I'm going to start working on my instrument rating. And, I thought Rod was single minded. I took that to be a fault. I just knew Rod was fixated on vengeance. Guess I was also.

Clay's self talk did not please him. Instead, it cast doubt on his judgment. Why didn't I think of something else? I could have gotten Manny to put a recording device on me, and had Rod admit he had them killed, and that he was going to kill me too. Rod would eventually have implicated himself. He couldn't have kept his mouth shut.

It was 3:40 a.m. when Clay approached Canney Field. He set in the Unicom frequency for the airport and clicked the transmit button on the radio once, and then again. The runway lights came on just bright enough that he could pick out the strip. He could have continued to brighten the lights but that might have called attention. Clay didn't want to repeat his landing performance from the previous touch down.

When he estimated he was less than 50 feet above the ground, Clay flipped on his landing light. It was a much better landing, and he turned the light off as the tires squeaked on the concrete surface. He rolled to midfield and took the exit that led onto the parking ramp, in the same spot he had left. He was pointed in the opposite direction, but that was preferable to any extra taxiing.

Clay shut down the engine and turned the interior lights and radio off. He had fuel remaining that he estimated to be approximately the five gallons he had poured into the tank on Gott's driveway. He crawled out of the cockpit, pushed the tail of the plane down, and pivoted it on the main landing gear for 180 degrees. He quickly attached his tie down lines and looked around. Not a soul was stirring anywhere in the vicinity.

Clay rushed the .45 and empty gas can to his company car. He fetched the two full cans from the trunk and threw the empty one in. He lugged the plastic cans to the plane and refueled with haste. The plane did not have a full load of gas, but had a sufficient amount to get him back to Byar with a reserve. He especially did not want to refuel at the same field where he had just filled up the day before.

As Clay was loading the empty cans back into the car, he noticed the bright quarter moon just starting to show above the tall pines east of the airport. He hopped in the car and sped out of the airport toward the hotel. He still needed to get rid of the empty cans. He pulled in behind a quick oil change shop and set out two of them, thinking someone would think they were lucky to find the jugs someone had accidentally left behind. At the hotel, Clay tossed the last one into the dumpster.

In his room at last, Clay field-stripped the .45 again. He still had to change out the extractor and the firing pin. They were the final parts that could leave a telltale mark on a cartridge case, though not as likely as the barrel or magazine. The chore required only the use of the new firing pin to depress the old pin and slide out the firing pin stop to remove the extractor and firing pin. The new parts went right in and the reassembly was completed in a couple of minutes. It was easy enough, but not something he had wanted to do in a poorly lit cockpit, while flying. He would dispose of the old parts on the way to the golf course. Clay set the alarm and fell on the bed, clothes and all. Maybe I'll get two hours sleep. Exhaustion overwhelmed his racing thoughts. Within minutes he was out. An hour later, he was checking the clock. Sleep was over before time was up. The body was tired but the mind wasn't resting. Clay gave it up, undressed and hit the shower. A long hot drenching helped wash away some of the fatigue from the muscles.

Clay sat on the edge of the bed in his slacks and knit shirt. Why is there no remorse? A man is dead. I went there to kill him, and now he is dead. But I'm not feeling for Rod Gott. It is me that I'm worried about. I didn't shoot him, but I would have. I am no better than Rod Gott. Maybe I do have the bad blood of Wild Bill Longley?

CHAPTER TWENTY-EIGHT

It was mid-morning on an otherwise normal Saturday when Manny's cell phone rang. He was sitting in a canvas camp chair with his wife along the sidelines watching their daughter's soccer game. It was going to be a good game – Brittany had scored the first goal for her team and they were leading two to zip. The call came from Sheriff Bell from Byar County.

"Lieutenant Rojas, hate to spoil your weekend, but we got something big up here."

"What is it, Sheriff?"

"Senator Rodney Gott has been killed. Shot dead sometime last night." The sheriff paused for a response.

"Gee!" It wasn't much of a response, but he couldn't say the first thing that came to his mind – Clay Longley took his revenge.

"Yeah. You might better come on up here. This may tie in with the on-going investigation."

"How and where did it happen?" Manny said. He figured Sheriff Bell had jumped to the same conclusion, or at least had harbored the thought that the conflict between the Longleys and Gotts, specifically the murder of Will and Elizabeth and now Rod Gott, were connected. The obvious connection would be Clay Longley.

"At the Gott place, right on his front porch. Their stableman found him this morning."

Manny scratched his neck. "Do you have the crime scene blocked off?"

"Well, I'm still out here at the house. We got the gate closed and we got the coroner's office and a couple of State Troopers here. News people gonna be all over this in no time."

"Don't disturb any thing. It'll take me a couple hours to get there. I'll call you back when I get close." Manny turned to his wife to say what she had already surmised.

"I know. You've got to go. Doesn't anybody take the weekend off?" she said.

"Well, crime doesn't. Tell Brittany I'm sorry to miss the rest of the game. I've got to go to Byar County."

"What now?" It had not been that long since they had been to Byar for the Longley funerals and Caye was familiar with the names of all the players in the investigation.

"Ah, a politician was shot last night." Just in case someone else may be overhearing the conversation, Manny wasn't going to mention any names.

Realizing the need for confidentiality at the moment, Caye spoke low.

"Who? Senator Gott?" She assumed that if anyone needed shooting, it would be Rodney Gott.

It was a twitch of the cheek, not really a wink, that told Caye she had guessed right. "Walk me to the car," Manny said, rather than confirm or deny his wife's comment. It didn't matter. Caye knew Manny far too well not to be able to read his face.

Manny had driven his official car to the game, as he normally did. Unless he was checked out on vacation, he was considered to be on duty and would respond anytime called. It wasn't that unusual to be called away in the middle of something – Caye and Brittany were used to it.

"I'll be back tonight," he said as he kissed his wife. As always, Manny left saying that he loved her. He called his office. He relayed briefly that he needed the forensic team to meet him in Byar. The crime scene specialist would also have to be called back in for weekend duty. This was a high visibility murder case. The Rangers could not take a chance on leaving it to local authorities to gather evidence for the investigation. Even though the sheriff had said there were a couple of DPS troopers on the scene, they were best at traffic accidents. This would be a Texas Ranger case. Manny did not have to make a stop by home or office on the way out of Houston. His gun and badge were always with him.

***

Everyone who has ever played the game of golf knows how physically and mentally demanding it can be, especially for a weekender who tends to be a perfectionist. Clay often told himself that it was just a game – *a friggin' game,* for fun and relaxation. Nevertheless, it was a continuous battle between his competitive spirit and his philosophy of golf. Clay had witnessed far too many otherwise sane and stable individuals driven to the brink of madness by that damn little white ball. But for him, it was not to be a day of long straight drives, measured chips and miraculous putts. Clay felt horrible, and his play matched it. Physical fatigue was not the worst of the maladies. His concentration was severely lacking. He had always mentally clicked through the golfers' checklist as he addressed the ball on the tee. Grip – head down – eye on the ball – keep the left arm straight – smooth back swing – shift the weight – don't try to kill it – let the club follow through. No use.

Clay could not get his mind off the previous night's work. He had tossed the old firing pin and the extractor out the car window along the highway. Even though he knew there was nothing that would tie his gun to the death of Rod Gott, his stomach was heaving and he felt his pulse racing. He wondered how he would respond to acquaintances when he got home. Could he believably fake surprise to the news that Rod Gott had been killed while he was up in Arkansas? Clay had to excuse himself after nine holes for a toilet break. The back nine was no better and he felt compelled to apologize to his partner for his poor play. He was never so glad as when the round was over.

Clay drove back to the hotel and got there a little after noon. He arranged for a late checkout and decided to try to sleep a couple of hours. No one had called his cell phone yet, so he turned it off. Again, Clay fell short of getting the planned amount of rest. By 2:00 p.m. he was checking out and headed for the airport. He filled in the paperwork, recording the mileage from the company car odometer. He had driven the car less than 30 miles. Clay dropped the keys off in the FBO office. The car would be retrieved by a Consolidated employee on Monday.

It was good that Clay could satisfy himself by taking his time to preflight the aircraft in full daylight. He found no damage from his hard landing. Everything looked good, and he was once again pleased with his choice of a well designed and strong kit plane. Weather was no factor. It was again clear all the way.

***

Manny arrived at the Rod Gott home close to the same time Clay had wrapped up the round of golf in Arkansas. The coroner had already removed the body, but Sheriff Bell had left a deputy to guard the gate. The Ranger had called the sheriff and within 15 minutes, Sheriff Bell returned to the scene. Manny casually looked over the area, trying not to disturb anything before the State Crime Lab forensic team arrived.

"Man, ain't this somethin'," Bell said, approaching Manny.

"Yes it is. Unbelievable."

"We got a lot of pictures before they removed the body. They'll be here in a few minutes. Printing them up now."

"Sheriff, tell me what you think happened," Manny said.

"Like I told you, Rod's stableman came in about 8:30 this morning. The gate was closed – he has an opener. Name is Ramon Rodrigues. Been working for the Gotts about three years. Comes in and takes care of the horses and barns and does some other things. Anyway, he finds Rod – dead up there on the porch by that column, just this side of the front door."

"Yes, I see where it is chalked," Manny said, referring to the white marks on the tile.

"Rod had a Ruger .44 Magnum layin' by his body. Three shots fired. Got it locked up in the trunk of my car."

Manny looked at Bell and said the obvious. "Then he came out shooting at someone."

The sheriff nodded yes, but said, "Actually he didn't come out the front door there. That door is still bolted from the inside. The side door back here was unlocked. My guess is he came out that side door, came up beside the house and then on to the porch. Who ever was here exchanged shots and Rod was the loser."

"You have a statement from the witness? You said his name is Ramon?" Manny was stalling, but at the same time making sure all the open squares had been filled. Within a few minutes, the two man forensic team arrived. Close behind them was the Mazda sports car of Marcus Franks.

"Here comes the news media," Sheriff Bell said, referring to Marcus' red roadster that he was accustomed to seeing when something happened in Byar County. "Aah, yeah – I got Ramon's statement, and everything is in the car."

Many excused himself from the sheriff and went over to meet the lab guys to get them started. Hank, the senior of the men, went to the porch while the other retrieved a metal detector from their van. He started sweeping the area in front of the porch and worked his way out.

Hank, on the porch, picked up a number of small bits of matter and placed each bit in a separate plastic container. Most of the bits were stained by dried blood and were easily spotted on the light colored tile deck.

"What happened here?" Marcus directed the question to Manny.

"Marcus, you know you've got to hold off until next of kin is notified," Sheriff Bell said.

"You mean Gott is dead? He was killed?" Marcus had picked up enough on the police scanner to know something was going on at the Gotts, but did not know what.

"Yes. Senator Rodney Gott was found dead of an apparent gunshot wound at about 8:30 a.m. today. At this time an investigation is underway by Sheriff Bell and the Texas Department of Public Safety, including the Texas Rangers." Manny said it as if it were a press release, which was exactly how he intended it. "Marcus, as the sheriff said, you've got to sit on this for a while."

"Yeah. Well, Mrs. Gott and the boy are in France, I hear," Marcus said.

"Right," Sheriff Bell said, and then continued. "We think we found the contact information in the house, a telephone number, and I have attempted to call Mrs. Gott but received no answer. I'll be trying again shortly."

"We'll let you know as soon as we're clear," Manny said.

"I already have a headline story for this week. County Judge called me in this morning for an exclusive."

"What does Mason have to say?" Manny asked.

"I'm sure it'll be leaked before we get the paper out Wednesday. Judge Griggs is resigning from office. Has plans for a small private practice. Says it's time for a change."

"Heck," Bell said. "We don't need any more changes around here."

"The Bodas," Manny said, reflecting a little. "Guess they did what they intended. They ran everything in the County, and now the era of the Bodas is over. Two dead and one resignation. Yep. Wild, huh?"

CHAPTER TWENTY-NINE

Sheriff Bell was in the house using the Gott phone for his overseas call when one of the State Crime Lab technicians made a discovery. He placed a small flag at the site of a shell casing in the grass. He flipped the spent shell into a clear plastic bag and presented it to Manny.

"Looks like a .45 ACP," Manny said, holding the bag up at eye level. It didn't surprise him. It was what he expected to find.

Marcus was still there, and slid up beside Manny to also peek at the potential piece of evidence, as the sheriff came out of the house.

"Marcus, you can run with the story. I just spoke to Mrs. Gott. You can be the front man to break this to the radio station."

"Since it is a State Senator, DPS in Austin will also do a news release," Manny said. "And Sheriff, we just came up with a .45 case in the grass over there."

Manny and the sheriff walked out to the marker flag while the lab tech continued to sweep the area with the metal detector. They gazed back at the house, trying to imagine a shot fired from that approximate position. It would be a reasonable shot for a pistol marksman.

"Check the house siding for any missed shots," Manny told the other tech who had otherwise finished on the porch.

Finally, the Ranger had to address his suspicion. "Marcus, have you seen Clay today?"

Sheriff Bell looked on intently, then spoke. "Hate to admit it, but Longley would be my number one suspect." His comment earned a disapproving look from the Ranger, in spite of his own suspicion. Clay Longley had the motive, and had also told Manny he owned a .45 semi-auto.

"Can't be," Marcus said. "Clay is up in Arkansas. Left yesterday morning – flew his plane. Said he would be back late today. I'm going to pick him up at the airport at six. He left his truck at Firestone for new tires and stuff."

Manny was glad to hear that, but experience and training told him that hearsay alibis had to be thoroughly checked. He did not want it to be Clay, and hoped it wasn't. But he would go wherever the evidence led him.

It took another half hour before the technician was confident no other cartridges were to be found in the grass, and Hank reported there were no bullet impacts on the front wall of the house.

Marcus had already departed, to start writing his two blockbusters for Byar County politics. He agreed to call a friend at the local radio station to break the story. Word would travel fast enough after that. Byar could expect news crews out of Houston and surrounding areas before the day was over. Since he had plenty of work for the remainder of the day, Marcus readily agreed to permit Manny to meet Clay at the airport in his place. He also agreed not to call Clay and tell him about Rod. Manny had already placed a call to Ranger Headquarters in Austin, and filed a preliminary report.

"Guess I'll be spending the rest of the weekend at the office," Sheriff Bell said. "Expect we'll be getting a ton of phone calls and some visitors."

"How about keeping a deputy stationed at the gate here," Manny said. "Just as soon none of your guests come snooping around the scene."

"Sure. We can do that for a day or so. Just let me know as soon as you can when we can call them off."

"Let's get a tape up around this whole area," Manny said, waiving a hand to indicate the house and the grass area out front. "None of the family is here right now, so it shouldn't be a problem for anyone."

The State technicians strung out the crime scene plastic tape that denoted the prohibited area. The yellow tape with black lettering ran from the right front corner of the house, around the silver Dodge, out to 75 feet north of the house, then east to a corner and back to the other end of the front porch. They also stretched tape across each doorway into the house, even though there was no reason to believe anything had transpired inside. When the techs had completed their work, they informed Manny they were on their way to the coroner's office. They hoped to gather any additional information there, since the body had been removed before their arrival.

It was still a while before Clay was due back at Byar County Airport, according to what Marcus had said. Manny figured he would be there early, just to be sure.

***

Clay lifted off early on his departure and thought he might have to wait for Marcus to pick him up, back at Byar. The plan was for Marcus to drop him off at the Firestone Tire Store so he could retrieve his pickup truck with new tires, oil change, and lube. Firestone had not called his cell phone on Friday, so the truck apparently didn't need anything else.

As nice as the warm and clear afternoon was, it was not a pleasurable flight for Clay. He had climbed out to 4,500 feet and the air was smooth. He throttled back to economy cruise. He was in no hurry, but his mind was far too busy to enjoy the green landscape passing slowly beneath him. He tried to think about Claire – about him and Claire. Again the question was, what would Claire think if she were to know what he had done? He tried to busy himself with his flight log. He had destroyed the one he had backtracked on from Arkansas to the Gott ranch. All he now had was the clean log he had filled out for the return flight. Eventually, he started his descent into Byar County Airport.

As Clay rolled off the runway onto the taxiway, he noted that Marcus' red sports car was not present, but another vehicle was. He also recognized Manny standing by the car. It caused a lump in his throat, and he feared there would be nervousness in his voice. Instead of taxiing up to his hangar, he passed it by, and pulled up to the gas pump a couple hundred feet down the taxiway, to refill. Clay pulled the mixture control to shut off the engine fuel supply, and let the engine die. He unstrapped and hoped he had full control of his demeanor. He wished it had been Marcus there, instead of Manny, to break the news to him about Rod Gott.

As Clay was crawling out of the cockpit, Manny walked up to the plane. Clay tried to give him an honest-to-goodness good-buddy smile. "What're you doing here? I was expecting Marcus."

"Marcus is busy. Rodney Gott was shot last night," the Ranger said.

"Shot!" Clay hoped it sounded like he was shocked. Quickly he realized that Manny did not say "killed." He instinctively knew Manny had said it that way intentionally, and was gauging his response and reaction. "Much as I'd like to, it wasn't me."

"Yeah, I know you would like to. How was your flight?" Manny's intent was to work on him slowly, and try not to damage their friendship needlessly.

"It was good. Is he dead? Is Rod dead?" Clay figured that was a safe question, and would be what someone who didn't know the outcome of the shooting just reported might ask.

"He's dead. His stableman found him this morning."

"Don't guess I'll grieve over him," Clay said, as he used his credit card at the gas pump. "How did it happen?" It was another good question, which Clay had planned to ask Marcus.

Manny kept his eyes focused on Clay's expression and body language. "There at his house. Sometime after the bar closed out at the Marina."

"What about his family, his wife and son?" Clay looked directly into Manny's gaze.

"Sheriff Bell has notified them. He also had to go over and break it to Gott's mother." Manny thought he detected a slight wince flash across Clay's face.

The mother. The thought deeply pained Clay. The mother, who lost both of her children in a matter of a couple of months, does not deserve this fate. Rod deserved what he got – his mother did not. It was also true for his wife and son. Clay was engrossed in his own thoughts as he pumped the gas. This was another burden on Claire.

Clay regained his composure just in time to stop the pump at twelve gallons. He had planned to stop at 10 gallons, and had calculated it would have taken fourteen and a half gallons. The trip from Arkansas would have taken only ten gallons, plus a few more sips. He had made his first mistake. He also wondered if Manny had said anything else.

"I really feel sorry for Mrs. Gott," Clay managed to utter. He didn't know what else might be appropriate.

"Yeah, that is really bad. I heard she was kind of fragile before this. It could send her over the edge."

"I need to call Claire and see how they're doing." While he knew his statement would seem odd if anyone knew it came from someone who intended to kill the old lady's son, Clay was sincere in his concern for the innocent.

"Twelve gallons, is that one way from Arkansas?" Manny said, a question asked ostensibly to satisfy his curiosity. "What kind of gas mileage is that?"

Clay held up the fuel nozzle, looking at it, thinking how best to reply. "Yeah, aah. With a plane we don't figure miles per gallon, although you can. We normally refer to gallons per hour. That's what we do for flight planning. Too many variables affecting what the ground speed is from one flight to the next." Clay figured that if Manny really wanted to get into solving a math problem, he could dig for the other data.

Manny nodded, thinking, then shot Clay a look. "Oh. Clay, you carry that .45 with you?"

"Yes. It's here in the plane," Clay said. He faked a puzzled look at Manny. "In fact, I've got two .45 pistols now. Got one in my car." Appearing forthright in response to the Ranger's inquiry was best on the subject of guns, he thought.

"Mind if I see it?"

"No. What for? I told you I didn't shoot Rod Gott." Clay thought he should be able to say that convincingly. It's the truth. I did *not* shoot Rod. He hung up the nozzle and opened the hatch. He reached across to the passenger seat and pulled the shop towel from under the seat. He unwrapped the 1911 Service Model and handed the gun to Manny, butt first. "It's loaded," Clay said as a precaution.

"Okay. We just want to be sure we rule everyone out." The Ranger accepted the pistol and took care to point it away from Clay. He held it up in his right hand, flipped the safety off, and pulled the slide back enough to slip a round into the chamber, and released it. "Mind if I let one off?" Manny didn't wait for Clay to answer. He walked a few yards from the concrete pad, a safe distance, he judged, from the fuel pump, and fired the semi-auto into the ground.

There was no chance of a ricochet. The plush grass and sandy soil absorbed the round and the spent case was ejected. Manny lowered the hammer and bent over and picked up the cartridge case. It was silver – different from the brass colored case picked up at the Gotts. He pressed the magazine release and dropped the clip into his left hand. The top round and the other rounds in the magazine, which he could see through the sides of the magazine, were all silver colored. Manny also noted the rounds were lead only, no copper jacket. He reseated the magazine, put the weapon on safety, and handed it back to Clay.

Clay was satisfied the Ranger had collected his evidence – evidence that clearly indicated Clay's weapon was not the one present at the Gott house at the time of the crime. He knew the Ranger was interested in the spent case, and was a little surprised when Manny pulled out a large liner-lock pocketknife, and dug in the ground for the slug. He knew there was no lead slug to compare ballistics against. He had fired one time, and it was into the air off to the west. Besides, it was a bullet that traveled down an old worn barrel, not the same one as Manny just tested. Manny picked the lead out of the black dirt and grass roots after digging about six inches down. It was slightly deformed, but all there. He wiped away the dirt and placed the bullet in his shirt pocket.

"You going to do a ballistics test on that?"

"No. It's just a sample. They do that by shooting into a water tank. Marcus is tied up and I told him I would fetch you over to get your truck," Manny said as if the handling and firing of the gun had not even occurred. "He's got stories to write. The other thing you missed is Marcus telling us that Mason is resigning as County Judge."

"No kidding! That is a surprise. Kind of hate to hear that." Clay had developed some respect for the judge after Mason had let him know about the Commissioners' meeting, and then him going against Rod Gott. Mason had gotten the new D.A. appointed. It was the D.A. who was going after Oliver Harrell. It looked like Mason was going to be part of the clean up of Byar County corruption. Clay took his credit card receipt from the gas pump, and realized he was shaking his head.

"Is that the way these fuel pumps are? Just slip in a credit card like for car gas?" Manny said.

"Most places are like that now. Seems like there aren't any line boys any more. It's not bad for this plane, though. I don't have to get a ladder to get on top of the wing like the Cessna I trained in." Clay figured correctly that the Ranger was still collecting data. He continued to do his best to act as if it was innocent conversation. "Let me get this thing over there and pushed into the hangar, and I'll be ready to go."

Clay crawled into the cockpit; Manny stepped back and started walking back over to Clay's hangar. Clay started the engine and let the aircraft roll away from the gas pump. It took less than a minute to cover the distance to the hangar. He cut the mixture, let the engine die and the plane roll to a stop. This time he picked up his shut down checklist and zipped through the items to make sure everything was turned off. Clay exited the aircraft, unlocked the side door of his one-plane hangar and opened the main door from inside.

Manny, not knowing how to help, stood by until he could determine what Clay was doing. He did note that the hangar was neat and clean. It was just as he would have surmised. He also took note that it was empty, no motor vehicle of any type – not even a moped. Finally, when he saw that Clay was holding down on the plane's tail, he lent a hand on the other side of the fuselage. Together they swung the plane around so the tail faced into the hangar, and slowly walked the light aircraft into its parking spot. The homebuilt was so light Clay often did it alone, but it was good to have some assistance.

"What did you do up in Arkansas?"

"It was a plant visit. That is the official reason, and then we played golf this morning," Clay said while motioning to the golf clubs behind the seat. He went ahead and pulled them out of the plane and leaned the bag against the workbench. "You Golf?"

"Nope. Never had time to start."

"If someone saw me play this morning, they'd think it was my first time." Clay reached back into the cockpit and retrieved his one piece of luggage, the .45 semi-auto, and the manila envelope, from the passenger seat. He unzipped the luggage and slipped the gun into the top. He took the gas receipt he had just gotten and put it into the envelope. "Expense report stuff," he said. "I do get to charge off some of this for company business. When you use your own vehicle they'll reimburse you for mileage or actual expenses."

"You normally fly your own plane on business?"

"No, but for an overnight trip like this we would normally forward the requirements to Atlanta, and the aviation department would either send a company plane or arrange a charter. With just one person traveling, that doesn't make economic sense. Besides, this is the fun part of traveling, getting to drive yourself."

"Mind if I see that?" Manny said referring to the envelope.

Clay's face took on a look of balking. "I am beginning to feel like I'm a suspect. Do you think I wasn't in Arkansas the last couple of days?" He handed over the envelope.

"Like I said, Clay, if I don't check everything, the Rangers can be subject to a lot of criticism. It's just the job." Manny was trying hard to be casual and friendly. But there was something in his gut that told him to keep digging. "I would like to make copies of this, that okay?"

"No problem. Get it back to me in a couple of days."

"Sure, you about ready to go?"

"Let me just close things up here," Clay said, as he punched the button again to lower the big hangar door. They exited out the side door with just Clay's travel bag, leaving the golf clubs to be picked up later.

"What are you getting done to the truck?" Manny felt compelled to make idle conversation as he drove.

"New tires, coolant flush, transmission service, oil and lube. Told them to check the shocks and replace if necessary. I used to do some of that stuff myself, but just don't have the time any more. Guess that isn't true. What time I have, I would rather spend flying or tinkering with the plane."

"Well, I still get my hands greasy from time to time."

"Let me bail my truck out and I'll buy you dinner," Clay offered just as Manny's cell phone rang.

"Rojas," Manny said, answering the call. He listened for a while and then replied. "Okay. See you there. Oh, how about call Sheriff Bell and ask him to meet us there." Manny returned the phone to the belt case. "Thanks, Clay. I'm going to have to pass on that offer. I've got to get back to Houston tonight." In a few moments, Manny pulled up to the tire store where Clay had directed him. They said goodbyes for then, and Manny said he would probably see Clay on Monday.

Manny left Clay standing outside the Firestone dealership. Clay felt confident he had handled himself adequately, and although the Ranger would check everything out, there was nothing to implicate him. God, I would so love to tell Manny the dumb prick shot himself.

CHAPTER THIRTY

It was Hank, the lead crime lab technician, who had called Manny. Upon leaving Clay to pick up his truck, Manny returned to the Gott ranch as requested. He wanted the sheriff to also be present to get the details and analysis from the lab guys. Sheriff Bell was already there, standing with the techs at the edge of the porch.

"We collected Rod Gott's shirt, additional blood samples, and the remains of the lead slug, from the Coroner's Office," Hank said. "Coroner said the bullet shattered his neck, killing him instantly. He had already determined that Senator Gott had a blood alcohol level nearly three times the legal limit at the time of his death. He was drunk."

"Not surprising," Manny said.

"The coroner also showed us that the vicinity of the wound contained tiny slivers of white rock." Hank pointed to the square rock column of the porch where the body had lain. "Look here on the back side of this rock." The technicians pointed out to Manny the point where a bullet had ricocheted off the back side of the rock column about 18 inches above the floor. "See the shiny specs in here?" Hank held a penlight, shining it into the indentation in the stone.

"Yeah, minute particles of lead," Manny said, confirming what Hank was showing him. As Manny drew back from looking, Sheriff Bell took his turn and shook his head in agreement.

"We'll pick out some sample to make sure," the tech said. "We also examined the slug recovered from the body." Hank motioned toward their van, where they had a traveling mini-lab located in the back. "The remains of the bullet weighed in at 307 grains. It didn't match up with the .45 casing found in the grass, for a couple of reasons. First, the bullet from the .45 would have been copper clad. Thought so anyway, and we verified that by microscopic examination of the inside of the casing. Secondly, the largest size lead bullet for a .45 ACP is 230 grains, far smaller than the fatal slug. The final detail, the .44 Magnum shells left in Senator Gott's gun are 330 grains – lose a few grains in the barrel rifling, some more in the stone column, and maybe a little in bone fragments, and it would be reasonable to have about 307 grains left over."

"Case solved? Rod Gott, in a drunker stupor, accidentally shot himself," Sheriff Bell said.

"Aah, let me show you something," Hank added, as he withdrew his automatic from its holster. He dropped the clip into his other hand and then cycled the slide to unload the weapon. Hank also produced two pencils for demonstration. "Now, Gott's pistol was a long barrel revolver, but this will give you an idea. While it is highly unlikely anyone would be hit by their own ricochet, it has happened." Hank inserted one pencil into the end of the barrel of his automatic and held it down to the level of the supposed indentation in the stone, and then held the other pencil as if to show the ricochet path of the bullet. "The bullet would have bounced out of this hole something like this," he said, as he wagged the second pencil around in a small arc.

"He would have had to be crouched down, or falling, at the time for the ricochet to hit him in the neck," Manny said as a conclusion.

"Right. I'd guess falling. And his revolver would have had to be pointed at an upward angle like this." Hank looked at Manny and the sheriff for their agreement to his analysis. "We'll do a paraffin test on this spot and I'll bet we find some gunshot residue."

"Let's be sure we check all the details before we make any announcements. You okay with that, Sheriff?" Manny said.

"We know by tomorrow?"

"We'll know in a couple of hours," Hank said.

"Well, case partially solved. What was Gott doing out on his porch in the middle of the night, and what, or who, was he shooting at?" Sheriff Bell said to no one in particular.

***

A prominent state senator being shot on his front porch was a hot item of conversation around the cafes and hardware stores of Byar by Saturday afternoon. Everybody had a theory about who wanted to whack Rod Gott. The leading supposition was that it was some political adversary who wanted to stop Gott from being elected Texas Attorney General or maybe even Governor. Others expanded on the conspiracy to include the imagined staged accident that had already killed Ray Gott. A few citizens suggested that Rod's wife, who had run off to France with the boy, was involved, somehow, in the murder. Had there been any bar rooms in Byar, a few drinks would certainly have stimulated even more interesting scenarios. But, thanks to the Gotts' stranglehold, the still private Lake Byar Restaurant and Marina remained the only watering hole in Byar County.

As soon as Clay was home he tried to call Claire. There was no answer. When he called her cell phone it was evidently turned off, so he left a message. Clay called Marcus to talk about the events because that's what he would normally do.

"Yeah. I was out there when Manny Rojas was there," Marcus started telling. "I didn't see the body. It was already gone. They had a couple of crime lab guys there, and they picked up a .45 caliber shell. Of course, they don't know if it was important or not. But Manny asked about you, and Jimmy Bell said something about you being a suspect. I told them you weren't even in town."

"Manny kind of quizzed me. I don't think he really believes it was me. He's just checking everything." Clay didn't mention that Manny had taken one of his spent shells and dug the bullet out of the ground. After all, Marcus was a reporter, and some of that detail might wind up in one of his stories. He would rather not have his name mentioned in relationship to the entire event.

Marcus said, "Manny tell you about Judge Griggs?"

"He mentioned it. What's the deal there?"

"He called me this morning and wanted to meet. He had told me in confidence that he wasn't running again and, that if I kept it quiet, he would let me know when to announce it. He kept his word on letting me know first, but this resignation was a surprise. He gave me a letter to put in the paper this week. It is addressed to the Citizens of Byar County. It has the normal appreciation for your support stuff, and then says he is going to take time off before opening a small legal practice in Byar."

"Maybe he'll reconsider the resignation now that this has happened to Rod," Clay thought out loud.

"Maybe." Marcus paused before continuing. "I called him this afternoon for a statement about Rod's murder. He didn't say anything about the resignation and I didn't think to broach that subject. That would kill one of my big stories, but if I'm going to lose a story, it's good to have an even bigger one at the same time."

"Do you have any theories? Has the sheriff said anything?"

"I was running all over town, talking to folks outside Wal-Mart, or wherever I could find a few people together. Lots of people are talking about it, but nobody really knows anything. The Sheriff's Office just has their official statement that the death is under investigation in conjunction with the Texas Rangers. And DPS put out a press release in Austin this afternoon. Same thing."

***

On Telephone Road, on the far south side of Houston, is a number of what many people would describe as the hangouts of the unsavory. Wild Willie's Icehouse was typical of the open environment pubs that are scattered among a few seedy strip clubs and run down motels.

Wild Willie's clientele consisted of over-the-hill bikers and the retired or otherwise non-working blue collars. They were the tired, burned out, and bummed out, most of whom spent more money on cigarettes and beer than on food. Weekends added additional faces to the normal afternoon crowd. It was warm enough that all of the roll-up industrial style doors were open, providing easy entry all across the front, and on the south side of the steel frame building. The floor was bare cement; there were two pool tables with shop lights hanging over them, and a number of crude tables and chairs scattered around.

The long rustic bar, situated across the back of the icehouse, offered half a dozen brands of beer in cans and longneck bottles. Draft beer was a little cheaper and the favorite of the locals. Willie also offered food. It was hamburger, or cheeseburger; you could get either one with jalapenos, plus your choice of greasy fries or onion rings.

There were already several motorcycles parked among the few old pickups when Reggie "Smudge" Bishop, and Freddy Harper pulled in on their Harleys. Each raced the engine a couple of times before killing it. It was the way they announced their arrival, a common trait of Harley riders.

Bishop had gained his nickname, originally "Smudge Pot," in junior high for putting black face under his eyes when playing sports, mimicking athletes he saw on TV. He might have done it in high school as well, but his formal education hadn't gone that far. He had sandy hair and an unshaven face. It would be difficult to describe his facial growth as a beard – it was never thick enough for that. The style of his hair was just "no haircut," and he had a bandana headband keeping it out of his face. His sidekick, Freddy, was the opposite. While Smudge was less than 150 pounds, Freddy was over 300, and his bald head was covered by a faded red doo-rag. The stubble on his fat face indicated he did shave occasionally. Both wore denim jeans, scruffy boots and black tee shirts. Smudge wore his shirt outside his pants and a black leather vest with plenty of shiny metal work on the front.

It was the fourth place Smudge and Freddy had stopped that Saturday afternoon. They found stools at the bar and ordered their normal Lone Star beers. The television sitting on a shelf behind the bar was tuned to a local channel, and the news was on. About half way through the second beer, there was a live report from Byar County. It caught Smudge's attention.

"Look at that, Freddy."

"Yeah. Byar, what an armpit." Freddy wasn't nearly as interested as Smudge.

The handsome on-scene TV reporter was standing at the entrance to Senator Rodney Gott's rural ranch estate. "This morning an employee found the body of Senator Gott on the front veranda of the mansion, located here in Byar County. Senator Gott had apparently been shot and killed sometime last night or the wee hours of the morning. This is the second bizarre murder to occur in Byar in just a few months."

At that point the video switched to a view of the Longley's home as viewed from the highway, while the reporter continued with his story. "Will and Elizabeth Longley, a retired couple who raised Longhorn cattle, no more than half a mile from the Gott's, were found murdered in their home. At the time the Longleys were killed, they were in a legal dispute with Byar County over the county attempting to take their ranch by eminent domain for the development of the proposed Lake Byar Convention Center. Senator Gott was probably the biggest, or certainly at least the most prominent proponent of the convention center project. The Longley murders remain unsolved. Byar County Sheriff Jimmy Bell and the Texas Rangers are investigating both crimes. People around here are beginning to wonder if there is some connection between these two gruesome murders. With big happenings in the normally quiet piney woods, this is Tad Cruz reporting from rural Byar County."

"That asshole got somebody else to do my job. That's why I never heard from him," Smudge said to Freddy, but loud enough for the bartender and anybody else to hear.

A barrel-chested urban redneck on the bar stool next to Smudge looked over and made an obvious smirk, as if to question the validity of the comment. "Yeah. They probably wanted it done right." Redneck had been watching the news story also, and thought he detected some boastfulness on the part of the small fry mouthing off next to him. He was surprised by the ire his comment raised in Smudge.

Smudge looked hard at the stranger on his left who had mocked him. "You mean somethin' by that, or you just flappin' your fat mouth?" Smudge leaned back toward Freddy as he spoke, separating himself from the confrontation that was to come, verbal or physical.

"Piss ant, you better go find some little girls to pick on. You gonna get hurt in here. Ridin' that hog don't make you big." The redneck spit and glared at what he considered a punk.

Smudge slid off the bar stool backward as he gave the much bigger guy a push with his left hand. He yelled, "What about this." Smudge reached behind his back with his right hand, under his shirt tail, for the .38 revolver tucked inside his belt. He planted his feet, squared off at his adversary.

Scrubby little punk's going for a weapon, Redneck knew. Like I can't tell when I'm havin' a knife or gun pulled on me. Bring it, punk, whatever ya got. With his half full mug, he took a wide backhand at Smudge's head, sloshing beer all over. Freddy got slopped on his barstool as the mug smashed into Smudge's face. His pistol was clearing his side when

Smudge felt an excruciating impact. *Crack!* His jawbone shattered. Three teeth shot to the far side of his mouth.

Smudge, still conscious, knees giving way, aimed his gun and fired. Anyone who hadn't yet noticed the fight, was now alerted. The shot was harmless. It hit the unfinished metal wall behind the bar.

Before patrons could flee, Freddy had climbed across the empty stool and grabbed the mug assailant. Smudge wasn't through. As he was falling he caught himself with his left hand. He pointed and fired again. He'd have been better off unconscious. His aim would have been good, but for Freddy bear hugging the other man, about to deck him. The shot caught Freddy in the side just below his outstretched left arm. The bullet splintered an upper rib, passed through two heart chambers and lodged against the breastbone.

Both big guys slumped to the floor. Smudge went on all fours, blood filling his mouth. A couple of pool shooters grabbed him from behind. They jerked him onto his back. One guy stomped on his gun hand. More cracking bones. Someone pulled the gun from his useless broken fingers. Smudge rolled to his right to spit blood and teeth.

Willie and a couple patrons were calling 911 on their cell phones. Smudge and Freddy had been at the icehouse for only 20 minutes. Smudge was painfully injured, and Freddy was dead.

CHAPTER THIRTY-ONE

Houston Police Department took statements from Wild Willie and his patrons, who all told essentially the same story. The little guy insulted the other beer drinker, and then pulled a gun on him. To defend himself, the other guy hit him with a beer mug, but the punk got off two shots. He inadvertently shot his own buddy, who was trying to help him. The investigating officers communicated to Smudge that he had evidently killed someone. Smudge was only able to grunt. Paramedics had stuffed his mouth with gauze in an attempt to stop the bleeding. The pain was so intense he did not attempt to lift his head.

Smudge and Freddy were hauled off in separate ambulances. Smudge was under arrest. There would be a number of charges against him. Freddy went straight to the morgue.

It was 8:00 p.m. before Smudge was able to talk with an investigating officer at the county hospital. Through muffled words, and finally some scribbling with his left hand, he conveyed to the police officer that he wanted to speak to someone about the murders in Byar County. The officer had caught the news item on the shooting of a State Senator that day and recognized it as a hot item. He called in to his precinct and relayed information that he had someone who had knowledge about the shooting.

It was near 10:00 p.m. when the phone rang at Lieutenant Manny Rojas's home. It was the duty officer from Company A. They had received a call from HPD. A man had been arrested in Houston who had information about the gun slaying in Byar County. He would have to talk to him in the county hospital. Manny asked the Ranger Office to relay back to HPD that he would be there early Sunday morning.

The new light on the case was disturbing to Manny. He put in a call to Sheriff Bell to tell him there were other developments, and that no statements would be issued on the investigation until further leads were checked.

Manny had reviewed Clay's receipts from his trip. If they were real, Clay definitely had been in Arkansas at the time of Rod Gott's death. He had bought 10.2 gallons of gas at Canney Field in Arkansas, and he had charged dinner on a credit card at 9:08 PM. Had Clay driven back to Byar in the middle of the night, that would have been a 400 and something mile round trip and taken all night. It was possible, but the company car provided to Clay had only been driven 30 miles. If Clay had flown back to Byar at night, he had no visible means of transportation from the airport to the Gott ranch. Besides he would have needed another 20 or so gallons of gas from Arkansas. Clay looked like he had a foolproof alibi.

Every detail perfectly documented. Too perfect? Manny planned to get all credit card records, and verify everything.

***

It was at 10:00 p.m. when Clay received a return call from Claire. "You've heard about Rod?" Claire said.

"Yes. I am so sorry for Mrs. Gott. How is she?"

"Sedated again. I don't know how she's going to get over this."

Clay could tell Claire was whimpering, causing him to squirm in his chair. "How about you? How are you handling…everything?"

"I don't know. Just trying to take care of one thing at a time," Claire said. It had been a long difficult day, and he heard it in her voice.

Clay wanted to say that he wished he could be there with her. It would have been a bad time to cut short on their agreed isolation. "Can I help you with anything?"

"I spoke to Margarette this afternoon. No arrangements will be made until she gets here. That'll be late tomorrow. When did you get back?" Claire said, remembering Clay had told her about the planned trip several times the previous week.

"Late this afternoon. It was a good trip. Nothing exciting." After a little more chitchat, they said goodbye. Clay had tried to not sound as exhausted as Claire obviously was. He had a secret he would never be able to share with her. That did not make him feel good.

The physical fatigue overcame Clay's mental anguish, and he slept soundly for several hours. At 3:00 a.m. he was lying wide awake. He replayed the details over and over. There was one thing he thought he had to clean up. The plane needed another three gallons of gas to be full. It didn't seem like a big detail, but what if somehow that fact came out. Manny had already seen him pump 12 gallons. It could all add up to him leaving Arkansas with less than a full tank. If the fuel situation unraveled, what else would start unraveling? Small details bugged Clay.

Four a.m. found him in the kitchen preparing a full breakfast. At five, Clay was turning lights on in the hangar at the airport. He opened the overhead door and rolled the plane out. Just before daylight he started the engine and taxied to the end of the runway. The orange tint to the eastern sky was his signal for takeoff.

By the time Clay had climbed out to 2,000 feet, the upper third of the Sun had climbed above the horizon. Clay flew around the perimeter of Lake Byar as the Sun rose in the morning sky, and eventually he returned to the airport. The airport was still quiet. It looked to Clay that he was the only soul stirring at that early hour. He pulled up to the gas pump, again using his credit card for fuel purchase. He filled the tank and took his receipt.

Clay maintained two flight logbooks. The first was the pilot log. It recorded his personal flight time, regardless of which plane he was flying. The other was the aircraft log. It recorded the number of hours of operation on the airframe, and the number of hours of operation of the aircraft engine. Neither logbook had been filled in since he had left for Arkansas. He made the entries in each, one for the flight to Arkansas, and one for the return – 2.1 hours up and 2.3 hours back. The Sunday morning flight was recorded with an extra half hour of time to account for the additional gas it took to fill the tank. Clay closed the logs and put them away in the hangar. Now he was not concerned if Manny, or anyone else, wanted to review them. Everything would add up. He called Marcus to see if he wanted to go flying around later in the morning. Of course Marcus did.

***

At the county hospital, Manny met HPD Homicide Detective Kelly Zajac. She had gotten the assignment late on Saturday, and it was her first meeting with the perpetrator. Detective Zajac had the rap sheet on Reginald "Smudge" Bishop – it was substantial, but mostly assaults and petty theft.

"Look at these," Kelly said to Manny showing him the rap sheet. "These old arrests are from Byar County. He started young."

"Yeah. I'm surprised I didn't know him back then. That's when I lived in Byar. It isn't a big place."

"Bet you didn't travel in the same circles," she said.

"Let's see what he has to say. I'm eager to get on with it."

A HPD patrolman had been stationed in the hallway outside the private room, but otherwise Bishop was not restrained in any way, other than the I.V. in his arm.

"I am Texas Ranger Lieutenant Manuel Rojas, and this is Detective Zajac of Houston Police Department," Manny said. The Ranger was in uniform, but Kelly Zajac was in street clothes, so she showed Bishop her badge. "I am the lead investigator for the killing in Byar County, and Detective Zajac is investigating yesterday's shooting here in Houston. We understand you have information on the Byar County incident."

"Yeah, I know something," Bishop said. His right jaw area was swollen, and he had black bruising just under the right eye. The packing had been removed from inside his mouth, and he was pumped up with pain medication. While some words got slurred, his speaking ability was satisfactory. "I'll tell you, somebody tried to hire me for a killing in Byar. Now, I want a lawyer and I want a deal. I ain't talkin' no more 'til I get a lawyer."

"Any kind of...deal, as you say, will depend on the accuracy of evidence you can provide, and your willingness to give testimony. The value of your evidence will be judged by Ranger Rojas," Detective Zajac said.

"Before we go any further, we have to get a better idea of what you're talking about," Manny said.

"He offered me five grand. I know him and can identify him. I know him from Byar 20 years ago. That's it. Nothin' else. Besides, you know I didn't mean to kill Freddy."

"Of course you have a right to an attorney. We'll see that you get representation, and we'll be back to see you," the detective said.

Once in the hallway, Kelly Zajac said to Manny, "I'll contact the D.A.'s Office and let them know what we have here. They'll get him a court appointed attorney."

"I want to get this wrapped up as soon as possible. Let me know when we can get something better out of him. Today, if possible," Manny said.

The Ranger left the hospital with his stomach knotted. This didn't look good. Sure, Clay had an alibi, probably a well-planned, well-documented alibi. Manny thought about the conversation at Clay's home, with Clay and Forest. It was the night after his parents had been murdered. Yes, it was pointed out that Rod Gott could not have done it because he had seen Forest in Austin that day, at the approximate time of the murders. A planned alibi?

It was late afternoon before Detective Zajac called Manny back. She had an Assistant D.A. in tow, and he had recruited a defense attorney to represent Bishop. The attorney's court appointment would be a formality that could wait until Monday morning. They all agreed to meet back at the hospital for the next phase with Bishop.

After half an hour of discussion in a conference room, the party was ready to approach Bishop in his hospital room. His new attorney went in first and introduced himself. He gave his client the rundown on what he could expect. The charge would be Manslaughter One. A plea bargain, including testimony in another case could get him a Man Two. He should expect to be sentenced six to twelve years, probably serve four. Not bad for killing someone. But it would be contingent on his testimony in the Byar County case.

Manny, Detective Zajac, and the Assistant D.A. entered the room when motioned in by the attorney. The A.D.A. was introduced to Bishop.

"My client accepts your offer and is prepared to give you a statement at this time."

"Is your name Reginald Bishop," Manny asked as a formality.

"Yeah. Everybody calls me Smudge. That's short for Smudge Pot. It ain't no racial thing."

"Okay, Mr. Bishop. You reported that you had information on the killing of Senator Rodney Gott in Byar County, Texas yesterday. Is that correct?"

"Gott? Hell no! I wasn't talkin' about Gott. I was talkin' about the Longleys. Those old people that was murdered."

"The Longleys?" Manny was stunned. He fully expected to hear something about who tried to hire Bishop to kill Rodney Gott. He privately feared that someone was Clay Longley.

"I seen it on TV. Somebody killed the Longleys, right?

"Yes, they did," Manny said.

"Ain't you investigating that too?" Smudge winced with a sudden shooting pain.

"Absolutely. What information do you have on the Longley murders?" Manny said.

Smudge huffed, shook his head clear of the pain, and tried to focus. "That old sheriff, Ollie Harrell, asked me to kill those old people. Said it would be easy. He would even furnish the gun. He said he would pay me five thousand dollars. I didn't do it. But Ollie Harrell is the one that wanted them killed."

Manny thought Smudge was telling the truth, but only part of it. What is he holding back? "How do you know former Sheriff Oliver Harrell?"

"Hell. He was the first guy who ever arrested me. For takin' a truck when I was fourteen. A couple months back he sees me in Huntsville. Says he has work for me and then I can leave the state. That's when he tells me about the Longleys and the house off the highway. I wouldn't do it and I never heard from him again. I been in Laredo since then and didn't know somebody had done the job until I seen it on TV." Smudge thought he had said enough. No need to tell them he'd have done the job if Harrell had agreed to his asking five grand for each hit – a total of ten thousand

Manny left the hospital, pleased with the expected cooperation from his newest witness. It wasn't testimony regarding the Gott killing. It was for the Longleys, and that was far more satisfying.

CHAPTER THIRTY-TWO

With the statement from Smudge Bishop, it was easy to obtain a search warrant for Oliver Harrell's home. After all, Harrell was already under a felony indictment for the extortion case concerning Clay Longley and Consolidated Industries. The warrant specified firearms, money, financial records, and misappropriated personal property.

Sheriff Bell, accompanied by Ranger Manny Rojas and two deputies, appeared at the Harrell house in late morning. Their appearance and the warrant caught Harrell by surprise.

"Ollie, we've got a search warrant for the premises," Sheriff Bell said, handing Harrell his copy of the paperwork.

"What kind of shit is this, Bell?"

"We are investigating the murders of William and Elizabeth Longley," Lieutenant Rojas said.

Oliver Harrell looked intently at Manny. He didn't swallow hard and he didn't blink. It was more a questioning look than one of fear. Manny looked for a body language clue, but could read nothing.

Harrell, with a lifetime of experience around police work, had his own agenda. He did not intend to give away anything. What do they have that brought them here? Why now? Did they get something from Gott's house that implicates me? With no other choice left, Harrell stepped back as if to invite them into the house. "Tell me what you're looking for and I can save us some time," he said.

"Like the warrant says, first off – financial records," Manny said.

"In my office back there," Harrell said, motioning with his head toward the rear of the house. Manny and the sheriff followed him through the kitchen into the den where Manny had sat with Harrell a couple months before. At one end of the den were the desk and file cabinets that Harrell referred to as his office.

"Checkbooks, bank statements, brokerage accounts, or what have you," Manny said.

"Don't have no stock broker. No savings account – just checking. I'm poor. Live on Social Security."

Manny picked up a checkbook from the desktop. The check register in the front was not up to date for the balance after several checks had been written. The Ranger noted that the balance could not be more than a couple hundred dollars. He thumbed to the back and removed one of the blank deposit slips so he would have the account number. Manny handed the ticket to one of the deputies so it could be cataloged with whatever other items that might be removed. There were other items on the desk Manny looked at. One was a folder that had the word "Med" written on the tab. Manny looked through the numerous papers, most of which were Medicare statements of benefits payments. His eyes fell on one that included the word "Oncologist." He pulled it out and held it toward Harrell.

"Oncologist?"

"Yeah. You can read." Harrell stared at him, arms folded.

Sheriff Bell had wandered off to look around other rooms of the small house, but returned at that time. "Ollie, how about opening this lock box in the bedroom?"

Harrell frowned, dug into his pants pocket and pulled out a set of keys. He fingered through the keys as he slowly walked toward the bedroom. The lock box was a portable fire safe that sat at the end of the dresser, just inside the doorway. The safe was a 15inch cube. With a small shiny key, Harrell bent down, unlocked the hasp and stood up. He waved with his hand as if to say, "have at it."

Sheriff Bell bent down over the safe and lifted the heavy fireproof lid. He thumbed through a number of folders that had tabs for Deed, Will, Insurance, and Investments. In the back was a white envelope lying on the bottom. It was stuffed. Sheriff Bell picked it up carefully with his rubber-gloved hand. The flap had been sealed, but the envelope had been cut open with a knife or letter opener. He held it up for Harrell to see.

"Lieutenant Rojas, we have something here," the sheriff said in a loud voice.

Manny stopped his inspection of the desk area and responded to the sheriff's summons. When he walked into the bedroom the sheriff was holding out the envelope. Without taking it in his hand, Manny could see that it was stuffed with cash. Manny took the envelope for closer examination. He held it by the edges. There was nothing written on the outside, and he could see that the contents were mostly $100 bills, with some twenties and fifties.

"Lots of money for a poor guy," Manny said to no one in particular. A deputy showed up and produced a plastic baggie. Manny inserted the envelope. The money would have to be counted later. Manny looked for Harrell, who had been standing outside the doorway. He was gone. "Where's Harrell?" he said with some excitement. The sheriff, deputy and Ranger were back out into the hallway and headed back toward the den. There they saw Harrell, with his back to them, doing something with his hands in front of him. Manny placed his right hand on his sidearm and hit the strap to unsnap it.

The sheriff was leading the way with Manny close behind. "Ollie," Sheriff Bell called out in a loud voice.

They took two steps closer. Harrell wheeled around to his right. He had a revolver pointed at them from not more than ten feet away.

Sheriff Bell had enough time to reach for his own weapon as he held up a palm signaling Harrell to stop. "No, Ollie!"

Fire came from the end of the barrel. The sound would have been deafening had the action not been so intense.

Manny, behind and just to the right of Bell, was drawing his gun and clicking off the safety. He'd grabbed Bell's collar and pulled him to the right, as Harrell fired. Not soon enough. The sheriff never got his gun out of the holster. The slug ripped through his left palm and struck him in the side, just below the rib cage.

Harrell saw Bell fall. He eyed the Ranger. Manny's pistol was directed at Harrell's gut. Harrell paused. They locked eyes for a whole second. He moved his aim toward the Ranger.

Manny had decided many years before that if he were ever in a life-or-death situation, and deadly force was necessary, he would not hesitate. He had accepted that as going with his choice of a career. There was no *talk them out of it, shoot to only wound* or the most preposterous of all *shoot the gun out of their hand'* No, you shoot to stop them – whatever it takes.

The Ranger squeezed off a round. It hit Harrell below the breastbone. It seemed to made him stand up straighter, rather than knocking him backward. The muzzle blast and recoil took the .45 off target and Manny had to pull it back on for the second insurance shot. This slug hit two inches below the first. Harrell crumpled over backward.

The deputy had just gotten his revolver clear of his holster when the assailant hit the floor.

There was no question in Manny's mind that he had done the right thing, but his first thought as he saw Harrell on the floor was he didn't want him to be dead. He wanted to talk to him.

"Oooh. Damn, damn, Oooh." The moaning came from Sheriff Bell. It broke a momentary silence where the only other sound Manny heard was ringing ears.

"Get an ambulance," Manny barked to the deputy, as the other officer came running into the room with gun drawn. "Get some clean towels from the bathroom!" Manny lowered the hammer, flipped on the safety of his weapon, and put it away. He slid away the revolver that had dropped from Harrell's hand, and started to check on Sheriff Bell.

The sheriff was clutching a painful hand injury. He also had an abdominal wound. Bell was lying on his right side, and Manny had to use his pocketknife to cut away the heavy shirt material to expose the bullet entry and exit wounds. The bullet had caught him below the rib cage, about two inches in from his side. The exit wound was relatively clean and not bleeding heavily. One of the deputies arrived with towels, and wrapped the bleeding hand.

Manny checked on Oliver Harrell. He was still alive; he looked into the eyes of the Ranger. Manny asked him in a clear and loud voice, "Did you kill William and Elizabeth Longley?" Manny grabbed the other deputy who had been communicating on his radio. He needed him to observe any responses he may get from Harrell. The other deputy, as well as Sheriff Bell, became quiet in attention.

"Yes," Harrell grunted. He kept his eyes locked on Manny.

"Did Rodney Gott pay you to kill the Longleys?" Manny knew Harrell was failing rapidly, and wanted as much testimony as he could get. If Harrell died, it would most likely be a very cold trail.

"Yes," The old sheriff gave a labored answer.

I've only got time for a few answers. "Where is the gun you used to kill the Longleys?"

"Tomatoes ... tomatoes," were the last words uttered by Oliver Harrell. He was dead. His open eyes were still fixed on Manny.

"I heard that all," the sheriff grunted through his own pain. "What did he mean by tomatoes?"

"I don't know," Manny said. "Go look for tomatoes – anywhere around here."

One of the deputies went to the kitchen to look around. While Manny stayed with the sheriff, the other deputy went out the back door to check outside. Within a few seconds he was back.

"Got four tomato bushes planted against the house, out back," he said.

The sheriff managed to give Manny a smile through his grimace. He tilted his head toward the deputy and said, "Dig 'em up."

Both deputies were off to look for a shovel, and had just located one when the ambulance arrived. Sheriff Bell was loaded on a gurney and headed to the local emergency room. The EMS techs had satisfied themselves that Harrell was dead. His body would wait for the arrival of the County Coroner. After the ambulance departed, Manny went out back to see what the deputies might be finding.

The plants, with a few green tomatoes, had been pulled out of the ground and one of the deputies was removing soil from the planter along the back of the house. A foot and a half into the dig, they found it. Manny reached into the hole and retrieved from the loose soil a plastic package further wrapped in duct tape. Even before unwrapping it, he was sure it was indeed a pistol. Without Harrell's dying confession, it was unlikely the gun would have ever been discovered.

With his pocketknife, Manny slit the plastic wrap and heavy gray tape to reveal a revolver. It was an older model Hi Standard, nine shot, .22 caliber, with a six-inch barrel. After determining the pistol was unloaded,

Manny wrapped the plastic covering back over the gun. Further examination would be left to the crime lab fellows.

***

In Austin, the Texas Rangers' Headquarters issued a press release. "Investigation by the Texas Ranger Company A in Houston, Texas, the Sheriff's Office of Byar County, and the Department of Public Safety State Crime Laboratory, has determined without question that the bullet that killed State Senator Rodney Gott came from his own gun as a result of a ricochet. The death has been classified as accidental by the Texas Rangers. Further determinations will await the results of the Byar County Coroner's Inquest." The report also noted that Senator Gott had a blood alcohol content far higher than would be permitted for driving. It further stated that the Rangers would continue to review the incident, but at the present, there was no specific evidence of criminal activity.

News of the death of Rod Gott brought Forest Donovan back to Byar to consult and visit with Clay. They were meeting in Clay's office at work.

"The damage suit on the cattle, I believe we should continue to pursue. It may take a while. It's still applicable against the estate, just as if Rodney Gott were alive," Forest said.

"Now, the County is still trying to force sale of the farm, aren't they?" Clay said.

"Yes. Unless Byar County acts to rescind the eminent domain claim, we must go forward with a suit to stop it."

"I've talked to several people around here that have said, 'why don't they take the Gott place instead?' And really, that piece of property would fit in with the Convention Center and development as well as Mom's place. Now that Rod Gott is dead and his wife and son are supposedly living in France, why not try to get Byar County to go after that property by eminent domain?"

"Clay, I understand the urge to have someone get a taste of their own medicine. But you can count me out if that's your plan. I'm with you all the way defending against the County taking your property for private development. And, for the very same reason, I'm against you if you promote taking someone else's property for private development. It being Rod Gott, or him being deceased, doesn't make any difference. Down in my bones, I know it's wrong."

"Yes, you're right," Clay said. "I've been talking to Claire. Remember you met her here when my folks died. She has kind of sold me on the idea of the convention center, and even having a golf course to go with it

– a hotel and all. It would be good for the area."

"That was never the question. Sure, it would be good for the economy. But it's bad precedent. Have you changed your mind about keeping the farm? You know, if you want to sell the farm, we can ask the County to withdraw the condemnation, and you can offer the property for sale."

"No. I want to keep the farm," Clay said.

The conversation was interrupted by Millie buzzing Clay's phone. She told him it was Manny Rojas. Clay took the call in Forest's presence. He felt they were all friends.

"Couple of things I wanted to let you know about," Manny said. "In case you haven't gotten the news, we issued a press release this morning that the death of Rod Gott was an accidental shooting. He was killed by the ricochet of his own bullet."

"Well good, Manny. Even if you had some doubts, I knew I didn't shoot him," Clay said half jokingly, then regretted replying so lightheartedly. After all, it was a matter of a death, and Rod Gott had not yet been buried.

Manny did not say so, but he still had some lingering doubts, suspicions. He ignored Clay's response, not intending to get into any kind of discussion on what he might think. The other bit of news was far more important. "The other thing is, former Byar County Sheriff Oliver Harrell was killed this morning in a shooting in his home. Before he died, he confessed to having killed your parents. We have also located what we believe to be the murder weapon."

"Oh, man!" The meaningless expression was followed by a short pause, after which he said, "I guess I was prepared to never find out who did it."

"Since we will never be able to keep this quiet, I'll tell you, Harrell also confessed that Rodney Gott gave him the money to do it."

"Thank you, Manny. Somehow, I thought Rod was behind it." Clay knew it for a certainty. Rod Gott had shouted out that he had those 'old people killed.'

"I hope this can give you closure. I know it is always better to know what happened. It's probably also better to know that the perpetrators got their just rewards."

"Who shot Harrell?" Clay asked out of curiosity.

"He shot Sheriff Bell and then turned his weapon on me. I had no choice but to fire myself. Sheriff Bell was wounded, but will be okay. Harrell died at the scene." Manny wanted to give only the bare facts. He didn't feel it necessary to describe how he saved the sheriff from receiving what would most likely have been a fatal bullet, or how Oliver Harrell had delayed long enough for him to shoot.

"Thanks again for calling." Clay ended the call and started relaying the details to Forest.

"That's a clear case of wrongful death," Forest said, thinking and speaking like a personal injury lawyer. "You've got a strong case against the Rodney Gott Estate. File it today."

CHAPTER THIRTY-THREE

The following Wednesday State Senator Rodney Gott was buried in Byar. Marcus Franks' lead article in the Byar County News that day focused more on the Gott's past in Byar than it did on announcing the death. By the time the News went to press, everyone was aware of the death, and the investigation had determined that Rod had been killed by accident, with a bullet from his own gun.

The story also recapped the recent tragic death of Rod's brother, Raymond, in a traffic accident, and the likelihood of Rod being a candidate for statewide office. Marcus had a thing against speaking evil of the decreased and was, at least in print, kind to the memory of the Gotts. Instead, he used some quotes from Mason, a few other local notables, and the Governor concerning Rod's political career and civic contributions. He mentioned the Gotts' strong support for the Byar County Convention Center project, but did not mention the conflict with the Longleys.

It was a full news week for the local paper. There was also the front-page story that got added near the deadline concerning the deadly confrontation between Sheriff Jimmy Bell and former Byar County Sheriff Harrell, that led to the wounding of Bell and the death of Harrell by Texas Ranger Lieutenant Manuel Rojas. The story was limited in detail, but did say that Byar County Sheriff's Office and the Texas Rangers were executing a search warrant at the home of Harrell when the former sheriff shot and wounded Sheriff Bell. Jimmy Bell was in satisfactory condition, and recovering at Byar County Regional Medical Center.

There was no mention of the resignation of Mason Griggs from his position as County Judge. Marcus had gotten back to him following Rod's death, and Mason had indeed reconsidered, asking Marcus to ignore their discussion. Marcus agreed to withhold any reporting of the matter.

The services for Rodney Gott were well attended, but not spectacular. Even less so was the service for Oliver Harrell, the day after. Now, with the last of the Gotts gone, there was no one left to kowtow to, and many county residents that had turned out for the Ray Gott funeral decided they could stay away. Clay toyed with the idea of not attending himself. He had neither love nor respect for the Gotts, and had Manny's report that Harrell had implicated Rod in his parents' death. However, as one of the more prominent business leaders in the community, Clay felt obliged to attend. He also thought about seeing Claire, and perhaps having an opportunity to speak without raising eyebrows of the more prudish locals. He felt a tinge of guilt, for his attendance was anything but mourning.

Forest had contacted a prominent personal injury lawyer in Houston, and the day following the Gott funeral a wrongful death suit was filed in Byar County naming the estates of Rodney Gott and Oliver Harrell. The urgency was to preclude Margarette Gott disposing of the estate and again leaving the country with liquid assets. The sum of the suit was an attention getting ten million dollars, a figure estimated to be about one-third of the net worth of the Rodney Gott fortune.

Poor Ollie Harrell had an estate estimated at only $91,000, and $18,760 of that was the suspicious cash found in his house the day of his death. The balance was the value of his modest home. Rodney left a wife and son and Ollie left only a daughter who had moved away years before.

Once the Coroner's Inquest on the violent deaths in Byar County had been concluded, Ranger Manny Rojas was free to reveal details of the investigations. He again met Clay in his office at Consolidated.

"As I had told you before, Harrell confessed to killing your parents. The State Crime Lab has determined that the gun we recovered at Harrell's was the murder weapon," Manny said to Clay.

"How did you know it was Harrell," Clay asked. He had read the report that the Byar County Sheriff and Texas Rangers were serving a search warrant when the shooting occurred, but it did not say why Harrell was being investigated.

"We got lucky. An incident in Houston – a plea bargain. We have a witness that Oliver Harrell had offered him $5,000 to do the job. He declined. We haven't been able to directly trace payments from Rod Gott to Harrell, but Harrell admitted that Gott paid to have them killed. We found an envelope of money at Harrell's, eighteen thousand plus change, not something you would figure he would have laying around. The envelope seal contained Rod Gott's DNA, he licked it. Of course that doesn't mean for certain that particular envelope originally contained the money. It probably did. My guess, Rod gave Harrell about 20K to hire someone. Harrell tried to get someone for a lot less, figuring to keep the difference. For some reason he decided to do the job himself and pocket the full amount."

"Doesn't make sense them being killed just for the ranch," Clay said, but then thought about himself. He fell silent. Manny figured Clay might be lamenting about his parents, but Clay was comparing what Oliver Harrell had done to what he had been prepared to do.

It wasn't for money or land. It was for self-preservation - or was it vengeance? Not vengeance – it was justice. Either way, the results were the same.

Manny broke the silence. "This was likely the worst thing Harrell ever did, probably Rod Gott, too. It's what happens to people who have little respect for the rights of others. They may fudge a little here and there, maybe minor violations of the letter of the law. As time goes by, and they get away with it, they move closer and closer to the edge of criminal activity. The bigger stuff, they rationalize some justification."

Rationalize justification? Clay knew it fit. He continued his silence. Manny took it as his cue to continue.

"By the way, I'm sure this wasn't common knowledge. Harrell was dying. He had cancer. We found medical records and followed up with his doctor. Even with aggressive treatment, they gave him only six months."

"That's why he pulled a gun on you and the sheriff." Clay made the comment as a conclusion rather than a question.

"Nothing to lose." Manny thought again about Harrell's momentary delay after he had shot Sheriff Bell. Maybe Harrell had a real hatred for Bell, since Bell had taken his job. Maybe he actually wanted to take Bell with him, but would he have fired again? Maybe, but he forced Manny to shoot. He dictated his own execution, Manny concluded. He would live with it just as he would live with the lingering doubt about Clay, and his part in Rod's death.

Manny had checked all of Clay's credit card records, the Fixed Base Operator at Canney Field in Arkansas, the motel, and even the Consolidated plant manager. There was absolutely no evidence that Clay could have been in Byar at the time of Gott's death. He had checked out Clay's new .45, the Glock semi-auto. There was also no evidence that Clay hired someone to take care of Rod. Manny had determined that there was no large sum of money missing from Clay's current assets that could have been used to pay for such a deed. The fact that he suspected his friend would continue to bother Manny for some time to come.

Clay had time to contemplate, after Manny had left. His guilt and regret were gnawing at him. He resolved that each time he thought about the events, he would remind himself, that he had not shot Rodney Gott. He could not change the facts – that would have to suffice.

***

Margarette Gott was interested in settling outstanding issues and obligations in Byar County. Her intent was to liquidate the estate as soon as possible, including the sale of the Gott mansion and ranch. Margarette and Todd had no plans to return to live in Byar. She approached Mason Griggs to dissolve the partnership of the Griggs and Gott legal practice. In turn, Mason contacted Claire, heir to the other partner, Ray Gott. Mason reached an agreement with the widows to assume full ownership, and in turn provide an annual payment to each widow for the next ten years.

One stipulation was that all monies due to Margarette would be held in escrow until the Longley suits were resolved. That inspired her to move quickly toward a resolution. She agreed to settle the issue of Todd having killed the Longhorns, for the full amount of the specified damages and cost. Forest called his fee "free money" and proclaimed he had never done so little work to earn so much.

Mason represented the estate in negotiations with Clay's lawyer in Houston on the wrongful death suit. The evidence and testimony was convincing enough that Mason advised Margarette it would be in the best interest of the estate not to go to court. If the suit made it to court, all of the details of the harassment of the Longleys would be revealed. The hiring of someone to kill the old couple would compel a jury to not only award actual damages, but the punitive damages permitted in Texas could take the entire estate. Margarette made an offer of six million dollars for a settlement.

"What do you think I should do," Clay asked Claire. It was on their first real date in twenty-five years, a low-key dinner at the Marina Restaurant, still the nicest place in town. Clay didn't count "telephone dating."

"What's fair?"

"Nothing is fair. It isn't fair they were killed. It isn't fair that people can buy their way out of trouble." Clay thought, it isn't fair that I get away with what I did and now face a financial windfall. He reminded himself, *I did not shoot Rodney Gott.*

"Mason is a reasonable person. Maybe you should just talk to him directly," Claire said.

"I want to do that. I'd like to settle it as much as they would. I want to put it behind us."

"Is the 'us' you and me?" After months of talking almost daily, Claire felt confident what Clay meant. She smiled. He smiled. It was like they were college students again.

"I think we both want that," Clay said

"We don't have to talk about the troubles. I don't want to talk about Ray or home building or any of that."

Clay reached across the table to hold her hand. He had Claire back and didn't want to let go. She didn't mind. They were tuning out anyone who might notice or care how they were acting. "I remember this feeling," Clay said. "I've been waiting for this chance." Clay was looking into Claire's eyes – he thought he could see joy there. "It's been too long."

"We've talked about that," Claire said. "All of that time is past. Let's talk about now – let's talk about the future."

"Now? Now I want to spend all of my free time with you."

"What if you get tired of me? What about your true love?"

"True love? There's nobody else." Clay knew Claire's question was in jest. Her eyes didn't lie and her tone wasn't accusatory.

"Do you know you talk about that airplane like it was a girl friend?" Claire had been mildly miffed to hear Clay mention the plane and flying so often during their conversations.

"Aah – you two need to meet."

"I want to know all of your friends – and you mine. They'll be our friends. No one or any thing gets thrown away."

"Of course" Clay figured it was a good starting point. "Our phone calls have been the high point of my days. I need to get use to being with you."

"You will," Claire said. At least for her part, she planned on being around. "Even if I have to share time with your plane." It was being an engineer and an Army officer all over again. Clay has obsessions, she thought. If the airplane was part of Clay's life, she had decided it would be just as important to her.

"It has a seat for you."

"Okay. And what will you do? Will you go to church with me, or dinner with a bunch of real estate agents?"

"I'll go wherever. I want everybody to know that I love you." While Claire continued her agreeable smiles, Clay paused, then added. "You don't go to operas do you?" It was more nervous jest - he wasn't really concerned. Had that been the case, Claire would have mentioned it long before now. Claire's commitment to her church had been revealed, but they had not discussed religion.

"Church is tomorrow. I don't care if anyone thinks it's too soon."

"I want to get on with our future." He emphasized the word *'our'* and pointed first to Claire and then himself. "We've lost too much time." People can change over the years, but in the last few months, Clay was satisfied that he and Claire were still compatible.

"Don't beat around the bush. I don't want to take a chance on any misunderstandings this time. What do you have in mind?" Claire was soft spoken, even loving, but direct and forthright enough that it made it easy for Clay.

"This really isn't a normal question for a first date, but will you marry me?" Clay knew what he had in mind. He had dwelled on it for months, but didn't anticipate it that evening.

"Thank you. Thank you. Yes. Yes. Yes." Claire was all smiles.

"I'm sorry, I wasn't prepared for this. I should have a ring for you.

This feels awkward." Clay blushed.

"I don't need a ring. Besides, I've still got your high school ring. I never gave it back to you. I hid it."

"I know. Subconsciously, I guess - I never wanted it back."

"One other thing. About Margarette; we don't need the money."

"I'm ready when you are. Let's set a date," Clay said.

"Let's be engaged for a while. I want to enjoy it. You have to take me out on dates. Maybe you'll get lucky sometime." Claire's unspoken thought was, Besides, I've still got Mama Gott. She had been pondering what to do about her. Mama Gott and Margarette had never been close and Claire was all she had.

The evening ended with reminiscing, hand holding and kissing, but not with Clay getting lucky.

***

The Mama Gott problem resolved itself three weeks later when she died in her sleep. She had outlived her husband, Junior Gott, for two and a half decades. It seemed a fate of Gott husbands to make early departures.

Sheriff Jimmy Bell recovered from his gunshot wounds and enjoyed a hero status after Marcus Franks had penned a series of articles detailing the violence that had been visited on Byar County. The sheriff made it a point to call Ranger Rojas and thank him profusely. He had been teetering on being nothing more than a has-been go-fer for the Gotts, much like his predecessor. Finally, he was his own man and intended to make the most of the opportunity to instill honor in his office.

***

The headline of the Byar County News read, *Longley Donates Former Gott Mansion.* Marcus Franks wrote a nice article.

'Byar County native son Clayton Longley has donated to Byar County the former Gott mansion and property that he received in settlement of a lawsuit against the estate of the late Rodney Gott. An out of court settlement with the Gott estate, handled by Griggs and Associates Law Firm, resulted in Clayton Longley, son of Will and Elizabeth Longley, assuming ownership of 160 acres of the horse ranch and the mansion valued at approximately 4.5 million dollars. Longley also donated the Lake Byar Marina and Restaurant, additional property gained from the settlement, valued at over 1.5 million dollars. Byar County Judge Mason Griggs announced the donated real estate would become an asset of the newly formed Lake Byar Convention Center Corporation. The new corporation owns 100% of the corporate stock, and will at some future date offer shares for sale to the public. Judge Griggs said that Byar County will withdraw an eminent domain claim on other property desired for the Convention Center project. Upon questioning, Judge Griggs stated, "It was a mistake for Byar County to condemn private property that would be turned over to private development."'

That last line was Marcus' idea, and he forced Mason to say it. The story did not mention that Claire had agreed to purchase the remaining 420 acres of the section of land left in Rod Gott's estate. She had ideas that it would be a good investment for the future.

Marcus also included a quote from Longley attorney, Forest Donovan. "In a way I'm sorry we didn't get to make a federal case out of this. I would love to demonstrate to the nation how morally corrupt this whole idea is of taking private property from one citizen and giving it to another more affluent citizen, or corporation, so they can make money off of it. In many respects, I see Byar County, Texas, as a microcosm of the nation."

Forest later mentions to Clay that Marcus had not written all that he had said. "I called the Gotts 'cynical, arrogant elitists trying to steal our property and our freedoms.' Marcus thought that a little too strong."

The smaller story on the front page was Clay's favorite. Marcus wrote it also. 'Mr. and Mrs. Clay Longley announced the foundation of the Will & Elizabeth Longley Texas Longhorn Museum. The museum will be housed in a new facility to be built on the site of the Longley's Longhorn Ranch. In conjunction with the museum, a new breeding program for prize Longhorns will be implemented. The ranch and museum managers, Freddie and Carla Roberts, say the ranch will be dedicated to education of the public on the history of Longhorn cattle, ensure the survival of the breed, and provide a legacy for Will and Elizabeth Longley.'

The Bodas were born, raised, and ran roughshod over Byar County. Only Mason escaped the clique to become his own man. If the Bodas left a legacy, it isn't something that is celebrated.

About the Author

Joe Crain grew of age in Merryville, Louisiana and Newton, Texas. He earned a B.A. in History from the University of Louisiana – Lafayette and a Masters of Education from Tulane University of New Orleans. Joe joined the Navy Reserve just prior to college graduation and subsequently attended Navy Officer Candidate School, followed by Navy Pilot Training. Joe served a total of 30 years as a Navy pilot on active duty and in the Navy Reserve, retiring as a Captain (O-6).

Joe married Donna Whatley of Lafayette, Louisiana and they subsequently had three children – Gary, Danette and Christopher. The great tragedy of their life was the 2004 loss of Danette in an auto accident caused by a drunk driver. The greatest joy of their life has been their children and grandchildren, Gary's sons Cameron and Matthew, Danette's daughter Brittany and Chris's son Joey.

Joe and Donna make their home on Lake Livingston in East Texas, a setting similar to the fictitious Lake Byar of Eminent Murder. Joe spent the twilight of his civilian work career with The Boeing Company, supporting the International Space Station Program at Johnson Space Center in Houston.

Eminent Murder is Joe's second novel. The first, Wind Ahead of the Wing, relied heavily upon Joe's flying experience in the Navy Hurricane Hunters and was published in March 2006. A couple more fiction works are in progress.

ALL THINGS THAT MATTER PRESS ™

FOR MORE INFORMATION ON TITLES AVAILABLE FROM
ALL THINGS THAT MATTER PRESS, GO TO
http://allthingsthatmatterpress.com
or contact us at
allthingsthatmatterpress@gmail.com

www.ingramcontent.com/pod-product-compliance
Lightning Source LLC
LaVergne TN
LVHW041925090826
845145LV00015B/689

* 9 7 8 0 9 8 4 2 5 9 4 5 8 *